Praise for the

"An artistic but deadly combination of brides, bank robberies, and blame, set against the quaint backdrop of the Vista Beach community. What's not to love about this Valentine's-themed cozy?"
— Jennifer J. Chow,
Agatha & Lefty Award-Nominated Author of *Death By Bubble Tea*

"*Ghosts of Painting Past* is a holly, jolly, oh-my-golly romp of a holiday mystery. Christmas spirit abounds, but in the surfer's paradise, Vista Beach, everyone, even the snowmen—I mean sandmen—have deeply buried secrets worth killing for. Sybil Johnson has created a tightly woven plot with a murderer who will keep you guessing until the end."
— Annette Dashofy,
USA Today best-selling author of the Zoe Chambers Mysteries

"Johnson paints characters with a folksy charm that makes them feel like family...Color me a fan!"
— Diane Vallere, Author of the
Material Witness, Style & Error, and Madison Night Mysteries

"Johnson has penned a charming mystery filled with colorful characters, clever plot twists and unexpected surprises that will keep you guessing whodunit right until the end. A rewarding read and a refreshing debut."
— Hannah Dennison,
Author of the Honeychurch Hall Mysteries

"With a smart, sympathetic protagonist, lots of colorful details, and even tips on creating trompe l'oeil paintings, *A Palette for Murder* is a work of art."
— Ellen Byron,
Agatha Award winning author of the Cajun Country Mysteries

"Rory is definitely a quirky character; she has the ability to draw the readers in so that they want to follow her through her adventures."
— *Suspense Magazine*

"Johnson has crafted a clever mystery with a colorful protagonist. Set along the vibrant Southern California coast, this story resonates with a rich understanding of the artistic as well as the homeless communities. A smooth read!"
— Daryl Wood Gerber,
National Bestselling Author of *Grilling the Subject*

"Johnson has an assured, steady hand in creating complex plotlines in *Fatal Brushstroke*. Readers will definitely want to revisit Vista Beach in Aurora's next outing of investigating."
— Naomi Hirahara,
Edgar Award-Winning Author of *Murder on Bamboo Lane*

"A fun and fast-paced romp with plenty of suspense and intrigue, colorful characters, infidelity and family secrets. *Fatal Brushstroke* is sure to please cozy readers, especially those who love crafts mixed with murder."
— Sue Ann Jaffarian,
Author of the Ghost of Granny Apples Mystery Series

The Aurora Anderson Mystery Series
by Sybil Johnson

Brush Up On Murder

An Aurora Anderson Mystery

Sybil Johnson

BRUSH UP ON MURDER: An Aurora Anderson Mystery

Vista Beach Press

Copyright © 2023 by Sybil Johnson

www.authorsybiljohnson.com

This is a work of fiction. The story, all names, characters, and incidents portrayed in this production are fictitious. No identification with actual persons (living or deceased), places, buildings, and products is intended or should be inferred.

Book Cover by Stephanie Savage

First edition 2023

Print ISBN: 979-8-9876606-0-7

eBook ISBN: 979-8-9876606-1-4

To Jina Tan Wong and Lia Biscoe, my decorative painting pals, gone but not forgotten.

Chapter 1

A chill filled the morning air and dark skies hovered over the city of Vista Beach as Rory Anderson walked along the streets downtown. A banner advertising the upcoming Love Run, now only two days away, stretched across the street, swaying in the ocean breeze. Pedestrians made their way down the sidewalks, hurrying to walk their dogs or finish their errands before rain arrived later that day, driving everyone inside.

Hands in the pockets of the hoodie she wore over a long-sleeved t-shirt, Rory hurried toward her destination, picking up her pace and averting her face when she passed the building housing Vista Beach Realty. She headed into the nearby park, a green oasis in the middle of the concrete block. Perched on a slight hill, it sloped down toward the street below. A half dozen benches scattered around the park enjoyed unobstructed views of the ocean. Rory walked across the grass toward the only occupied bench and slipped into the seat next to a thirty-something woman with paper bags around her feet.

Teresa Mut smiled and held out a bag filled to the brim with green boxes. "The kids were excited to get your order. You're one of our best customers."

Rory exchanged money for the bag and peeked inside. Her face lit up when she viewed its contents. "I'm just glad to find someone to feed my habit." She dropped her voice. "If you see Liz, don't tell her I bought these, okay?"

A quizzical look appeared on Teresa's face, soon replaced by a soft smirk. "Too late."

Rory looked around to find her best friend, a petite woman with dark brown hair fashioned in a pixie cut, standing beside the bench, hands on her hips, a disappointed expression on her face. Dressed in black pants, a faux leather jacket and a lightweight animal print sweater, Elizabeth Dexter shook her head in disbelief.

Rory mentally kicked herself. Liz must have spotted her when she walked by her real estate office. She knew she should have taken a different route.

"What's in the bag?" Liz said.

Rory hugged it tightly to her chest. "Nothing." She squirmed under her friend's intense gaze. "Okay, fine, you caught me. I bought some Thin Mints."

Before Liz could say anything else, Teresa held up one of the other bags. "You're both so strange. Twenty please."

Rory's mouth gaped open. Her gaze shifted from one to the other and back again. "Wait. You're buying Girl Scout cookies too?"

Liz gave a sheepish grin and handed a bill to Teresa. "So much for keeping each other on a diet."

Teresa's gaze swept from the six-foot-tall Rory to the almost foot shorter Liz. "Why are you two on a diet? Neither of you needs to lose weight. Being healthy, that's the most important thing. That's what I always tell my kids."

"We want to make sure we still fit into our bridesmaid dresses for Solange and Xander's wedding," Liz said. "We ordered them months ago and ate way too much over the holidays. Or at least I did."

"That's right. You're part of their I Do Crew. You don't look like you've gained weight to me, but better safe than sorry, I suppose."

Rory looked wistfully at her bag filled with cookies. "Guess I'll have to wait until after Valentine's Day for my fix."

Teresa pushed her glasses up her nose. "You can probably have one or two without causing any damage. You can freeze the rest for later, you know. We've been doing that for years."

"Me too. Nothing beats the taste of frozen Thin Mints."

"How's the wedding planning going?" Liz said. "Do you need us to do anything?"

"Everything's on track. Much better than some of the weddings I've put together over the years."

"But?" Rory said, sensing something was wrong.

"It's nothing, really. The florist almost ordered the wrong flowers. And there was an accidental cancellation of hotel rooms for out of town guests. Both easy to fix."

"That kind of thing happens?" Liz asked.

"On occasion. That's why I double check everything. Still, I feel ...uneasy." Teresa looked up at the darkening sky. "Maybe it's the weather." She made a notation on the outside of an envelope, stuffed the money inside and put it in her purse. "I'd better get going. I've got cookies to drop off and some last-minute things to take care of for tomorrow night's party."

"You're planning that too?"

"I'm a full-service wedding planning business. Anything to do with the wedding and I'm there. Makes it easier that both the party and the reception are at the Akaw," Teresa said, naming a hotel in downtown Vista Beach. She picked up the last bag and stood up. "Thanks for buying the cookies. My kids and I appreciate it. See you tomorrow." She waved and walked across the grass toward the street behind them.

Liz sank down on the bench while Rory opened a box of Thin Mints. "Just two each."

They munched on their cookies and stared at the waves crashing onto the sand while they talked about the upcoming wedding. They'd met the bride-to-be in a painting class the year before, bonding instantly over their love of decorative painting. Before long, they felt as if they'd known each other for years. Over the last year, they'd witnessed Solange and Xander's whirlwind romance. Three months after meeting, the couple became engaged. When Solange had asked Rory and Liz to be in the wedding party, they'd immediately accepted.

"Have you talked to the Blushing Bride recently? How's she holding up?" Liz said between bites.

"She's fine. A bit nervous, I think, but that's to be expected with the wedding only two weeks away. Hiring Teresa to do the wedding planning has been a big help. Solange can concentrate on her tax preparation business and the online painting magazine."

"At least she's got you to do a lot of the work for the magazine. She doesn't have to worry about the website and the nitty gritty of putting together *BrushToBrush* with you on the job." Liz wiped her dainty fingers on a tissue she pulled out of her pocket. "Do you know what you're going to say in your toast at the party?"

Rory closed up the box of cookies and put it back in the bag. "I have some ideas, but nothing concrete yet."

"If you need someone to bounce ideas off of, I'm available. Or you can ask the others at the makeup rehearsal tomorrow afternoon."

Friday afternoon, right before the party at the Akaw, the bridesmaids were getting together in a room at the hotel to try out the makeup for the wedding.

A chime sounded and Liz frowned at her phone. "I got an alert from the city. There's been another bank robbery. The downtown branch of Vista Beach Savings."

"I was just there getting cash for the cookies," Rory said.

They looked in the direction of the bank less than half a dozen blocks away from the park.

"Did you go inside?"

"No, I used the ATM. Do you think it was happening while I was there?"

"The alert didn't give many details. This is, what, the third bank that's been hit in the area in the last few weeks?"

"Something like that. I know it's a very common crime in L.A. County, but still..."

"What does Dashing D say?" Liz asked, referring to Rory's boyfriend, Vista Beach police detective Martin Green.

"He hasn't told me much, but I don't think they have any leads."

"The paper came out today," Liz said. "Too late for anything about *this* robbery, but I bet there's an article on the others."

Rory made a mental note to grab a copy of the city's weekly newspaper, *The Vista Beach View*, on her way home. Her own cell phone quacked, indicating the arrival of a text. She glanced down at the display. "Solange wants to see me about the magazine. I'd better get home. She's meeting me there in twenty minutes."

Rory replied to the text and the two friends went their separate ways.

Rory and Solange Fournier sat side by side in front of the computer in the work area of Rory's house, one half of the great room that spanned the front of the twelve-hundred-square-foot structure. Muted sunlight came in through the window that looked out onto the narrow street beyond. Except for the occasional passing car, little movement could be seen on Seagull Lane. They went down the to-do list, going over the March issue of the online decorative painting magazine that Solange had recently founded.

"Why, oh why, did I ever agree to a Valentine's Day wedding?" Solange scrunched down in her seat, arching her neck back and addressing the ceiling for an answer to her question.

Rory took her hands off the keyboard and swiveled her desk chair so she faced the bride-to-be. "It's romantic. Besides, I thought that's what you've dreamed of ever since you were a little girl."

Solange sat up straight. "That was before I started doing taxes for a living. This is the busiest time of year for me. It's not like I can put off the work either. Uncle Sam is picky about deadlines."

"Why didn't you do it later in the year then?"

"I suggested it, but Xan looked so disappointed I couldn't say no." A soft smile played about her face. "He's such a hopeless romantic."

"Not a bad thing to be."

Solange nudged Rory's arm with her elbow. "I bet that man of yours is too. He gives off that vibe. Any idea what he's planning for you for Valentine's Day? Besides going to our wedding."

"Martin says he has something planned, but he wouldn't tell me what. He's being very secretive."

"I bet it's good. You'll have to tell me all about it." Solange spun her chair, her gaze sweeping the work area and the adjoining living room. "Where's your cat? She usually comes over to say hi."

"Sekhmet's around somewhere. She got into some catnip I spilled on the ground earlier. I think she's sleeping it off."

Solange's curly hair bounced as she laughed. "I bet that was a sight." She turned her attention back to the computer screen. "At least I have you helping me out with *BrushToBrush*. I don't want to see it fail. I have big plans for it."

"Don't worry. I've got your back. Now, what else did you want to talk about?"

The two of them spent the next half hour going over the rest of the notes about the upcoming issue. After they'd covered everything, Rory said, "You could have talked to me about this over the phone. What's really going on? Is it the wedding?"

"No. Teresa's doing a great job. I'm so glad you suggested I hire her. Honestly, I just wanted to see a friendly face."

"Are you still having problems with Xander's dad?"

"I think he's afraid we won't last. He doesn't like the age difference. Thinks his son should marry someone older. Then, when I told him I wasn't changing my last name, he went through the roof."

"Neither of those things has anything to do with whether a marriage lasts or not. Ten years is not a lot at our age. It's not like you're sixteen. The difference between twenty-nine and forty is no big deal."

"I know, but I'm questioning everything right now. Xan's been ...different the last few weeks. I feel like he's pulling away from me and I don't know why. The closer we get to the wedding, the worse it gets. Makes me wonder if he's getting cold feet. Maybe he's realizing I'm not really his type. All of his other girlfriends have been short and petite. Look at me." Solange swept her arm down her body. "I'm tall and what my mother always called big boned."

"You're smart and beautiful and a lot of fun to be around. Xander is lucky to have you."

"Thanks. I needed that."

"I'm sure whatever's going on with him, it has nothing to do with you. Where is all this coming from? This isn't like you. You're usually so confident."

"I don't know. Pre-wedding jitters, I guess. I always pictured my engagement and wedding as a joyous event where my husband's family welcomed me with open arms. I've missed that, having a family." Sadness spread across her face.

Rory ached for her friend whose parents had died within a few months of each other while she was still in middle school. The aunt and uncle who took her in had passed away less than ten years later. Ever since, she'd been searching for a new family.

"Don't worry. Xander's dad will come around."

Solange's face brightened. "Zeke did clear his schedule so he could be here and help out until the wedding. And he is throwing us the party tomorrow night. He can't be all that upset. You and Martin are coming, right?"

"Wouldn't miss it. How come it's at the hotel and not at Xander's restaurant?"

"We all decided it would be better this way. Saves a lot of arguments. They're both very stubborn. If it's at the restaurant, Xan will want to take control of the party and his dad wouldn't go for that. This way, Zeke can do whatever he wants. Plus he's staying at the hotel while he's in town, so it's convenient for him."

"Xander's okay with that?"

"Not really, but I convinced him it was for the best." Solange looked at the time on her phone. "Yikes. I didn't realize it was this late. I've got a lot of work to do before tonight. I promised I'd help out with this wine and chocolate tasting at the restaurant. It's the first one and everybody's nervous."

"I saw the ad for it. I tried to get tickets, but it had already sold out." A wistful expression appeared on Rory's face.

"They went fast. Don't worry, if it goes well, there'll be another. I'll make sure you get into that one." Solange gathered her things, giving Rory a quick hug before she left.

Not long after the bride-to-be was out the door, Rory received a text from Liz to come outside.

When she opened her front door, she spotted a four-seat golf cart parked in her driveway behind her own sedan. A sign attached to the side of the cart advertised Vista Beach Realty. Liz, now dressed in a long-sleeved t-shirt and running leggings, stood next to the cart, stretching her arms over her head.

Rory raised an eyebrow. "What's with the golf cart? Where's your car?"

"Isn't it a beauty? The office just got it. I'm taking it for a spin." A determined look on her face, Liz walked across the lawn toward the front door. "We're going on a run. We need to work off those extra calories we ate today."

"We only had two cookies each."

"Then think of it as training for the 5K we're running on Saturday."

"We were already out earlier this week. Besides, we're walking it. And I don't think I need any more training. I'm not planning on competing for the top spot or anything."

A brown Abyssinian cat poked her head out of the front door. Before Rory could stop her, Sekhmet bounded out the door toward Liz, stopping to sniff at her legs.

Liz bent down to pet her. "See, even Sekhmet thinks it's a good idea." With a finger, she bopped the cat gently on her nose. "Would you like to come along? You probably don't need the exercise the way you run around inside, but we'd enjoy your company."

Sekhmet meowed in response.

Liz looked over at Rory. "I think that was a no leash request."

"I know better than to try that. I think that meow was more of an I'd rather stay home comment. She's still recovering from a bout with catnip."

The cat rubbed against Liz's legs one last time before running back toward the house.

Rory closed the door as soon as the cat was safely inside. "See, Sekhmet knows the value of staying home."

"Come on. It'll be fun. Just down to the pier and back. We don't have to run. We can walk." Liz gestured to the gray hoodie, jeans and t-shirt Rory had on. "You don't even have to change your clothes. What you're wearing is fine."

Rory eyed the threatening clouds in the sky and considered the idea. "I could use some fresh air. It's supposed to rain later. We should go while we can." She locked the front door and zipped up her hoodie. "I hope the weather cooperates for the race."

"The rain's supposed to be gone before then."

As they walked across the lawn, Liz directed her attention to the partially framed house across the street from Rory's single-story stucco home. "What's going on there? I thought they'd be further along."

"Construction's on hold. I'm not sure why. The new owners may have changed their minds about what they plan on building. Whatever the reason, both Sekhmet and I are happy to have a break from the noise."

"I bet Granny G is glad they're not littering the street anymore," Liz said, naming Rory's seventy-six-year-old neighbor, Winifred Griswold.

"She wasn't happy about them leaving their lunch trash around, that's for sure. It was nice of her to pick it up. She didn't have to do that. I'm not sure she's worrying all that much about what's going on here right now. She's out of town, visiting her sister who's recovering from an operation."

Side by side, the two made their way toward downtown Vista Beach, Rory taking one step for every two her much shorter friend took. Along the way, they caught up on the latest news.

"How was your meeting with Solange?"

"Good. The next issue is coming along." Rory crinkled her face in worry. "I hope the wedding goes smoothly."

"Is she still having problems with her future father-in-law?"

"You know about that?"

"She told me about it a while back. I know he hasn't always agreed with Xander's life choices, but I think he likes Solange. Or I hope so. From what I can tell, he cares about his son, so I don't think he'll cause any real problems for them."

"They were estranged for a while, weren't they?"

"That's right," Liz said. "He didn't agree with Xander's decision to quit medical school and become a chef. Now that he's so well-known and his restaurant is doing well, his father seems to have come around."

"Better late than never. Probably doesn't hurt there's talk Xander might get a TV cooking show."

"I heard about that too. Fingers crossed he gets it." They paused at a red light and Liz pushed the walk button. "The next couple weeks are going to be busy."

Rory spotted a stray candy bar wrapper on the sidewalk, picked it up and tossed it into a nearby trash can. "I'll have to spend a lot of late nights working to fit it all in." She ticked off the items on her fingers. "We've got the party tomorrow night at the Akaw—"

"And the makeup rehearsal beforehand."

"Then we've got the Love Run on Saturday, the wedding favor painting on Sunday and the rehearsal dinner right before the wedding." Rory frowned. "I'm forgetting something."

"The spa day a week from Saturday for the bridesmaids and the bridal shower the following day."

"Oh, right. I'm looking forward to getting to know that friend of Solange's."

"You're talking about Jade, right?"

"That's right. Jade McIntyre," Rory said.

"Do you know much about her?"

"Just what Solange had me put on the wedding website I created for them. That was two weeks ago when she replaced the bridesmaid who dropped out."

When they stopped at another light, Liz brought the couple's website up on her phone's browser. "There's no photo of her."

"Solange never gave me one. Something about Jade not being able to find one that satisfied her."

"We'll meet her tomorrow at the makeup party. We can grill her then."

Less than ten minutes later, they were at the top of the hill leading down to the ocean. From their vantage point, they could see a lone protester marching back and forth in front of the entrance to the pier, holding a sign high in the air. Rory couldn't make out what was on it until they were almost at the bottom. On white poster board was a drawing of a heart shaped padlock and the words "Save Love" beneath it.

Rory cocked her head. "What do you think that's about?"

Liz pointed to a bunch of people clustered around a section of the pier railing. "Maybe they know something."

As they crossed the bike path onto the pier, the group parted, exposing the railing. Attached to it were silver and gold padlocks in varying sizes, including a few heart-shaped ones as well as two that were intertwined. The number of love locks had grown considerably since Rory had first seen the symbols of eternal love a week ago.

"There were only a dozen here last week," she said. "Must be over a hundred now."

"With more to come, I'm sure," Liz said. "Valentine's Day seems to have brought out the romance in everyone."

They watched a young couple in their twenties clip a lock to the railing, deposit the key in a nearby trash can and kiss. A woman with a red streak in her black hair and a nose ring, clad in distressed jeans and a light sweater, took a picture of the couple, jotting down their information in a small spiral bound notepad.

Rory gestured toward the woman. "Veronica's here. She must be writing an article for the paper."

"Or for *Vista Beach Confidential*," Liz said, naming the blog the newspaper reporter maintained on events in and around the city.

As soon as the couple left, Rory and Liz walked over to Veronica Justice who was now taking close-ups of a few of the padlocks, all with either initials or first names on them, some also including a date. A handful were decorated with hearts and flowers in a variety of colors.

Veronica checked the pictures she'd taken, then put her camera and notepad in the tote bag that served as her purse. "Get a look while you can. They're going down soon," she said in a raspy voice.

"What do you mean?" Rory said.

"The city's worried the railing will collapse under the weight of all the locks like it did in France."

Rory eyed the pier railing. "Doesn't seem in danger of collapsing right now. There were a lot more love locks on the Pont des Arts."

"It's early days yet. Word is spreading. The mayor's expecting more people to add locks, especially with Valentine's Day right around the corner. She's trying to prevent a problem before it becomes a reality."

"She probably doesn't like the idea of people throwing the padlock keys in the ocean either," Liz said.

"At least the couple we saw used the trash can. But, I suppose, that's not always the case," Rory said.

"The city's erecting a metal tree next to the fountain by city hall that will withstand the weight of thousands of locks and directing people there instead." Veronica gestured toward the padlocks on the railing. "They're planning on cutting all of these off and throwing them away."

Rory looked back to the base of the pier where the protester was still walking back and forth, waving her sign. "Is that what the sign's about? Did you talk to her?"

"Not sure about that one. She thinks as long as her lock stays fastened, her love will last. Once the city cuts it off—poof!—there goes her relationship."

"She really believes that?"

Veronica shrugged. "Some people are really into symbolism. I've talked to others who agree with her. But there are just as many who think the locks are an eyesore and want them down. Could get ugly."

"There's nothing anyone can do about keeping them?" Liz said.

"They're on public property so the city can take them down if they want."

"That's not right." Liz's expression turned thoughtful. "I might have an idea."

"You should tell the folks at city hall. I'm sure they'd welcome a better solution." Veronica glanced at her phone. "I've got places to go and people to see. Catch you two later." She waved and made her way toward the entrance of the pier.

"What's your idea?" Rory said.

"I'm not ready to talk about it yet. I don't want to jinx it. Do you mind if I go by city hall on our way back to your place?"

"I want to stop off at my mom's store, anyway. Why don't you meet me there after you're done?"

Their plans made, the two walked back up the hill, separating at the top to do their respective errands.

Chapter 2

The bell over the front door tinkled when Rory stepped inside Arika's Scrap 'n Paint a short time later. A feeling of contentment washed over her as she breathed in the pleasing scent of unfinished wood. Prominently displayed near the cash register were padlocks in all shapes and sizes, all of them painted with designs that included hearts and flowers. Next to them was a sign that read: *Initials painted on free of charge with purchase.*

A young couple examined the locks while half a dozen other customers perused racks of painting and scrapbook supplies. The sound of voices drew Rory to the neighboring classroom where she found her mother sitting at one of the two eight-foot tables that filled the room, painting a red heart on a padlock. Sitting by her mother's side was a handsome man dressed in a suit and tie. A pen and small notepad sat on the table in front of him.

As she stepped inside the classroom, she heard the word "sweetheart."

Detective Martin Green's face brightened when he saw her.

Arika Anderson stopped talking and looked up from her painting task. She smiled at her daughter. "What brings you by?"

Rory kissed Martin hello before slipping into a seat across from them. "Liz and I took a walk down to the pier and looked at the love locks. Did I hear you say something about sweetheart?"

"The Sweetheart Robber. That's what the press is calling him. Martin and I were just talking about the article in today's paper." Arika pushed a copy of the *Vista Beach View* across the table toward her daughter.

On the front page was a piece on the bank robber that had struck several times in the area in the last three weeks. Accompanying the article was a grainy photo of the culprit, a man with a short beard, wearing sunglasses and a ball cap that partially obscured his face. After studying the photo, Rory read the article. It described how the robber silently handed a heart made out of red construction paper to the teller with the words "Give me all your money" printed on it. He always struck when only a handful of customers were inside. The whole event was so quiet and took so little time, few people in the bank even knew what was happening until it was over.

Rory directed a question at Martin. "Is all of this true? The bit about the paper heart too?"

"It's accurate as far as it goes," he said in a deep voice.

"The teller never puts up a fight?"

"They're trained to hand the money over. There's a better chance no one will get hurt that way."

"Martin is asking all the store owners in town if we saw anything suspicious this morning," Arika said. "You heard about today's robbery?"

"I did. Did you see anything?"

"No. I hadn't gotten to the store yet. We're far enough from the bank I'm not sure I would have seen anything even if I'd been here at the time."

"What about you? Were you in the area?" Martin said to Rory.

"You'll probably see me on the footage from the ATM camera if you haven't already," she said. "I got some cash this morning from the bank where the robbery occurred."

He looked at her, heightened interest on his face. "What time were you there?"

Rory considered the question. "I'm not sure exactly. I left home around nine, so I probably got to the bank fifteen minutes later. Hold on." She pulled her wallet out of her jeans pocket and drew out an ATM receipt. "This says 9:16."

He jotted down the information in his notebook. "Did you see anything unusual?"

Rory cast her mind back to the visit to the ATM, picturing the scene in her mind. All she remembered was getting the money and thinking about a programming project she was working on. "Sorry, I don't remember anything that'll help you."

"What about anyone hanging around the area?"

"There were a few customers waiting in line at the ATM. Maybe a couple people walking by. I can't tell you who any of them were. I'm pretty sure none of them looked like this guy, though. I don't remember much else." She looked with concern at Martin. "Was I in any danger?"

He reached across the table and squeezed her hand. "Not that I can tell. It was just a note job." When she stared at him in confusion, he added, "The robber hands a note to the teller. Not even a suggestion of a gun. Do you remember anything else?"

Rory thought for a moment before shaking her head. "I don't think so. Do you have any leads?"

"Nothing definite."

"How much does the robber get each time?"

"Two or three thousand."

"Why would someone take such a chance for so little?"

"Sometimes people are desperate. And two or three thousand might not seem much to you, but to others it's a fortune." Martin put his notebook and pen back in his jacket pocket and stood up. "Thanks for your help, both of you." On his way out of the room, he leaned down and spoke softly to Rory. "Are we still on for tonight? I have something special planned."

Her face crinkled in pleasure. "I'm looking forward to it." As she watched him leave, she wondered what he had in mind for the evening. Moments later, she heard the bell over the front door tinkle. With some effort, Rory brought her mind back to the present. She gestured toward the padlock her mother had finished painting. "How long have you been carrying these? I don't remember seeing them before."

"Not long. I figured I'd get in on the craze. Other stores are selling them too, but I'm the only one who's adding decorations and painting on the initials." Arika pushed an unadorned padlock toward her daughter. "Help me paint the rest of these. Put hearts or anything else you want on them. Just make sure to leave space for initials to be added later."

Using an already completed lock as her guide, Rory began painting hearts and flowers on a silver padlock, adding a few flourishes of her own. "Did you know the city is planning on getting rid of the locks on the pier?"

"I've heard rumors. It's definite, then?"

"Veronica seems to think so."

"Sounds like I should move up my photo shoot." Arika explained how she planned on taking photos in front of the locks to use in an ad for the store. "Veronica agreed to take the pictures for me."

"She didn't mention that to us, but she did say the city is putting up a metal structure in front of city hall for people to use instead. You could always take the pictures there if the pier doesn't work out."

Arika placed a finished lock to one side and picked up another. "Too bad the locks on the pier couldn't be saved, but at least the city is providing a place for people to put new ones."

The two continued their task in companionable silence. They were working on the final padlocks when the bell over the front door tinkled wildly. Moments later, Liz breezed into the classroom and plopped down on a chair, a triumphant look on her face.

"How'd your errand go?" Rory said.

"Couldn't have gone better. I saved the love locks."

"The ones on the pier?"

Liz nodded. "The city agreed to my proposal to move them to the structure by city hall."

"That was fast," Rory said. "I would have thought the city council would have to okay it or something."

"I talked to the mayor herself. She's known my family for a long time and was happy to help. I suspect she's also thinking it'll be good for her re-election prospects."

"How are you going to move them?" Arika said. "No one has the keys anymore. They've all been tossed."

"That's where my lock sporting group comes in."

Arika raised an eyebrow. "Lock sporting?"

"We pick locks for fun. Don't worry, we have a very strict code of ethics. We make sure we don't do anything illegal. We're allowed to relocate locks on public property as long as we have permission and put them somewhere else."

"So you're going to pick the locks and move them to the new structure in front of city hall?" Rory asked. "The city really agreed to that?"

"The mayor thought it was a good idea. She talked to Chief Marshall first to make sure no laws were going to be broken. I'm putting together a group for next week. She wanted it done ASAP."

Arika painted the last stroke of a pink rose on a padlock and put her brush down. "There. Another batch done."

Liz studied the locks on the table. "These all look really nice. Better than the plain ones. You should promote them more."

"I plan to." Rory's mother held up a piece of paper with a picture of a decorated padlock in the center surrounded by the words *Love Locks Sold Here*. "This is going in the front window, and I'm putting together some ads for the paper. I'm doing a photo shoot in front of the love locks."

"I like that idea."

"Did you see the article in the *View* about the bank robberies?" Rory said.

Liz picked up the paper from the table and studied it. "The Sweetheart Robber. So that's what they're calling him. Hard to tell anything from the photo. Average build, beard. Can't really see his face. Not enough details for a positive ID." She put the paper down. "I wish the police would catch him, whoever he is. It's getting so I don't want to be anywhere near a bank."

"I don't think anyone's in real danger. Martin said no gun was used and the tellers are told to hand over the money."

"When did you talk to him?"

"He was just here asking about the robbery."

"Did he have anything new to add?"

"Unfortunately not."

Liz flipped through the paper, stopping at an inside page. "Here's the route for the race on Saturday." She turned the paper so Rory and her mother could see the map.

They bent their heads over the page to study the route. Participants had the choice of going the full 10K or opting for half the distance. Both courses went down the same streets at the beginning with the 5K turning back to the pier halfway through while the 10K continued on.

"I didn't realize it goes right by the store," Rory said.

"Your dad and I will make sure we're here rooting you all on. That reminds me. I'll be right back. I want to show you both something." Rory's mother went into the back room and returned moments later with a poster board sign with *Congratulations Solange and Xander* painted on a white background, surrounded by wedding bells, hearts and flowers. She held it up so they could see it. "What do you think?"

"Looks great," Rory said.

"They'll really appreciate it," Liz said. "You know what we should do. Get people to sign it."

"That's a good idea," Arika said. "I'm sure some of my customers will want to. A lot of them have known Solange for a while and subscribe to *BrushToBrush*."

"We can get the I Do Crew to sign it at tomorrow night's party too."

Rory frowned. "But Solange and Xander will be there. We should try to keep this a surprise."

Liz tapped a finger on the table. "I'll come up with something to make sure they don't find out. Leave it to me."

"We can pick the sign up tomorrow afternoon on the way to the makeup rehearsal," Rory said.

"I'll have it ready for you." Arika leaned the sign against the classroom wall and sat back down. "Besides you two and the bride and groom, who else is participating in the race?"

"As far as I know, the entire wedding party," Rory said. "The plan is for all of us to walk together as a group, at least at the beginning. Not sure how long that will last."

"A few might find the pace too slow," Liz said. "But I think it'll be more fun staying with the group."

Arika gently touched the paint on the padlocks. "These are ready to put out."

The three picked up the finished locks and put them in the display on the sales floor. A short while later, the two friends were walking up the driveway of Rory's house when Liz pointed to the front door. "There's something on the doorstep."

Rory hurried across the lawn to find a bouquet of red roses encased in a plastic sleeve. She smiled when she read the accompanying card. "It's from Martin."

"Duh. Who else would it be from? What's it say?"

"He's picking me up at seven. I'm supposed to dress up."

"Do you have any idea where you're going?"

Rory put the card back in the envelope. "It's a surprise."

"I bet it's something good." Liz touched one of the roses with the tip of a finger and stared at it, a wistful expression on her face. "These are so beautiful. I wish I had someone to give me flowers." She straightened her shoulders. "Not like I *need* a man. It would be nice, though. I've tried some dating apps, but haven't had much luck with them. I think I prefer the face-to-face approach."

"What about the groomsmen? I think at least one of them is single."

"Maybe. I haven't spent time with any of them."

"You can scope them out at the party."

"I've also got that speed date and paint event on Tuesday."

Twice a month at his restaurant, Xander held a speed painting event, similar to speed dating, but instead of talking for a short period of time before moving on to the next date, participants got to know each other by collaborating on a piece of art.

Liz checked her watch. "I'd better get back to the office. I'm meeting a client in half an hour." She hopped into the golf cart and soon was on her way.

Rory brought the roses inside and put them in a vase on her desk. Before getting back to work, she called Martin. "I got the flowers," she said as soon as he picked up. "They're beautiful. Thank you."

"It's only the beginning."

"More flowers?"

"You'll see. I plan on making this a memorable Valentine's Day."

"It's two weeks away."

"Doesn't mean I can't stretch it out."

Rory pictured Martin grinning into the phone. She grinned back on her end. "So where are we going tonight?" She made her voice casual, hoping he'd let something slip about their destination.

"You'll have to wait and see. Just a sec." Rory could hear him talking to someone in the background but couldn't make out any of the words. When he came back on the line, he said, "Sorry. I need to go. See you later tonight."

Rory settled down in her work area, smiling every time she looked up from her computer screen and saw the roses. She was concentrating on a change to some code when the patter of drops against glass made her look up. Outside the skies had opened up and a deluge of rain was coming down. She went around her house, closing the few windows that were open, then sat back down in front of her computer and watched the rain fall. Sekhmet jumped up on the desk and, after a quick sniff at the roses, stared outside. Rory stroked the cat's fine fur. "I bet you're glad you're not out in this." She frowned as a sudden thought struck her. "I hope this doesn't change our plans for the evening."

She watched the rain come down for a few more minutes before returning to work.

By seven p.m., the rain had stopped, leaving a freshness in the air. Precisely at the top of the hour, a knock sounded on the front door.

Wearing black dress pants and a royal blue silk blouse, Rory walked to the front door, narrowly avoiding Sekhmet who was racing around the great room batting a toy across the wood floor. As soon as Martin appeared in the doorway, the cat trotted toward him, a ratty looking catnip mouse in her mouth, and dropped it at his feet.

He scratched Sekhmet behind the ears, then tossed the mouse down the hallway. He cocked his head and looked thoughtfully at the cat as she raced after it. "Is that...?"

"Yep. It's the toy we got her for Christmas."

"She's still playing with it? I'd have thought she'd have gotten tired of it by now."

"It's seen better days, but she doesn't seem to mind."

They looked at the playing cat for a few moments before Martin turned to her. "Ready?"

Rory put on a raincoat, popped her cell phone and keys in her clutch and stepped outside. As soon as they were in the car, Martin handed her a piece of black cloth. She looked inquiringly at him before realizing what he wanted her to do. "A blindfold? Really? You can't just tell me where you're taking me?"

"It's a surprise. Come on, humor me."

"Okay." She put the blindfold on with his help and settled back in her seat. She tried to figure out where they were going, but soon lost track of all the twists and turns. When the car stopped and the engine turned off, Martin said, "You can look now."

Rory took off the blindfold and peered through the windshield at the darkness beyond. It took a moment for her to figure out they were parked on the street facing Zephy's, the fine dining restaurant owned by Solange's fiancé, named after his recently deceased mother. Specializing in fish and seafood, the restaurant had been open for less than six months but had quickly become one of the most sought-after dining experiences in the city.

Light beamed out of the single-story building onto the street. She could see people inside, sitting at tables covered in white cloths.

Rory turned to Martin, a surprised look on her face. "I've been wanting to come here for a while. Solange said she'd get us in, but I never took her up on the offer. I guess you did."

"She may have given me the idea."

They followed a couple dressed in semi-formal attire toward the front door. A murmur of voices greeted them as soon as they stepped inside. Her gaze swept the area, noting with interest the dining room to the right and a framed article from the *Vista Beach View* displayed on the wall to her left. The headline read "Local Chef Opens New Restaurant." Below it was a photo of Xander in his chef's coat, tattoo-covered arms folded in front of his chest, beaming for the camera.

Instead of going toward the host stand and the main body of the restaurant, they turned down a hallway, following signs for the wine and chocolate tasting event.

"We need tickets for this," she whispered to Martin as they joined the line waiting to enter the banquet room.

"I know." He gave his name to the man standing at the doorway who checked them off a list and ushered them inside.

Several long tables covered in white cloths were scattered around the room, all facing a podium and a board next to it listing chocolate and wine tasting pairs. A dozen couples were already in the room, milling around and talking while they waited for the event to begin.

"How did you get tickets? I thought it was sold out."

"Someone may have helped me." Martin looked toward the entrance where a clean-shaven man wearing a white chef's coat stood, scanning the room, a satisfied look on his face. Electricity filled the air as soon as he stepped inside. Everybody's gaze followed him as he made his way toward them.

Xander Axelrod kissed Rory on both cheeks before shaking Martin's hand. "I'm glad you both could come."

"I hear we have you to thank for getting us in tonight," Rory said.

"The least I could do with everything you're doing for Solange."

"Speaking of Solange, she told me she was going to help out, but I don't see her. Is she here yet?"

"She has too much on her plate these days with work and the wedding so close. I told her not to worry about it. My sister is helping instead." Xander pointed toward the entrance where a woman whose features closely resembled his own was consulting with the man who'd been checking off names. Naomi Axelrod waved at them, then motioned for her brother to join her.

"Excuse me," Xander said. "I'm needed up front. Enjoy yourselves."

The chef and his sister made their way toward the podium and stood side by side facing the group.

Naomi picked up the microphone. "It's time to start. Please take your seats."

Rory and Martin found two empty places next to each other at the table nearest the door. He helped her out of her coat, which she draped over the back of her chair before sitting down. She glanced at the sheet of paper in front of her that listed the wine and chocolate pairings for the evening before turning her attention to the podium.

"I'll be conducting the tasting tonight," Naomi said into the microphone. "Before we begin, Chef Axelrod wanted to say a few words." She handed the microphone to her brother. Enthusiastic applause broke out, lasting until he raised a hand to quiet them.

As soon as the noise died down, Xander began his remarks. "I'll keep this short since I'm sure you're all eager to get started. Welcome to our first chocolate and wine pairing event. I'm hoping this will be the first of many such events here at Zephy's. Thank you all for coming. Naomi here, my sister and partner in this restaurant, will be your host tonight. She's going to do a bang-up job. I hope you all have fun."

He turned the microphone back over to Naomi and waved as he left the room to return to his duties in the kitchen.

An air of disappointment hung over the group for a moment. Naomi seemed to sense the change in mood. In a cheery voice, she said, "Chef will be back at the end of the tasting, but right now he needs to work his magic in the kitchen."

A string of waiters fanned out around the room, placing empty wine glasses in front of each participant along with rectangular plates containing pieces of chocolate. As the waiters distributed the plates and glasses and poured the wine, Naomi continued to talk. "Tonight we'll be tasting four chocolates and four fine wines. I'll be guiding you through the tasting process. I know you're all eager to get started, but please don't eat or drink until I tell you. You'll get more out of the experience that way."

Rory glanced at the plate a waiter set in front of her. Four pieces of chocolate stared at her temptingly from the plate.

"Hard to resist, isn't it?" Martin whispered to her.

"I know," she whispered back.

"While everything's getting set up, let's start with some fun facts about chocolate. These are things you can wow people with at your next party. First, did you know chocolate was very popular in Colonial America? Benjamin Franklin sold chocolate along with stationery supplies and bibles in his print shop in Philadelphia as early as 1739. And did you know that it takes four hundred cocoa beans to make one pound of chocolate? Each cacao tree produces approximately 2,500 beans."

"Where are all of the beans grown?" someone asked.

"Seventy percent comes from West Africa. The average size of those farms is seven to ten acres." Naomi continued to dispense tidbits while the staff finished distributing the squares of chocolate and pouring the wine. As soon as they had completed their task, she began the tasting.

"We'll be working our way from the chocolate with the least percentage of cocoa to the most. Let's start with the chocolate on the far left of your plate. It's a citrus-infused white chocolate. We're pairing it with a Sauvignon Blanc. Tasting is a sensory experience. Before you taste it, rub the chocolate gently to release its aroma. Now smell it. What does it smell like to you?"

They all rubbed their pieces of chocolate and sniffed.

"That's good. Now take a small bite and slowly let it melt on your tongue. What do you taste? You don't have to raise your hands. Just shout out what you think."

The tangy taste of lemon filled Rory's mouth as the chocolate melted. She and Martin spoke quietly to each other, comparing notes, while some of the others voiced their thoughts out loud.

"Now, pick up the glass of wine. Look at it first. Notice the color. Swirl your glass and take a sniff. Take another bite of the chocolate and a sip of the wine right after. Notice how they create a new flavor on your palate."

The group continued with the pairings, discussing each as they went. All during the last pairing of dark sea salt chocolate and Cabernet Sauvignon, Naomi periodically glanced at the door. When the tasting was over, she said to the group, "Chef should be here soon."

Raised voices sounded in the hallway. She looked nervously toward the entrance to the banquet room. "Let me go see what's keeping him."

The raised voices silenced as soon as she stepped out of the room. Naomi returned moments later, an uneasy expression appearing momentarily on her face, soon replaced with a bright smile. "I'm afraid Chef isn't available. He's needed in the kitchen. But he wanted me to thank you for coming once again and ask you to fill out the comment cards we left at each of your seats."

Another wave of disappointment swept over the group, but no one complained. Naomi stood at the entrance to the room and collected the cards as the couples exited.

Rory and Martin hung back, waiting until the room had emptied before handing in their cards.

"That was a lot of fun." Rory looked at Naomi with concern. "Is everything okay?"

"Everything's fine. We ran out of an ingredient so Xander had to change the menu. Minor issue. Happens all the time."

"One of the problems of running a restaurant, I suppose," Martin said.

"It's never a dull moment around here."

Rory sensed there was more to it than that. As they walked down the hallway toward the entrance, she wondered if whatever problems the restaurant had were the cause of Xander's recent change in attitude or if something else was going on he didn't want Solange to know about.

Chapter 3

The next afternoon, Rory entered the Akaw through automatic doors that whooshed open as she approached. Perched on a hill overlooking the ocean, the hotel was in the heart of downtown Vista Beach, only steps away from dozens of shops and restaurants. Between the tropical plants scattered around the lobby and the hotel staff dressed in Aloha shirts and Hawaiian print dresses, she felt as if she had been transported to Hawaii.

Her gaze swept the lobby lit by a combination of strategically placed skylights and overhead lighting, studying each of the faces she saw. Satisfied neither the bride nor groom were in the area, she texted Liz the coast was clear. Moments later, her friend entered the hotel carrying a bag containing her clothes for the evening in one hand and the sign Rory's mother had made in the other. Signatures and heartfelt wishes for the couple's future from customers of Arika's Scrap 'n Paint now covered half of it.

"What are you planning on doing with the sign?" Rory asked.

"I thought we'd ask at the front desk if they could stash it somewhere. We can tell the bridal party, on the hush-hush, to come out to the lobby and sign it."

"That sounds good."

The two went toward the front desk where a couple was checking in and another was waiting patiently for their turn. They were about to join the short line when a woman dressed in a Hawaiian print dress, with a name tag that indicated she was the hotel manager, came out from behind the desk and greeted them by name.

Nell Fremont walked the short distance toward them. "You're here for the makeup party, right? Let me check on the room number for you." She went back behind the counter, looked up the room number on a computer and wrote it down on a Post-it note. She came back around and handed it over. "Here you go."

"Is Solange here yet?" Liz asked.

"I thought I saw her go up, but honestly she's been in and out of the hotel a lot in the last few days. I could be mistaken."

"Maybe you can help us. We have this poster we want all of the wedding party to sign, but we don't want Solange or Xander to know anything about it." Liz held up the large piece of poster board. "Is there some place you can put this so we can send people to sign it tonight?"

"How fun. I think the best place for it is behind the front desk. I'll be here all night, making sure everything's running smoothly. You can send people to me and I'll bring them around. I have some Sharpies in the office they can use."

"Thanks so much."

"How's it going?" Rory glanced around her. Half a dozen guests occupied bamboo chairs scattered around the lobby while others hustled in and out of the hotel through the front entrance or the elevators to the underground parking. "The hotel seems busy."

"Everything's great. We're fully booked these days." Nell led them over to a quieter area. She lowered her voice, excitement in her eyes. "Don't tell anyone, but I might have a new job."

"Here at the Akaw?" Rory said, surprised. "You're already the manager. What else is there?"

"Not here. A big hotel chain." A sad expression flitted across Nell's face. "I'd have to move. I'll miss it here, but it's a great opportunity."

"Do you know when you'll be leaving?" Liz asked.

"No. It's not a done deal yet."

"Our fingers are crossed for you," Rory said.

"Let me know if you need a referral for a real estate agent where you're moving," Liz said. "I have contacts all over the country."

"I'll be sure to do that. I'll put your poster away. You can send people to me."

While Nell returned to the front desk, Rory and Liz made their way to the bank of elevators and up to the second floor where they found the door to their room propped open, voices coming from inside.

Rory knocked before they entered. Inside, they found Solange sitting on a couch next to a slender woman dressed in casual attire.

"It was awful. Just awful," the woman said.

Solange patted her hand.

"What was awful?" Rory asked.

Solange ran over to hug them. "I'm so glad you two are here. We were talking about the bank robbery at Vista Beach Savings while we waited for the rest of you to arrive."

"Oh?" Rory said. "Is there any news? Did they catch the robber?"

"No," Solange said. "But Paris here works there. She was the teller who received the note demanding money."

"You must have been scared," Rory said.

Paris looked up at them, doe eyes wide with remembered fear. "I was. It was the first time that it happened to me. I've been in the bank when other tellers have received...requests for money, but it's not the same when it happens to you."

"Have you talked to the police?"

"Right after it happened. I wish I could have been more help, but I was in a tizzy."

"Tell us about it," Solange said. "Maybe you'll remember something new."

"I should have realized something was going on. He seemed nervous. And he didn't say a thing when I greeted him," Paris said.

"Smart," Liz said. "That way no one can recognize his voice."

"The bank was pretty quiet. Only a couple people in line." She took a deep breath. "When he handed me the paper heart, I thought he was hitting on me, you know."

"Does that happen very often?" Liz asked.

Paris tossed her long hair. "On occasion. When I asked how I could help him, he pointed to the heart. On it was a demand for money. Then he put a bag on the counter and pointed to it. I froze for a second, then did what I'd been trained to do. I put the money in the bag. As soon as I was done, he grabbed it along with the heart and blew me a kiss. Then he walked out the door."

"Wow," they all said when she was finished, unsure how to respond.

"Where are my manners?" Solange said, breaking the awkward silence. "You can hang up your clothes in the closet and help yourself to a drink." She gestured to a table where cans of soda along with glasses and a bottle of red wine and one of white were laid out. An open box of heart-shaped chocolate truffles nestled in red wrappers sat next to the drinks. "Food should be here soon. I ordered some appetizers to hold us over until the party."

No sooner had they hung up their clothes than a tall woman with carefully applied makeup entered the room, wheeling a case behind her. "Hello," she said. "Sorry I'm late."

"You're right on time," Solange said. "Let me introduce you. This is Harmony Wells, the best makeup artist in the world. You should have seen what she came up with for her kids' school play."

Harmony blushed at the compliment. "I'll only be a moment setting up." She pulled various brushes, bottles and powders in a variety of shades out of the case and arranged them on a table. After everything was laid out to her satisfaction, she moved a chair into position and patted its seat. "Who's first?"

Solange indicated Paris should take the seat. "You go. You've had a tough week."

Paris sat down and faced the makeup artist who said, "Tough week, huh?" as she studied her face.

"She works at the bank that was robbed," Solange said.

Harmony gasped and her eyes opened wide. "That must have been terrifying. I'm glad I wasn't there. I don't know what I would have done. Let's not think about that now. It's all in the past. This is supposed to be fun. Here's what I'd like to do."

While the two discussed makeup, the others sat around, helping themselves to the drinks and chocolates, and made small talk while they waited for their turn in the chair. Solange periodically glanced at her phone.

"Anything wrong?" Rory said.

"Jade was supposed to be here by now. I think I'll go down to the lobby and check." She was walking across the room when Teresa Mut came in the door with a petite woman wearing a t-shirt, yoga pants and blinged out pale blue casual shoes.

"I found one of your bridesmaids in the lobby looking lost," Teresa said.

"Jade, there you are. I was getting worried about you," Solange said.

"So sorry, so sorry. You know me. I'm always forgetting things. I couldn't remember where you told me to go." Jade McIntyre threw a dress and impossibly high heels on the bed before standing on tiptoe and draping herself around the bride's neck.

Solange patted the other woman on the back, then gently pushed her away.

"So that's Jade," Liz said quietly so only Rory could hear. She stuck her hand out. "I'm Liz and this is Rory. Nice to meet you."

A vacant look on her face, Jade gave them each a limp handshake.

"This is my oldest friend, Jade. We've known each other since high school."

Liz studied the petite woman for a moment. "Have we met before? You seem familiar."

She gave a tinkly laugh. "I don't think so. People are always telling me I have one of those faces."

"Do you live here in Vista Beach?" Rory said. "Maybe you've seen each other around town."

The woman's gaze locked in on the box of chocolates on the table. "Ooh, truffles." She popped two in her mouth in quick succession, carelessly tossing the wrappers aside.

Solange gestured for her to replace Paris in the makeup chair. "Why don't you go next?"

After making sure everything was going smoothly, Teresa left the room, holding the door open for a room service waiter pushing a cart in front of her. Purple hair arranged in a bubble cut, she wore a waiter's uniform of black pants, white shirt and black vest.

Rory's mouth dropped open at the sight of the private investigator who had helped them out on a number of occasions. "Candy?"

Something in the woman's eyes told her not to say anything else. Rory shook her head slightly at Liz who had opened her mouth to speak. They silently watched Candy place the plates of appetizers next to the drinks. After pocketing the tip Solange gave her, the PI mouthed the word "later" to the two of them as she passed by.

They exchanged puzzled glances, then turned their attention back to the others.

After inviting them all to eat, Solange checked her phone, then closed the door to the room before addressing the group. "That's all of us. Unfortunately, Naomi won't be able to make it. Something came up."

"That's your beau's sister, right?" Jade said from her place at the makeup table. "I was looking forward to meeting her."

"Don't worry, you'll see her at the party." Solange handed each of them a piece of paper while Jade traded places with Liz. "Here's the schedule for the next couple weeks. After the party tonight, there's the Love Run tomorrow morning."

Jade frowned. "Seems early to get up after partying all night."

Solange's lips tightened. "I know it's early, but it's important to me that you're all there."

They assured her they'd show up at the race the next day and continued to study the paper.

"One last thing. Don't forget to pick up your bridesmaid dresses if you haven't already." Solange directed her attention to Jade. "Your dress is in. You need to go in for that fitting you missed."

"Did I? Sorry. Don't worry, I'll take care of it first thing next week."

Solange checked the time again. "All right. We'd better get going. Rory, why don't you go next."

"But you haven't had your makeup done yet."

Solange waved her hand. "It's fine. I'll get dressed and fix my hair first."

Moments later, Rory replaced Liz in the makeup chair. "How long have you been doing makeup?" she asked while Harmony studied her face.

"It's been an interest of mine for as long as I can remember, but I only started doing it for bridal parties about a year ago. You have a lovely complexion and great cheekbones. And those blue eyes of yours. You don't need much makeup at all." She continued talking as she worked. "Teresa's kids and my kids go to school together, so when Solange was looking for someone to do the makeup for the wedding Teresa suggested me."

Rory opened her mouth to say something else, but Harmony cut her off. "It's much better if you don't talk."

After that, Rory sat quietly and listened to the swirl of conversation around her. While the others got ready, they talked about painting the coasters on Sunday. When Jade complained she didn't know anything about painting, Solange told her in a resigned voice that she didn't need to come.

At the end of the makeup session, as she had for everyone else, Harmony handed Rory a card with a list of the makeup she'd used and the URL for her website where the products could be purchased.

Hair and makeup done, they'd all slipped into their party clothes when Teresa entered the room, a twinkle in her eyes, and handed Rory a long jewelry box. "For you."

The women clustered around her as she opened the box. Inside was a silver necklace with a charm in the shape of a painter's palette. Chips of brightly colored gems were arranged around it representing blobs of different colors of paint.

"It's beautiful." Rory looked at Teresa. "Did Martin give this to you?"

Teresa grinned. "He's waiting for you downstairs."

"Dashing D sure is pulling out all the stops," Liz said. "It goes perfectly with your dress."

Solange helped Rory put it on, then turned to Harmony who was packing up her supplies and invited her to join the party, saying she could leave her bag in the room and pick it up later.

They all went out the door and were almost at the elevator when Rory stopped in the middle of the hall and checked her clutch. "I forgot my phone in the room."

Solange dug around in her purse and produced a keycard. "Here, take this one. I got a couple extras. Thought they might come in handy."

"Thanks. I won't be long. You don't have to wait for me."

"I'll come with you," Liz said, then mouthed something that Rory couldn't quite make out.

"See you two down there." Solange waved her hand and the rest of the group continued toward the elevator.

Rory waited until they were inside the room and the door was closed behind them before saying anything. "What was that about?" she said as she grabbed her phone off the table where she'd left it. "Did you want to talk about something?"

"Candy."

"Oh, I see." Rory sank down on the bed. "That was odd, wasn't it?"

"Do you think she's working a case?"

"If she is, Nell would probably know."

"Maybe not. Candy could be undercover."

"Wouldn't Nell find it suspicious that a private investigator wants to work here?"

"Candy's smart. I'm sure she could come up with some excuse." Liz screwed up her face in thought. "She told me once she spent some time as a cater waiter. She has the skills the hotel needs. Maybe that was her in."

"I'd hate to think there's something wrong at the hotel. That wouldn't reflect well on Nell and might jeopardize her chances for that new job." Rory dropped her cell into her clutch along with the room key and stood up. "Let's get going."

When they exited the elevator, Rory spotted Jade in the far corner of the lobby talking to a man with streaks of gray in his hair. Anger radiated off him. When he lifted a hand as if to strike Jade, Rory looked around for someone in hotel security. Jade stepped closer to him and whispered something in his ear. He pushed her away and stomped out the front door. She turned around, a smug smile on her face that soon morphed into a vacant expression.

Rory had a bad feeling about the encounter. She wondered if Jade was the source of the uneasiness Teresa had mentioned the previous day.

Rory pushed the idea to the back of her mind and continued her survey of the area, her gaze sweeping from the entrance past the hotel manager who stood in the center of the lobby greeting guests to the far corner. "I thought Martin would be down here. I don't see him, do you?"

"He's probably in the little boy's room. Let's go talk to Nell."

As they passed by the entrance to the hotel's restaurant, The Perfect Wave, an older couple stopped to stare at a menu posted next to a statue of a surfer. Disappointment filled their faces as they turned away. Nell approached them, handing them a piece of paper. "Sorry for the inconvenience. Here's a list of nearby restaurants, all within walking distance. I'm sure you'll find something you'll enjoy."

Looking happier, the couple walked out the door into the streets of downtown Vista Beach.

"They looked disappointed," Rory said.

"Can't be helped. Your party's taking over the restaurant."

Rory glanced over at its entrance and, for the first time, noticed the sign on a pedestal that read *Closed for Private Party*. She stared at Nell in disbelief. "Xander's father booked the *entire* restaurant? I thought we had one of the hotel's banquet rooms."

"He preferred the restaurant. Said it was a more intimate environment. And he was willing to pay a considerable amount of money for exclusive use of it." Nell glanced over at the front desk. "I've got to go. Have fun at the party."

Moments later, Rory heard a low whistle followed by a deep voice saying, "Hello, gorgeous."

She turned to find Martin standing next to her dressed in a suit and tie.

"I see you got my present."

She fingered the necklace. "I love it. Thank you."

He kissed her on the cheek and cast an admiring look at the slim-fitting black dress and heels she was wearing, then waved a hand in greeting to Liz. "You look nice too."

"Thanks."

The three of them got in line at the restaurant. Solange, Xander and his father, Zeke Axelrod, stood at the entrance, greeting each of the guests in turn.

Zeke and his son exchanged puzzled looks when Jade stepped up to greet them. After a brief hello, her lips twitching in amusement, she walked into the restaurant.

Martin squeezed Rory's hand and they moved forward for their turn.

Chapter 4

By the time Rory, Martin and Liz entered the main body of the restaurant, lines had already formed at both the buffet and the hosted bar on opposite sides of the room from each other. An area near the front had been cleared of tables, replaced with a temporary dance floor. A DJ was setting up nearby while a photographer moved around the room taking pictures.

The three sat down at an empty table on the side of the room where two sets of sliding glass doors led to a heated patio.

"Can I get you two something to drink?" Martin asked.

They gave him their drink orders and he went to stand in line at the bar. Moments later, Candy came up to the table carrying a pitcher of water.

"Ladies." She filled their glasses before setting the pitcher in the center of the table.

Rory looked around to make sure no one was paying attention to them. "Hi, Candy. Are you...working?"

"I'm trying."

"We mean...you know, working working," Liz said in a quiet voice.

"Oh, I see." Candy lowered her own voice. "Can you two keep a secret?"

Eager expressions on their faces, Rory and Liz leaned forward.

"The PI business hasn't been that great recently, so Nell's giving me some work helping out at events. She's short-staffed and I can use the extra money. You know I used to be a cater waiter, right?"

"We heard," Rory said.

Disappointment washed over Liz's face. "We thought..."

"That something juicy was going on? Understandable. I'd better get back to it."

"Do you believe her?" Liz said once Candy was out of earshot.

Rory studied the woman who was delivering water to another table. "I don't know. I feel like there's something she's not telling us, but I'm not sure what."

"Saying business was slow could be her excuse for applying for a job here and a way for her to investigate what's going on at the hotel."

"If that's true, who's she working for?"

"*That* is a good question."

Before either of them could say anything else, Martin returned with their drinks. "Is that Candy waiting tables?"

"She's making some extra money working events here." Rory took a sip of the Pinot Grigio he'd gotten for her.

"Before I eat, I'm going to make sure the rest of the I Do Crew knows about the poster," Liz said.

Rory whispered to her, "Here's your chance to check out the groomsmen."

"Exactly what I was thinking." Liz grinned and headed to a nearby table.

Martin cocked an eyebrow. "Poster?"

While Rory told him about the sign her mother had made, Liz walked around the room, quietly telling each member of the wedding party where to go to sign it.

After she returned, they helped themselves to the buffet. While they ate, music played softly in the background, low enough not to interfere with any conversations. Throughout the evening, Rory noticed several of the bridesmaids and groomsmen leave the restaurant to go out into the lobby, returning a few minutes later.

They'd moved on to dessert when Teresa Mut tapped on the microphone the DJ had set up earlier in the evening. "Could I have your attention? We'll have a few remarks shortly and dancing soon after. Make sure you have a drink to toast with."

Rory told Martin and Liz she was going out to the patio to gather her thoughts for the toast she'd been asked to make. She stepped through

BRUSH UP ON MURDER   39

the sliding glass doors and looked around for a quiet spot to sit. Heat lamps warmed the area, but no one had ventured outside so she had her pick of tables. She chose one away from the entrance where a potted plant shielded her from the rest of the patio.

She'd rehearsed her short speech several times when she heard voices. Rory parted the leaves of the plant to see Xander and Jade standing close by, engaged in an earnest conversation. Although she couldn't hear what they were saying, she could tell from his posture and the look of anger on his face that the conversation wasn't a pleasant one.

Rory wasn't sure if she should say or do something to make them aware of her presence. Curiosity won out and she stayed where she was, as still as she could, to see how the conversation played out. She strained to hear what they were saying. Before long, words drifted over to her on the ocean breeze.

"I asked you what you're playing at." Xander's voice rose a notch.

"I don't know what you mean. I'm helping out an old friend."

Rory looked through the leaves again at the woman whose face appeared calm with a hint of amusement.

Xander snorted. "Old friend? You didn't know each other in high school. I'm sure of that. Only I can't figure out why you're both lying."

"What about you? What are you keeping from your bride?"

"I haven't lied to her."

"One of omission, perhaps." She stepped closer to him and touched his cheek in an intimate gesture. "What about us?"

Xander stepped back and his face filled with anger. "There is no us."

"Really? Are you sure?" Jade brushed up against him and walked into the main part of the restaurant, seemingly unconcerned about the heated conversation. He composed his face into a more pleasant expression and followed her inside.

Rory wondered if there was something going on between the two of them and if that's why his attitude toward Solange had changed in the last few weeks. She had a hard time believing it. He'd never struck her as the kind of man who would cheat. Both this conversation and the heated exchange Jade had with the man in the lobby made Rory uneasy.

The automatic doors near her whooshed open and Teresa and Liz walked onto the patio.

"There you are," Teresa said. "What are you doing out here?"

"Gathering my thoughts, trying to figure out what to say."

Liz gave Rory a questioning glance.

"Gather them quickly. We're about to start the speeches," Teresa said, leading the way into the main body of the restaurant.

Liz stopped short of going inside, placing a restraining hand on Rory's arm, and whispered so only Rory could hear. "What's going on? Was that Jade and Xander I saw going back into the restaurant?"

"It was. Their conversation was very...suggestive." Rory quietly related what she'd overheard.

"So they know each other? Do you think they're seeing each other behind Solange's back?" Liz's hands balled into tight fists. "The rat."

"Let's not jump to conclusions. We should give Xander the benefit of the doubt for now. She came onto him and he immediately rebuffed her. I think she's a troublemaker."

"Why do you say that?"

"I saw her in the lobby with another man right before we went into the restaurant. He did not look happy."

"Who's the man? Is he here?"

"He left the hotel right after talking to her. Seemed angry about something. I haven't seen him since."

Teresa Mut looked through the patio doors and gestured for them to follow her.

Rory focused her thoughts on her speech as they went inside.

Rory was still thinking about the previous evening's puzzling conversation when Liz picked her up in the golf cart fifteen minutes before the scheduled meeting time Saturday morning. The threatening skies from earlier in the week were gone and a cool breeze blew in off the ocean, perfect weather for the Love Run.

Liz's face brightened when she saw the long-sleeved t-shirt Rory was wearing. On its back was an ad for Liz's real estate services featuring her picture with her full name, Elizabeth Tamiko Dexter, below it. "Good. You're wearing the shirt I got you. Thanks for doing that."

"Happy to do it. It's a good way to advertise your services. Besides, it's a very nice shirt. I see you've got yours on too." Rory slipped her ID in the pocket of her sweats and checked to make sure she had what she needed for the race before taking her seat.

As soon as they were buckled in, Liz stepped on the gas, driving the cart as fast as it would go toward downtown and the starting line of the race.

Rory clutched the seat as Liz took a corner. "How close are we going to be able to park?"

"Pretty close. My office has a dedicated spot for the cart."

"I thought the streets were closed near there for the race."

"No one's on the course yet. Don't worry, we'll get through."

As they got closer to downtown, the streets became more crowded. Liz slowed down, maneuvering the golf cart around cars backing into parking spaces and pedestrians walking across the street without looking. When they got to the street where her office was located, they found wooden barricades blocking access to it.

"Now what? There's not enough room to get through the barricade," Rory said.

"Sure there is. Hang on." Ignoring the road closed signs, Liz drove the golf cart onto the sidewalk, around the barricade and onto the street beyond. A few minutes later, she slid into a parking spot next to Vista Beach Realty. "Easy peasy. I told you I had a way in." She consulted her watch. "We still have five minutes before we're supposed to meet. Plenty of time to get there. Do you have your race bib?"

The two of them affixed the bibs to the front of their t-shirts before joining the stream of people dressed in running gear or casual clothes, making their way down the hill toward the parking lot above the pier. Booths set up around the perimeter of the lot featured people selling athletic wear, health care professionals advertising their services and companies giving out samples of nutrition bars and energy drinks.

At the entrance to the lot, Liz stood on tiptoe and looked around. "Do you see them?"

Rory scanned the crowd gathered in front of the registration tent. "No."

They grabbed sample bottles of a sports drink as they made their way through the crowd toward the railing overlooking the ocean.

"I see someone." Rory pointed at the pier below them where Paris and two of the groomsmen stood in front of the love locks while Veronica took their photo. "Looks like we're not the first ones here."

When the group glanced up, Rory waved at them. They returned the wave and started up the hill. They'd barely reached the parking lot when Xander and Solange emerged from the registration tent, carrying numbered race bibs and an eco-friendly bag. Dressed in sweats and matching long-sleeved t-shirts with white caps that identified them as *Bride* and *Groom*, they hurried toward the group.

Solange raised a hand in greeting. "Thanks for coming out for this. I know it's awfully early."

"Martin's going to join us," Rory said. "I hope you don't mind."

"The more the merrier. But we don't have a cap for him. Those are only for the bridal party."

"No problem."

Solange started pulling light blue ball caps with *I Do Crew* written across the front out of a bag and distributing them to the group. "We're missing your sister, Xan." She checked the time on her phone. "She'd better get here soon if she wants to pick up her race bib in time for the start."

"Don't worry. She picked it up yesterday. Besides, they changed the order of events. The 10K is going first. The 5K doesn't start until eight thirty. She's got plenty of time."

"That's right. I forgot you told me. I should have changed the meeting time."

"Better early than late," he said.

"What about Jade?" Rory asked. "I don't see her anywhere."

"I gave her a cap last night. I don't expect to see her until right before the race starts."

"May I have your attention, please," a man said through a bullhorn. "The 10K will be starting soon. Be sure to pin your race bibs on securely. They need to be flat against your body for the timing strip to work properly. No crumpling them up."

Moments later, the countdown began, and the first participants started along the course.

After the crowd thinned out, Martin appeared at Rory's side. "Sorry I'm late."

"No worries. Our race hasn't started yet." A frown on his face, Xander looked around. "I wonder where Naomi is. I expected to see her by now."

The five-minute warning had sounded for the next race when his sister hurried over to them. Looking frazzled, she put the last pin in her bib, attaching it to her shirt. "Sorry," she said. "My alarm didn't go off. But I'm here now."

Solange handed her a cap.

"Get ready. The 5K participants will be starting in only a couple minutes," the man with the bullhorn said. "Remember, no baby joggers or dogs are allowed on the course for everyone's safety. And, if you're walking, please start near the back of the pack to allow the joggers to head out first."

The bridal party minus Jade grouped themselves near the back. As soon as the horn sounded, the crowd surged forward. Several minutes passed before the group made it across the start line.

"Don't worry," a man told his friend when he complained about the wait. "They don't start timing you until you cross the start line. That's what the timing strip in your bib is for."

Before long, the participants spread out, filling the width of the closed off street. The course took them up the hill and onto a street paralleling the ocean. They made their way through the business district, passing restaurants and shops closed at that early hour. People lined the streets, cheering the participants on. Someone dressed in a T. rex costume lumbered past, chasing a group of playfully screaming men and women. A young boy, about five years old, stood on the sidewalk next to his father holding a sign that read "You can do it,

Mommy!" He cheered when he spotted his mother in the crowd. Bolstered by the encouragement, she blew him a kiss and sped up.

Some people ran or walked fast, clearly concerned about their race time, while others, including the bridal party, took a more leisurely pace. When they passed Arika's Scrap 'n Paint, Rory waved at her parents who stood on the sidewalk in front of the store holding up the sign that congratulated Xander and Solange on their upcoming wedding. The bride and groom laughed in delight at the unexpected sight and ran over to Rory's parents, giving each of them a hug before returning to their party and continuing down the street.

"This is going too slow," Naomi complained. "I'm going to jog the course. See you at the finish line." She waved and took off, maneuvering around the walkers that filled the street. She was soon lost in the crowd.

"You can go ahead and run too, if you want," Solange said to the rest of the group. "We don't mind."

They opted to stay with the bride and groom until the couple stopped so often along the course to take photos with people they knew, they insisted the rest of the I Do Crew go on ahead. When the course turned a corner and continued into a residential area of the city, the number of onlookers dwindled to almost nothing. They made a loop back toward the start, returning on a more level path. Soon they could see the pier off in the distance, a banner proclaiming *Finish Line* fluttering in the breeze. The sound of cheering reached their ears. Moments later, Solange and Xander ran up and rejoined the group.

Four blocks from the finish line, Rory noticed a cap like the one she was wearing lying on the side of the road. It puzzled her for a moment. She hadn't seen another bridal party in the race. Then she remembered Naomi jogging ahead.

Figuring Xander's sister had lost the cap, Rory hurried over to pick it up. When she bent down, she caught a glimpse of a blinged-out pale blue shoe sticking out from a nearby alley. Worried that Naomi had collapsed, Rory abandoned the cap and ran over, followed by Martin and the rest of the group.

In the space between two buildings, she found a woman wearing a t-shirt and yoga pants sitting against the wall, her legs out in front of her.

Rory's gaze riveted on the knife sticking out of the woman's chest, affixing a red paper heart to her breast.

Chapter 5

The I Do Crew clustered together at the mouth of the alley to see what Rory had found. Gasps and exclamations of shock and surprise rippled through the group.

"Is that...?" someone said.

"It's Jade, all right," someone else replied.

Rory averted her gaze from the knife sticking out of Jade's chest, focusing instead on the ground and the alley beyond. Red bits of paper peeked out from under the woman's leg. A trail of twenty-dollar bills covered in red splotches led to a nearby trash can. The building on the right side housed half a dozen businesses, their names painted on the back doors that opened onto the alley, all currently closed. With a start, Rory realized Xander's restaurant was one of them.

Before she could notice anything else, Martin insisted they all move to the adjoining street. When Xander leaned over to pick up the hat that had led to the discovery, the detective said in a commanding voice, "Leave it."

Xander straightened up and joined the group that now stood off to one side. Martin took out his phone and dialed. Before long, two uniformed officers had joined them and secured the scene.

He studied the group and began his questioning. "Did anyone see Ms. McIntyre today?"

One by one they shook their heads.

"None of you? Not even a phone call or a text?"

"She said she'd meet us at the pier for the start of the race," Solange said. "But she never showed up. She must have been on the way when..." Her voice trailed off and her eyes filled with tears. Xander put a reassuring arm around her shoulder.

"What about the hat?" The detective pointed at the ground where the discarded hat still lay. "Did you have any extras?"

Solange wiped her eyes and cleared her throat. "It must be hers. I only had enough for the bridal party. I gave one to her last night before we left the hotel."

Martin made a note in his cell phone. "Was that the last time you saw her?"

"Yes. She was going up to the room to change out of her party clothes."

"This is a guest room at the Akaw?"

"That's right," Solange said.

"Do you know where she went after that?"

"I think she stayed in the room last night. It was available to anyone who felt they'd had too much to drink. From what I saw, she'd been partying pretty hard. I don't think she could have made it home on her own."

Martin looked at the others. "Did anyone else stay in the room?"

After they all said no, Rory said, "I left my clothes there when I changed for the party. So did some of the other bridesmaids. Jade wasn't in the room when Liz and I picked ours up right before we left the hotel."

"So no one can say for sure that she spent the entire night there?"

Rory cast her mind back to the makeup rehearsal the previous evening. "She's wearing the same clothes she had on when we were getting our makeup done," she finally said.

"You're sure?"

"Absolutely. There's something else. Right before the party, I saw Jade in the lobby arguing with a man."

"Did you recognize him?"

"No. Never saw him before."

He wrote the information down. "I'll look into it."

"None of us can tell you anything more," Xander said. "Can we finish the race? My dad is waiting for us at the pier. He's going to be worried if we don't get there soon."

"All of you except Xander and Solange can go now. I may have more questions for you later."

A scowl appeared on Xander's face. "But—"

"I won't keep you long."

The bridal party minus the bride and groom continued along the course, more subdued than they'd been at the beginning of the race. Rory and Liz brought up the rear.

"Can we stop?" Liz said. "I've lost all of my enthusiasm for this."

"Me too. I'd rather walk over to mom's store and tell her about the race."

They said goodbye to the rest of the group and started up the hill. Along the way, they picked up bits of wrappers and tissues people had dropped in their eagerness to get to the pier, depositing them in nearby trash cans. At the top, they met Teresa Mut and Harmony Wells on their way down, tote bags slung over their shoulders.

"Finished already?" The smile on Teresa's face faded. "What is it?"

"Something...happened." Rory took a deep breath. "We found Jade's body."

Teresa and Harmony gasped.

"You mean she's...dead?" Teresa said once she'd had the chance to take in the news.

Rory and Liz nodded.

"She seemed healthy last night. Did she have a heart condition or something?" Harmony scratched her wrist and tugged the sleeves of her sweatshirt down.

"She was stabbed," Rory said without thinking, immediately regretting revealing the information.

"Stabbed?" Teresa and Harmony said at the same time.

Harmony paled. "My kids are walking the race."

"So are mine," Teresa said.

"I'm sure it was an isolated incident." Rory hurried to reassure them even though she couldn't swear to the truth of the statement.

Harmony pulled at Teresa's arm. "Let's go. I want to make sure my kids are okay."

They hurried toward the pier, concern written all over their faces.

"I didn't mean to scare them."

"Don't worry. They'll be okay. Let's go see your mom."

Rory spotted a tissue with a piece of tape attached to it on the ground. She picked it up and stuffed it in the pocket of her sweats, intending to throw it in the trash later.

Rory and Liz made their way along an oddly empty Main Street, not yet open to traffic. All of the spectators that lined the street at the beginning of the race had either walked down to the finish line or gone home.

When they reached Arika's Scrap 'n Paint, they found the lights off and the front door locked.

Rory cupped her hands around her eyes and peered into the store. "I don't see anyone."

"It's only nine thirty. The store's not set to open for half an hour," Liz said. "Maybe your parents went out for coffee."

"Or my mom could be in her office. Let's go around back." Rory led the way toward the alley behind her mother's store.

As soon as they stepped inside the unlocked back door, Rory called out, "Mom, are you here?"

"I'm in the classroom," her mother's voice answered.

Rory and Liz walked into the adjoining room, sandwiched between the back area of the store and the sales floor, where they found Arika unpacking a box of unpainted heart-shaped wood pieces.

"Are those for the wedding favors?" Rory gestured toward the coasters stacked in piles of five.

"They are. I'm just making sure the order's complete." Arika glanced at her watch. "Are you done with the race already? I thought you'd spend more time down at the pier celebrating."

Rory and Liz sat down at the table.

"We didn't exactly finish," Rory said in a subdued tone.

Arika frowned. "Why?"

Between the two of them, they caught Rory's mother up on the discovery of Jade's body.

Arika sat down heavily on a chair across from them. "Murdered? Are you sure?"

"I don't see any other explanation," Rory said.

"Do the police know what happened?"

"Not yet. Martin was there when we found her. He's taking statements."

"I'm sure he'll figure it out," Arika said. "He's very capable. How is Solange doing? Jade was one of her bridesmaids, wasn't she? They must have been close."

"They'd known each other for a long time," Rory said. "I'm sure it's been quite a shock. I'm not sure she's had time to process it yet."

"She seems to be hanging in there," Liz said. "Xander's with her."

"That's good," Arika said. "Where are they now?"

"They were still talking to the police when we left," Rory said.

Before she could say anything else, they heard a knock on the front door.

"I'll see who that is." Arika left the room and returned moments later with Solange. Her face, which had been so happy that morning, now radiated sadness.

Rory leapt up from her chair and hugged her. "How are you doing?"

Solange stayed in the embrace for a moment longer than usual, then sank down on a nearby chair. She brushed a tear away from her eye. "I'm okay. But I don't understand how such a terrible thing could happen to someone I know. Doesn't seem real."

"How's Xander?" Liz asked.

"He's shocked. But he'd only recently met her so..." Her voice cracked as it trailed off.

Rory and Liz exchanged puzzled glances.

"Are you sure about that?" Rory asked.

"What do you mean?"

"I overheard a conversation between Xander and Jade at the party last night. I got the impression they knew each other."

Solange frowned. "I'm sure you misunderstood."

Rory thought back to the previous evening, trying to remember the details. "Maybe," she finally said, not totally convinced she'd misinterpreted what she'd heard.

"Have you told the police about it?"

"Not yet."

"Let me talk to Xan first. I'm sure it's all a big misunderstanding."

Rory didn't like keeping information from Martin, but she figured waiting a day or so wouldn't matter.

"I'll wait," she finally said.

Solange's shoulders relaxed. "I'm sure it's nothing."

"What did Martin ask you about after we left?"

"He wanted to know about next of kin. Unfortunately, I couldn't tell him much."

"But you've known each other a long time."

"We lost track for a while. It's a lot of years since college. Even then, I never really knew her family."

"I thought it was high school."

Solange closed her eyes for a moment. "Yes, I meant high school. This has all been such a shock." She turned to Arika. "I stopped by to make sure we can still borrow this room tomorrow afternoon for painting the favors. It's not an imposition, is it?"

"Not at all. I'm closed on Sunday. You'll have free use of the store. I was just counting the coasters now."

"You're moving forward with everything, then?" Liz asked.

"For now," Solange said. "I don't know what else to do. I think Jade would have wanted us to."

Arika was showing the bride-to-be the unpainted wood pieces for the painting project when another knock sounded on the front door.

Liz peeked around the doorway that led to the sales floor. "It's Veronica. She'll go away soon."

Arika checked her watch. "It's time for me to open. I'll be in the front if you need anything." She moved about the sales floor checking to make sure everything was ready before unlocking the door.

Moments later, Veronica burst into the classroom from the direction of the back room. "I knew you were in here."

"If you want to buy something, you should go through the front door, not the back," Rory said.

"I'm not here to shop. I'm here to talk."

"What do you want to talk about?" Rory said, a cautious note in her voice.

"The murder. What else?" Veronica shook her head in disbelief, her nose ring trembling with each movement. "You found the body, right?" An eager look on her face, she directed the question at Rory.

"I noticed her in the alley. We were all there. It's not like I go out of my way to look for bodies."

"I know, I know. Tell me what you saw." Veronica pulled a small notepad and pen out of the tote bag slung over her shoulder.

"Weren't you there?" Liz asked. "I saw you at the race taking pictures of Paris and some of the groomsmen."

"The police wouldn't let me near enough to see anything."

"I think you should get the information from them," Rory said.

Veronica turned her attention to Solange. "What about you? The victim was in your wedding party. What can you tell me about her?"

Solange pursed her lips. "No comment."

"Sounds like I'm not getting anything here." Veronica popped the pad and pen in her bag. "I'll go and find out about the bank robbery then."

Everyone's mouth gaped open in astonishment.

"There was another robbery?" Rory said.

"It happened during the race, right after the bank opened at nine. It's not far from the alley where the body was found."

"That would explain..." Rory clamped her mouth shut when she realized she'd said the words out loud.

"Explain what?" The eager expression returned to Veronica's face.

"Never mind. It's not important."

She continued to badger them with questions, but they all refused to answer. When she realized no one was going to say anything else, Veronica left through the back door.

"Do you think the two crimes are related?" Liz said after she heard the door close.

"There was some money and a paper heart at the scene. Maybe Jade ran into the robber when he fled."

"That's it, then," Solange said. "She was simply at the wrong place at the wrong time."

"Looks like it, but we'll have to see if the police agree." Even with the heart and the money found at the scene, Rory wondered if it could be that easy.

Chapter 6

A murmur of voices from the sales floor captured their attention. Rory and Liz poked their heads around the doorway and studied the scene in the front of the store.

"Seems busier than usual," Rory said.

"The race did bring a lot of people downtown," Liz replied.

When they heard a group of women clustered around Arika utter the bride-to-be's name, they quietly withdrew into the classroom.

"What is it?" Solange said.

"Looks like some people are asking about you. They must have heard about your connection to the murder."

"I don't want to talk to anyone right now. I can't."

"Hold on. I may have a solution." Rory looked out the back door into the alley, happy to see no one was lurking outside. She reported the news to the others. "Go out the back. No one's around to bother you."

Solange hastily stood up. "I'd better go before someone remembers there's another entrance. Could you pack up the coasters for me? And tell your mother I'll pick them up later today after things quiet down."

"No problem. Go." Rory gently pushed her toward the back door.

After they put the coasters in boxes, Rory walked onto the sales floor where her mother was finishing ringing up a customer. The group of women who'd been talking about Solange was nowhere in sight.

"Did Solange leave?" Arika asked. "A number of people were asking about her."

"We heard. She went out the back."

"That's good. They were too nosy for my taste."

"We packed up the coasters and left them on the table. Solange said she'd come and pick them up later. I think she wants to do some prep work before our painting session tomorrow."

"No problem." Arika glanced out the front window at the sidewalk where a small group had gathered. "You should probably go out the back too. They were asking about you as well."

Rory and Liz made their escape into the alley unobserved and walked toward Vista Beach Realty where they'd parked the golf cart.

"Do you think it's strange Solange couldn't tell us much about Jade?" Liz asked.

"Or maybe wouldn't."

"What are you getting at?"

"I have this feeling she's hiding something," Rory said.

"We don't know much about Jade. We don't even know where she lived."

"Martin will have that info from her driver's license. I'll ask him about it later. I'm not sure he'll tell me anything, but I can ask."

"Maybe we can find something out on the internet. We can use the computer in my office."

Rory knew she should probably leave the investigating to the professionals, but maybe they would discover something helpful. "Don't you have work to do? A showing or something?"

"I have an open house, but it's not until this afternoon. We have loads of time."

A short while later, they walked in the door of Vista Beach Realty to find a handful of people in the office picking up paperwork to take to clients.

By the time they sat down at Liz's desk, they had the place to themselves.

They started their search by typing Jade's first and last names into a browser window.

"She's tagged a lot on social media," Liz said as she scrolled through the results. "I think they're all weddings."

They looked at all of the posts that were public. Jade was a bridesmaid in every single one of them.

"They can't possibly all be her," Rory said.

"I don't know. I know some women who are serial bridesmaids with something like a dozen bridesmaid dresses in their closet. Took up so much room they ended up donating most of them to charity."

"Let's look at the photos again. See if they're really her."

They looked in more detail at each of the pictures. All of the women had a resemblance to each other and to Jade.

"That one's Jade for sure." Liz pointed to a photo on the screen of a formal shot of a wedding party. "But what about this one?"

Rory studied a candid of a different wedding in another window on the display. "Hair's a different color and style, but I think it's her."

"Holy smokes! I went to that wedding!" Liz slapped her hand on the desk. "That's why I thought she looked familiar."

"Why didn't you remember her name?"

"I didn't really know the couple. I went as a plus one. Doing a favor for a friend."

Rory looked at several other photos. "She sure is a chameleon. What about the other search results?"

Liz kept scrolling and came across a website with Jade's name in the URL. When she directed the browser at the site, a professional headshot popped up on the screen.

"She's an actress," Liz said. "That explains the different looks. She probably changed her hair for a role around the time of each of the weddings."

"That would explain it."

They looked through some of the other results but didn't find anything else of interest.

Rory sat back in her chair. "Are the Vista Beach High yearbooks online? Solange said they went to high school together. I assume that means they graduated the same year."

"I think so." Liz found the appropriate site and, after figuring out the year Solange graduated based on her age, they brought up the correct yearbook.

They quickly found her graduation photo, but not Jade's. Her name wasn't even in the appendix where all students were listed by grade.

"Maybe she changed her name for her job," Rory said. "Or got married at some point. I didn't notice a ring on her finger, but she could have gotten divorced and never changed back to her maiden name. Let's look at the rest of the yearbook. She might be in a different class. Could've been a sophomore or junior."

But even after searching each page, studying every single photo, they saw no one that even remotely resembled the woman they were looking for.

"Guess she didn't get her picture taken," Liz said after they'd finished their search.

"Unusual, but not unheard of. Maybe she dropped out to pursue acting or graduated early. Or she could be a year older."

They brought up the yearbook for the graduating class before Solange's, but didn't find Jade in it either.

Liz closed the browser window and swiveled her chair to face Rory. "What's next? I still have some time before I have to go home and change for the open house."

Rory steepled her fingers below her chin and stared at the desk, trying to figure out who else they might approach for information. She lifted her head. "Candy. I don't know why I didn't think of her sooner. We should see if she can help. She might have noticed something at the party Friday night. And we could ask her to look into Jade's background for us."

"Good idea, but I think we need to pay for her services this time. Sounds like she could use the work right now."

"That could get expensive."

"She doesn't have to spend too much time on it. We can pool our resources and hire her for a couple hours. We can afford that."

Rory indicated her agreement.

Liz locked up and the two of them headed to the PI's office located above a clothing store on a street that paralleled the ocean. When they reached their destination, they discovered the lights out and the office locked. They knocked several times and called Candy on her cell but didn't get an answer either way.

"That's disappointing," Rory said as they went back down the stairs.

"Maybe she's at the Akaw. She could be working an event there and not be able to answer her phone."

"It's worth a shot."

When they entered the hotel lobby a short time later, they spotted Nell talking to the concierge. A big smile on her face, she turned and faced them when they called her name.

"You seem happy," Rory said.

Liz looked around to make sure no one was within earshot, then said in a quiet voice, "Did you get that job?"

"I don't know yet, but I have a good feeling about it." Nell's gaze focused on the numbers still pinned to their chests. "I see you ran the 5K this morning. How was it?"

Surprised by the comment, Rory said, "Didn't you hear? I thought one of your guests would have told you by now. We found a body on the course."

Shock registered in Nell's eyes when she took in the news. "A body? I saw some police cars race by earlier, but I had no idea. That must have been awful. Who was it?"

"One of Solange Fournier's bridesmaids, Jade McIntyre. You must have seen her Friday night at the party."

Nell frowned as if trying to picture the woman in her mind. "I'm sorry. I don't remember her. Which one was she?"

Rory and Liz described the petite woman as best they could, then told Nell about how they found the body while walking the course that morning.

"And the police don't know who did it yet?"

"Not yet."

"I hope they find out soon. Thanks for telling me. At least now I know about it in case someone mentions it."

Raised voices at the front desk caused them all to direct their attention to a man on crutches and his companion complaining to a hotel employee.

"...not making it up, and I'm not mistaken," the man said. "It's missing."

Nell looked with concern at the scene before returning her attention to them. "Now, you must have come here for a reason. What can I do for you?"

"We're actually looking for Candy. We went by her office and tried her cell, but she's not answering either one. We thought maybe she's working an event here today."

"Not today. She's not answering her phone, you say? I wonder..."

"What is it?"

"They were both at the party last night. You don't think...well, that Ms. McIntyre's death and Candy being missing could be related? Maybe they both overheard or saw something they shouldn't have."

Rory and Liz exchanged horrified glances.

"I'm sorry. I didn't mean to worry you. My imagination's working overtime. I'm sure everything's okay." The hotel employee who was dealing with the complaining guest motioned to Nell. "Listen, I need to take care of this. Thanks for letting me know about what happened. Forget what I said about Candy. I'm sure she's fine." With a wave goodbye, she walked over to the front desk.

Rory sank down on a nearby bamboo chair. Liz took the seat next to her.

"Now I'm really worried," Rory said. "I think I'll call Martin and see if the police know anything. Maybe she had an accident or something."

"I'll try her cell again and leave a message."

When Rory dialed Martin's number, she half expected it to go immediately to voicemail, but instead his deep voice came on the line. "I only have a few minutes," he said. "Is everything okay?"

"I'm fine. I'm concerned about Candy. We can't find her. She's not at the office and isn't answering her cell. After earlier, we got worried. Have you heard anything?" Rory held her breath.

"Finally, a mystery I can solve. Don't worry. She's fine. She was here talking to us about what she saw at the party Friday night."

Rory felt her shoulders relax. "Thank goodness." She mouthed the words "she's okay" to Liz who responded with a thumbs up.

"She left the station a couple minutes ago. You'll probably hear from her soon."

Right on cue, Liz's phone rang, and Candy's name flashed on the display.

"I've got to get back to it," Martin said to Rory. "I'll talk to you later, okay?"

"Wait. Did she tell you anything useful?"

"I've really got to go."

As soon as Liz was off the phone, Rory said to her, "Did Candy tell the police anything new about Jade?"

"She didn't say. She was in a hurry. She did tell me she'd be in her office for the next hour if we wanted to stop by." Liz stood up. "You're going to have to handle it. I've got to change before the open house. Do you want me to take you home?"

"That's okay. I can walk. I'll go over to talk to her right now."

"Let me know what she says."

Rory retraced the now familiar route to Candy's office. This time, when she climbed the stairs, she saw a line of light beneath the door. She opened it to find herself in an empty outer office, large enough to hold a desk and two chairs for clients to sit in while waiting. A copier sat on a table next to the desk, filing cabinets behind it. At the back of the room was a door leading into an inner office.

Candy came through the doorway, a yellow Post-it note in her hand. "Rory. Liz told me you might be stopping by." She placed the Post-it in the middle of the receptionist's desk. "Let's go into my office and talk."

Candy sat down behind her desk and gestured for Rory to take the seat across from her. She glanced ruefully at the surface covered with file folders and papers. "Sorry about the mess. My receptionist has been out for a few days. She usually keeps the clutter down to a minimum." She cleared off an area in front of her and leaned her elbows on the desk. "Now, I understand you have some questions about the party on Friday. I take it you want to know what I told the police."

Rory only had time to nod confirmation before Candy continued. "I hear you know the woman who died. Jade. That was her name, right? Very sorry for your loss."

"That's the problem. I only met her yesterday and no one can tell me much about her."

"Not even the bride?"

"They'd lost touch for a while. Only recently reconnected."

"What did you want to know about the party on Friday?" Candy said.

"We were wondering if you heard anything that could tell us more about Jade or point to who killed her."

"And your interest is...?"

"Solange, the bride-to-be, is a good friend of mine. She's really upset. She's already stressed out enough with her work and the upcoming wedding. I want to do whatever I can to relieve that stress and get her some answers."

Candy cocked an eyebrow. "You don't trust the police? Seems odd given your involvement with that detective."

"It's not that..." Rory hesitated, unsure what to say.

Candy waved her hand. "Never mind. I can see it's a sensitive situation. I can respect that. I'll tell you what I told the police, which wasn't much. There were some, shall we say, interesting conversations, but nothing that pertains to this Jade."

"What about what you saw? Who was she with?"

"No one in particular, except..." She paused to glance at Rory. "I did see her on the patio with a man. The groom, I believe."

"But you didn't hear what they said?"

"It was too far away."

"Did you tell the police that?"

"I did."

Disappointment washed over Rory when she realized Candy didn't seem to know anything that would help.

"Is there anything else? I have to leave soon."

"We were wondering if you could look into Jade's background for us. We haven't been able to find out much on our own so far."

Candy leaned back in her chair and studied Rory for a moment before answering. "I'm sure the police are doing that."

"We'd pay you. We can afford a couple hours of your services."

"You know I don't like to get involved in murder investigations. I also have a full plate right now. But leave me the details and I'll think about it." She took a pad of paper out of a desk drawer and handed it to Rory along with a pen. "There is one thing I can do that might help you. I'll give you the names of all the waitstaff I worked with. They might have seen something. I'm sure the police have interviewed them already, but I'm not sure how cooperative they'll be. They're a tough bunch to crack."

Candy moved papers around on her desk until she came up with the one she wanted. "Be right back. I'll make a copy for you." She went into the outer office.

Rory picked up the pen, moving a stack of file folders to one side to give herself a flat surface to write on, inadvertently sweeping some of them onto the floor. She bent down and gathered up the loose papers that had scattered all over the carpet, looking at each piece, hoping something on it would help her put it back in the appropriate place. She placed a photo of a young man with the name *Laith* written on the back into the folder with *L. Hayward* on it, crossing her fingers that's where it belonged and not in the one labeled *Newark*. She hesitated when she came across a piece of paper with *Akaw* written across its top. Before she could take a closer look at it, she heard footsteps coming toward her. She shoved it into a folder with the hotel's name on it and replaced everything on the desk, then put pen to paper and hastily wrote down the little she knew about Jade.

Candy handed Rory a typed sheet of names. "Hope this helps."

Rory barely glanced at it before folding it and putting it in the pocket of her sweats. "Thanks. I appreciate it. I left Jade's info on your desk." She pointed to the pad of paper she'd put on top of a stack of folders, hoping Candy wouldn't notice things weren't exactly as she'd left them.

"I'll let you know if I find anything."

On the walk home, Rory thought about everything that had happened that day from the discovery of Jade's body to her recent conversation with the private investigator. Questions filled her mind. The only thing she knew for sure—even after all of their digging, Jade still remained a mystery.

Chapter 7

As soon as Rory got home, she changed, removing everything from the pockets of her sweats before tossing them into the laundry hamper. She dumped the litter she'd picked up off the street into a trash can and studied Candy's list before settling down at her desk with a sandwich to get a couple hours of work in. She was finishing a particularly tricky bit of code when Liz called.

Rory glanced at the time on her computer screen. Late afternoon already. The hours had flown by. "How'd the open house go?"

"Good. Got a fair amount of traffic and some interest. I might have picked up a new client too. We'll see if they follow through and contact me. What I really want to know about is Candy. What did she say?"

"That was pretty much a bust. She didn't overhear or see anything I didn't myself."

"Did you ask her about looking into Jade?"

"That was kind of odd," Rory said. "She told me she had a full plate right now but would get to it when she could."

"I thought she was starving for business. You told her we'd pay, right?"

"It didn't seem to make a difference."

"Maybe she got some new clients."

"I saw a couple folders on her desk. Maybe those are new cases. She gave me a list of all the waitstaff who worked the event with her. Come to think of it, that was strange too."

"What do you mean?"

"She had a typed copy of all the names right on her desk. And then there was a folder on the Akaw." Rory told her friend about what she'd seen.

"I knew it! She *is* on the job. She's looking into something at the hotel."

"We don't know that for sure. I hope everything's okay there. Otherwise it might jeopardize Nell getting that new job." Rory sat bolt upright. "Wait. Maybe that's it. Maybe her new employer hired Candy to see how she runs the hotel, make sure she's a good manager."

"That could be." Liz sounded disappointed at the prospect. "There's another possibility. Candy could have done some work for the Akaw before. That's why she had a file folder on the hotel and maybe why she decided to ask about a temporary job there."

"That's certainly possible."

They discussed the different scenarios before hanging up. Rory was straightening up her desk when she heard a knock on the door. She opened it to find a tired-looking Martin on the front doorstep. He'd changed from the casual clothes he'd worn that morning for the 5K into a suit and tie.

As soon as he was inside and the door was closed behind him, he enveloped her in a big hug.

"What was that for?" Rory said when they finally broke apart. "Not that it's not welcome."

"I needed it after the day I've had," he said as they sat down on the couch in the living room.

Sekhmet wandered into the room and jumped up beside Rory, walking across her legs to curl up on Martin's lap.

"Guess she likes you better," Rory said, amusement in her voice.

"I think she has a crush on me." He absently stroked the cat's fur as they talked.

"How's the investigation going? Or should I ask?"

"It's going. We're still gathering information."

"Did you find out any more about the guy in the lobby?"

"Not yet."

"The security cameras didn't help?"

"Not a good enough angle to get a picture of his face," he said. "Don't worry. We're on it."

"I hear there was another bank robbery this morning. Do you think the two crimes are related?"

He looked at her curiously. "What makes you say that?"

"I saw the heart." Rory shuddered as she visualized the knife sticking out of Jade's chest, skewering a red paper heart to her breast. "Doesn't the bank robber hand a paper heart to the teller?"

"You saw that." He paused as if considering how much to say. "This will all be in the paper soon. The robbery did happen not far away from where we found her and, as far as we know right now, around the same time she was killed."

"I saw some money too. Was that from the bank?"

"You were very observant. I shouldn't be surprised."

"You're not going to tell me anything else, are you?"

"I will say that we're looking into all angles, including that Jade saw the robber run down the alley."

"Wrong place, wrong time."

"Sometimes the solution is as simple as that."

"Are you hungry?" Rory asked. "I can make you a sandwich."

"That would be nice."

She went into the kitchen and came back a short while later with a turkey sandwich and a glass of water. Sekhmet perked up when the food arrived.

"Can I give her some?" Martin asked.

"Go ahead. But not too much."

He tore off a piece of turkey and gave it to the cat who happily ate the treat. After he finished, Martin put the empty plate on the coffee table. "Thanks. Didn't have a chance to eat lunch." He looked at her with concern. "How are you? The morning was more...eventful than you expected. Did you get hold of Candy?"

"She called. I'm glad she's okay. Silly of me to be worried."

"From what I hear, she's pretty careful, but she does snoop for a living so who knows what can happen."

"Have you heard anything about trouble at the Akaw?"

"No. Something I should know about?"

"No. I was wondering why Candy is working as a waiter there."

He raised an eyebrow. "You think she's on the job?"

"Maybe. She says her PI business is slow, but I'm not sure I'm buying that."

"I'll keep my ear to the ground." Martin pulled a notebook and pen out of his jacket pocket. "Speaking of the Akaw, I need to ask you some questions about the party on Friday."

Rory sat on the edge of the couch, her hands folded in her lap, and angled her body to face him. "What do you need to know?"

"I was with you most of the time, but I was wondering if you saw anything the few times we were apart. I seem to recall you went out on the patio for a while."

"What kind of things are you interested in?" she said, stalling while she decided if she should tell him about the puzzling conversation between the murdered woman and the groom.

"I'm most interested in where Jade was throughout the night. Did you see her out on the patio?"

"Yes," Rory said in a reluctant tone.

"And..."

"I saw her talking to Xander."

"Did you hear what they said?"

"Some of it." She recounted the conversation the best she could.

"Do you know anything about their relationship?"

"Nothing. I thought they'd only met last night, but that conversation suggested something else. I'm still not sure what to make of it."

Martin nodded and, after asking a few more questions, left to continue his investigation, promising to check in with her later.

As Rory closed the door behind him, she wondered if it was a mistake to tell him what she'd overheard. A part of her knew it was the right thing to do, but she still felt as if she'd betrayed her friends.

Chapter 8

After church the next morning, Liz came over to Rory's house to get some lock-picking practice in before their afternoon painting session. Rory placed a blindfold around Liz's eyes then sat down at the kitchen table across from her. Holding a locked padlock in one hand and lock-picking tools in the other, Liz mentally prepared herself for her first attempt to open the lock.

Rory pulled up the timer app on her cell phone. "Ready?"

"Hold on." Liz readjusted the blindfold. "Okay, now I'm ready."

"Ready. Set. Go." Rory hit the start button on the stopwatch and studied her friend's movements, mimicking them on an invisible padlock of her own.

Without warning, Sekhmet jumped onto the table and nudged Liz's hands.

"Time out," Liz said. She pulled off her blindfold and wagged a finger at the cat. "That's not fair. This is serious stuff."

"She's not supposed to be on the table." Rory picked up the cat and held her on her lap. "She's usually pretty good about it, but sometimes she can't resist. Stay right here while Liz practices, okay." She stroked the cat's fur. Before long, Sekhmet was fast asleep.

"Do you want to try again?" Rory said.

Liz replaced the blindfold and picked up the padlock along with the tension wrench and pick. "Ready."

As soon as Rory gave the word, Liz's hands got to work, and in no time, she had the lock open. After two more tries, she ripped off her blindfold, raised both arms in victory and declared the practice session over.

Rory wrote the last time on a notepad and pushed it across the table.

Liz studied the list of times and frowned. "I'm usually faster than this. I think I've lost my lock-picking mojo."

"Why are you practicing blindfolded? You can keep your eyes open when you're relocating the love locks on the pier."

"It helps me focus. I'm trying to improve my sense of touch. It's important in picking locks." Liz returned her tools to their case and stuffed it into her purse. "You should come along."

"I won't be much help. I don't know anything about picking locks. That's your department."

"You don't have to pick them. You can help transport them to their new location and put them on the structure."

"That I can do. Count me in."

The two discussed the date and time and Rory entered the information into her calendar. Then they headed downtown to join the others at Arika's Scrap 'n Paint where they planned on painting the sixty heart-shaped coasters the bride and groom would give out to their guests. When they arrived, Solange, Teresa and Arika were already in the classroom arranging the paint, brushes and other supplies they needed for the project.

"Sorry we're late," Rory said. "We got caught up in something."

"You're not late," Solange said. "We all got here early."

Rory looked around the assembled party. "Is anyone else coming? I thought Naomi and Paris would be here."

"They're not painters, so I told them they didn't have to come." Solange gestured toward the coasters spread out on the table, each of them covered with pale blue paint. "Couldn't sleep last night, so I sealed and basecoated all of them. I stenciled *Love* on about half of them before I ran out of steam."

"Thinking about yesterday?" Rory cast a sympathetic glance in her direction.

"Jade. The wedding. It all feels so surreal. Then there's Xander's mother's death a few months ago. I'm beginning to wonder if our relationship is cursed."

"Don't say that," Rory said. "It's only a bump in the road. You've had no control over anything that's happened."

"There's something I need to say before we begin. I'm canceling the shower and spa day. Doesn't seem right to have them. I'll send out an email to everyone later today."

"Whatever you think is best."

"Is the wedding still on?" Liz asked.

"Yes. We decided Jade would want that to continue."

Rory studied the picture of the finished coaster that was on the table. Besides stenciling the rest of the wood pieces, they had a design of roses and leaves to put on.

"I thought about those step-by-step photos you need for the article on the coasters for *BrushToBrush*." Liz took a piece of paper out of her purse and handed it to Solange. "Here's the list of photos I thought we should take for it."

Solange looked over the list, running her finger down the page as she read. "Looks good to me. Who's taking the pictures?"

"Would you like me to do it?" Arika asked. "That way you can all concentrate on finishing the coasters."

"I wouldn't want to put you out."

"It's no problem." Arika looked at her watch. "I don't have to be anywhere for a couple hours. You have me until then."

"Thank you. Here, use my phone." Solange handed over her cell. "Okay, let's get to it."

Liz went over the list of shots with Rory's mother who worked on stenciling until she was needed to take a photo of the next stage in the project. The others concentrated on painting the flowers, placing finished coasters on the other table in the room to dry.

"Harmony did a good job on our makeup the other night," Rory said to Teresa who was sitting in the chair beside her. "She said your kids go to school together. Is that how you met?"

"It is. She's a really nice person. Makes me sad what she's going through right now."

"What do you mean?"

"Her oldest is very sick. It's been hard on the family. I've encouraged her to develop her makeup business. It helps keep her mind off things. If you like the products she used, consider getting them from her instead of another source. You'll be helping her out."

Rory made a mental note to place her order soon.

They'd been working for an hour with little conversation when Solange placed a coaster to one side and set down her paintbrush. She rubbed her temples. "All I can think about is poor Jade. Hard to believe that something like that could happen in Vista Beach."

"Especially to someone you knew," Rory's mother said. "If you're not up to helping with the ad photo shoot tomorrow, I understand."

Solange lifted her chin. "Don't worry, I'll be there. I always honor my commitments."

"I appreciate that." Arika stood up. "Let's take a break. I have tea and coffee in the back. I might even be able to rustle up some cookies."

"No need. I brought snacks," a male voice said from the direction of the back room.

Solange's face broke out in a smile. "Xan! What are you doing here?"

"I thought you all might want something to eat. I brought petit fours and macarons. I was stress baking."

They cleared space on one end of the table for the boxes of goodies. Soon they all had tea or coffee and were settling down to eat.

Teresa had finished her third macaron when she received a text. "I'm afraid I have to leave for a while. I'll be back as soon as I can."

"Everything okay?" Arika asked.

"Minor emergency. Trent can't find something one of the kids needs to finish her homework so Mommy to the rescue." She rolled her eyes. "He's probably staring right at it."

Arika consulted the list of photos. "The pictures are all done so I'm off too. Unless you need me for something else?"

"Go. You've done enough already," Solange said.

"You can leave the coasters on the table to dry overnight. I'll pack them up tomorrow and keep them until you're ready to pick them up. No hurry."

"Don't you need the room for a class?"

"Not until Tuesday." Arika turned to Rory. "You've got the key?"

"Don't worry. I'll lock up after we're done."

"Have fun," Arika said as she left.

They were about to go back to work when a knock sounded on the front door. Rory let Martin in, locking the door behind him. "You must have a sixth sense for food. Xander brought over a bunch of goodies."

"Nothing so exciting. One of his employees said he was coming over here. Is he still here? I need to speak with him."

Her pleasure at seeing him faded when she took in the serious expression on his face. "Is everything okay?"

"I need to speak with him. Could you get him for me?"

"Sure." She went into the classroom and returned moments later with the chef and his fiancée. Rory hovered in the background, straightening a shelf that didn't really need straightening, listening in on the conversation as she worked.

The detective frowned when he saw Solange. "I'd like to speak with Mr. Axelrod alone, please."

"Whatever you have to say to me you can say in front of Solange. I have nothing to hide from her."

"Very well." The detective produced a knife from an evidence bag and showed it to him. "Do you recognize this?"

Xander stared at it for a moment. "It looks like one of the knives we use at the restaurant. Where did you find it?"

"Would it surprise you to learn it has your fingerprints on it?"

"Not really, if it's from the restaurant. Wait. Is this the knife that...Jade?"

"It is. Any thoughts on those fingerprints now?"

Rory gasped and almost dropped the bottle of varnish she was holding. Martin frowned at her. She waved the bottle in the air and went toward the classroom, stopping near the doorway in a spot where she thought she was out of the detective's sight, but close enough she could still hear the rest of the conversation.

"I didn't kill her if that's what you mean. I couldn't have. I was with Solange all night and morning including at the race. There are lots of witnesses."

"Is that true?" Martin looked at Solange who nodded her head in confirmation. "You're sure?"

"Yes. There's no way he could do that."

"So how do you explain the knife, then?"

"Can I see it again?" Xander examined it in more detail. "This is the one I threw out."

"Knives are expensive. Why would you get rid of it?"

"I had a...meltdown at the restaurant the other day. I was frustrated. I ended up throwing it out in the garbage can in the alley." He held up both hands. "I know, I know, not the best way to dispose of it. Whoever killed Jade must have found it there and used it."

"Can anyone verify your story?"

"My kitchen staff."

"I'll check with them, then. How well did you know Ms. McIntyre?"

"Not at all. We only recently met."

"Really? Someone overheard a conversation you had with her that seemed to indicate you knew each other before the party."

"I don't know what they overheard, but they were mistaken."

Another frown from Martin. Rory returned to the classroom and, without a word, resumed her painting task. Liz sent her friend a questioning glance. Rory indicated she'd tell her what was going on later.

They bent over their tasks, placing completed coasters on the other table to be varnished after the paint fully dried. A short time later, the bell over the front door tinkled and Solange returned to the classroom, looking worried.

"Everything okay?" Rory asked. "I'm sorry about telling Martin about the conversation, but he already knew about it. I didn't feel I could lie."

"It's okay. I understand." Solange examined the completed pieces, avoiding their gaze. "Now, where are we?"

Rory cast an occasional glance toward the sales floor, expecting any minute for Xander to appear in the doorway. After she felt enough time had passed, she finally said to Solange, "Where's Xander?"

Without looking up, she said, "He had to leave."

Rory waited for her to elaborate, but Solange simply pursed her lips and kept her attention on the piece she was painting. They continued working in silence and, before long, all the coasters were finished.

"Do you want help varnishing these?" Rory's gaze swept over the coasters spread over the table. "I'm available later this week if you need me."

"I'd be happy to help too," Liz chimed in. "With the three of us working on them, it won't take long. How many coats did you want to put on?"

"I don't know." A defeated look in her eyes, Solange slumped down in her chair and stared down at the table. "I'm worried. The police are looking at Xan as a suspect. All because of his temper and that stupid knife."

"He has an explanation for that," Rory said.

"There's something else."

"What is it?"

Solange took a deep breath. "Jade didn't go to high school with me," she said in a rush. "I didn't even know her. We only met a couple weeks ago. I hired her to be a bridesmaid."

Rory raised an eyebrow. "You hired her? I didn't know that was a thing."

"It's not that unusual," Solange said defensively. "There's a company downtown, I Do For You, that hires out bridesmaids and groomsmen."

"Why did you hire her?" Liz asked.

"I needed someone to round out the numbers. Xan has a lot of friends he wanted as groomsmen, and I didn't want to disappoint him. When one of my friends dropped out because of a death in her family and I couldn't find anyone to replace her, I didn't know what to do until I saw the ad in the newspaper. It's not cheap. Xan has been concerned about how much money we're spending on the wedding so I paid for it out of my personal account and decided not to tell him."

"I'm sure he would have understood," Liz said.

"I know, I know. I should have told him."

"You need to tell Martin the truth about Jade. It could have something to do with her death," Rory said.

"Can you tell him for me?"

"It would be better coming from you. What about the conversation I overheard? Did you ask Xander about it?"

"He insists he doesn't know her. A friend of his warned him about her. That she was bad business, that she was a flirt and liked to shake things up. Apparently, she'd tried to break up a number of relationships. He admitted she came onto him, but he immediately pushed her away. He didn't tell me because he didn't want to upset me."

That matched what she'd seen, but Rory couldn't help thinking there was more to it than that. "You believe him?"

A hint of uncertainty shown in her eyes. "He wouldn't lie to me."

"Is there anything else we can do to help?" Rory said gently. "You know you can ask us to do anything."

Solange stared at them for a moment before seeming to come to a decision. "I'd like you to look into Jade's death for me. After that knife turning up where it did, I'm worried the police will be so focused on Xan they won't look at anyone else and the real murderer is going to get away with it. I know Jade and I weren't friends, but I still want to see her get justice."

"You need to give the police more credit. There's other evidence that seems to indicate she was stabbed by the bank robber," Rory said.

"I've been thinking about that. Would the robber leave the heart behind? He never has before. And use it in a way that brought attention to him?"

Rory considered the question. "He has been very careful to take it with him."

"There's something else," Solange said. "Xan got into some trouble a while back. A bar fight. He's been working on getting his temper under control since then, but I'm not sure the police will believe that."

"Maybe they don't know about it."

"They know, all right. He was arrested, but the charges were later dropped. It's bound to be a mark against him," Solange said. "I don't know. I feel like there's something he isn't telling me."

"We've actually been looking into Jade but haven't found much. That was before we knew she was a bridesmaid-for-hire," Rory said.

Solange looked at them with pleading eyes. "Please try again."

Rory looked a question at Liz who indicated her agreement. "We'll see what we can do. But whatever we find out, I'm taking to the police. Good or bad. Okay?"

"That seems fair."

"Do you remember anything about her that might help? Something she mentioned in passing?"

"Not that I can think of. We didn't spend that much time together. Truth be told, I learned pretty fast not to give her anything important to do. She was very forgetful. Didn't even show up to her dress fitting."

"Did you complain about her?"

"No. I'd just have to start over with someone new and I'd be the bride that two bridesmaids quit on."

"There was a man in the lobby I saw her with before the party. Do you know who that could be?"

"No idea. I didn't see him."

"That's all I can think of to ask. We'll let you know if we find out anything."

A look of relief on her face, Solange walked out the front door.

Rory locked the door behind her and returned to the classroom where Liz was busy writing on a blank sheet of paper.

"What are you doing?"

"Writing down everything we know about Jade so far. We've got to do our ABCs."

"ABCs?" Rory wondered what the alphabet had to do with murder.

"Assume nothing. Believe nothing. Check everything. The ABCs."

"Where did you hear that?"

"I've been watching episodes of *Midsomer Murders*. Research. It's a good show. You should watch it." Liz frowned at the paper. "I'm not sure what else to put down."

Rory slipped into the seat across the table. "What have you got?"

"We know she was an actress and, now, a bridesmaid-for-hire. And that she stayed at the Akaw the night before she was killed." Liz pointed to each item on the list as she talked. "We also know she didn't go to school with Solange. We don't even know if they're the same age."

"That explains why we couldn't find her in the yearbook."

"That's all I have so far on Jade."

"What about suspects? There's Xander. The police seem to be focused on him."

"The murder weapon was his knife, and he went to medical school."

Rory cocked her head. "Do you think that matters? The school part."

Liz shrugged. "I don't know. Maybe she was stabbed in a place that would be hard for anybody other than someone with medical training to find."

"There's also the robber. Jade could have seen him come down the alley."

Liz added "unknown robber" to the suspect list. "And there's the guy you saw her with in the lobby."

Rory stared at the piece of paper. "That's a pretty short list."

"I know. We know so little about Jade. There could be a lot of other people she ticked off."

They were discussing next steps when Teresa returned. She looked surprised when she saw only the two of them in the classroom. "Where'd everybody go? Did you already finish?"

"All done," Rory said. "Teresa, you know all about the wedding plans, right?"

"I'd better. I wouldn't be a very good wedding planner if I didn't know every detail."

"Did you know Jade was a bridesmaid-for-hire?" Liz said.

Teresa sat down at the table and took in the information. "No, but I should have. They didn't seem to know each other well. I chalked that up to not having seen each other in years."

"What do you know about I Do For You?"

"Is that the company Solange used? They have a good reputation. I haven't used them myself, but I haven't heard any complaints about them. They're pretty close-mouthed about the people who work for them."

"Are bridesmaids-for-hire common?"

"They're not uncommon, but I wouldn't say they're the norm either. If you don't need me, I'll be off." Teresa left through the back door.

Liz stared at her notes once again. "It's not much, is it?"

"Our best bet is this company Jade worked for. We should see what they know about her," Rory said. "I can make an appointment to pitch my website services to them. See what I can find out."

"From what Teresa said, they probably won't tell you much." An excited look came over Liz's face. "I know. We could say you're getting married and need a bridesmaid to round out the numbers."

"Whoa. Why do I have to be the bride? What if Martin gets wind of it? What will he think?"

Liz made a tsking sound. "He won't, but if you're worried, we'll say I'm the bride and you're my maid of honor."

Rory thought it over. "That could work." She brought up the company's website on her phone. "They're not open now, but I'll leave a message asking for an appointment as soon as possible."

After Rory made the call, Liz said, "What do we do now? We can't do anything until they call you back."

"Let's do a little research on the company. That way we'll be prepared for the appointment when we get one. I'll look online. You went to a wedding where Jade was a bridesmaid, right? Can you call your friend and see what he knows?"

"On it."

Rory checked out I Do For You online, reading reviews of the company, all positive, as well as others in the same business. She was surprised to discover how many people used their services.

A few phone calls later, Liz had some answers. "She was a bridesmaid-for-hire at the wedding I went to too. Always polite, always on time, never forgot a thing."

"Doesn't sound like the Jade we saw or that Solange described. I wonder what was so different about this wedding."

"Maybe she was intentionally screwing up for some reason. Hopefully, we'll find out more at our appointment." Liz looked at her watch. "What do you want to do now? We've got the rest of the evening unless you have plans."

"I'm free. Martin's working late. The first forty-eight hours are critical in a murder investigation."

"So I've heard."

"We have that list of waitstaff Candy gave me. There's no contact info, only names, but it could still be helpful. We could go to the Akaw and see if any of them are working today."

Liz bobbed her head in agreement. "Let's have an early dinner at the restaurant. One of them might be there. Where's the list now? Do you have it with you?"

"I left it at home."

Liz stood up. "Let's go and get it."

Chapter 9

Rory held the menu in front of her face, occasionally peeking over it at the waitstaff circulating around the sparsely populated restaurant. She sent out a silent plea for them to pass close enough she'd be able to read their name tags, but the universe wasn't cooperating.

"Do you recognize any of the waiters?" she said to Liz who was sitting across the table from her, studying her own menu.

"I'm not sure. How about I make a circuit of the room? I can pretend to be looking at the pictures on the walls. I should be able to read some of the name tags." Liz laid her menu on the table.

"Wait until after we order. Maybe we'll get lucky with our waiter."

Moments later, a twenty-something woman approached their table, a pleasant expression on her face. Rory noted the name on her tag.

"Welcome to The Perfect Wave. What can I get you to drink?" The waiter wrote down their order, giving them a curious look before she left.

Rory brought out the typed list of waitstaff Candy had given her and looked at the names. "We don't have a last name, but this must be our server." She pointed to a line on the list.

"Sunny is an unusual enough name," Liz said. "I bet it's the same person."

The waiter returned with their drinks a short time later. After taking their food order, she said to Rory, "Were you one of the bridesmaids at the party Friday night?"

Rory feigned surprise. "We both were."

"I thought I recognized you."

"You were working the party, right? I had a feeling I'd seen you before too, but I couldn't remember where."

A dreamy look came into Sunny's eyes. "You're so lucky to know Chef Axelrod. He's so handsome, and a whiz in the kitchen too."

"Have you eaten at his restaurant?"

"Not yet, but my dad said he'd take me there on my birthday." She looked over at a customer who was beckoning to her from a nearby table. "Excuse me. I'll put this order in for you."

"We didn't even get a chance to ask her about the party," Liz grumbled after she left.

"Don't worry. She'll be back. We can talk to her then."

After their orders were delivered and they'd had a chance to sample their salads, Sunny returned. "How's everything?"

They both gave her a thumbs up.

She squatted down next to the table, her fingers resting lightly on its edge to steady herself. In a subdued tone, she said, "Is it true one of the bridesmaids died?"

Rory swallowed and dabbed her mouth with a napkin. "That's right."

"You know the body that was found at the Love Run?" Liz said.

Sunny gripped the table tighter. "*That* was her? Which one was she?"

After they described Jade, she said, "I remember her. She was...busy."

"What do you mean?" Rory asked.

Sunny looked around as if to make sure no one was listening. "She was making the rounds of a lot of the men, especially the nicely dressed ones."

"Oh?" Rory said. "Anyone in particular?"

"There was this one guy. On the older side. She was talking to him on the patio. They looked like they were having a serious conversation."

"Did you hear any of it?" Liz asked.

"No. Maybe one of the other servers did."

"Are any of them working today?" Rory said.

"Not in the restaurant, at least not right now. They might be working an event." She stood up. "Sorry about your friend. Enjoy your meal."

Rory and Liz dug into their food and speculated about who the older man could have been.

"It depends on what she considers older." Liz popped a piece of broccoli in her mouth and chewed thoughtfully. "She looks young. Probably still in college."

"It wasn't Xander. She'd have recognized him."

"She does seem to have a crush on him. Maybe it was the man from the lobby. Too bad we don't have a picture of him." Liz pushed her empty plate to one side.

"She's only one of the waiters on our list. Let's see if we can find any of the others. They might know more."

"How are we going to do that? Nell?"

"I don't want to bother her again. I'm sure she has a lot on her mind." Rory thought back to the other times she'd been in the hotel. "The kitchen. That's where we need to go. I'm pretty sure there's a way into the area from the loading dock."

They quickly paid their bill and left. Instead of leaving the hotel through the front door, they went down a hallway lined with ballrooms and exited through a side door. Rory led the way past the dumpsters around the corner to the loading dock entrance. She stopped when she saw a man dressed in a waiter's uniform, leaning against the wall, smoking.

He stared at them curiously. "You two lost?"

Rory glanced at his name tag and took a step forward. "Actually, we were hoping to talk to you."

"Why?"

"You were working the party at the restaurant Friday night, right?"

He took a drag on his cigarette and blew smoke in her direction.

Rory coughed and took a step to one side. "We were wondering if you saw anything unusual that night."

"Unusual?" He cocked his head, a puzzled look on his face, then his expression turned angry. He dropped the cigarette, putting it out with his heel, using more pressure than necessary. "Do you two work for her?"

"Her?" Rory and Liz said at the same time, confused by his reaction.

"Candy." He practically spit out the name.

"Why would we be working for her? Doesn't she work here?"

"You really don't know?"

"Know what?" Rory said.

"We—the rest of the staff and me—are pretty sure she's lying about why she's here. We think she's investigating us."

"Why do you say that?"

"She's been real nosy ever since she got hired. Asking all sorts of questions. Poking her head in places she shouldn't be."

"Maybe she's a naturally curious person," Rory said.

"Or she wants to change careers and get into the hospitality business," Liz added. "She might want to see how everything runs."

"Maybe. But you know she's a PI, right? She says she's fallen on hard times, but I'm not buying it. She gets special treatment. Even some gifts. And she's had a number of meetings with the hotel manager. Too many. They don't think we see them—"

"Sebastian!" a sharp voice said from the direction of the loading dock entrance.

They all turned to see Nell standing nearby, her arms crossed in front of her chest, a stern look on her face. "Break's over. I hope you weren't smoking. You know it's not allowed."

Head bent down, he mumbled something, brushed past the hotel manager and hurried inside.

The stern expression on Nell's face deepened. "You two. Come with me."

They meekly followed her to her office near the front desk. Neat and tidy, it was bare bones and functional, devoid of personal items except for a single framed photo on the desk. In it, a younger Nell stood beside three other people, all smiling into the camera.

Closing the door behind them, Nell sat down behind her desk and indicated they should take the seats across from her.

"What a great family photo," Liz said. "Is that your brother?"

Rory doubted the attempt at distraction would work, but she mentally applauded Liz for the effort.

Nell put the photo in a drawer before Rory could get a good look at it. She folded her hands and placed them on her desk. "You've been questioning my staff."

"We just want to find out more about Jade and what she was doing in the hours before she died," Rory said.

"Why didn't you come to me?"

"We didn't want to bother you," Liz said.

Nell sat back in her chair. "I can't have you questioning people. It's disrupting my hotel."

"We're sorry," Rory said.

"What did Sebastian tell you?"

"He said Candy had been asking a lot of questions. That you've been giving her gifts and meeting with her on a regular basis. She's not working here because her business is slow, is she?"

"I knew I should've hired someone else. I don't know why I thought it would work. The whole town knows she's a PI. Any time I had info to give her I put it in a box. Didn't consider that someone would think it a gift. I tried to keep the meetings to a minimum. I really didn't think anyone would notice." Nell stared down at her desk for a moment, then seemed to come to a decision. "There's something going on in this hotel. I hired Candy to find out what she could. I'll have to let her go now."

"We didn't mean to get her fired," Liz said.

"I was already thinking about it. She hasn't found out anything useful. And now the staff are talking about her. She's lost her effectiveness."

"Do you have any idea what's going on?"

"I don't want to say."

"Drugs?"

"Heavens, no. That's all I need right now. I've said too much." Nell stood up. "I'd appreciate it if you wouldn't mention this to anyone, especially the police. If any of this comes out, I could lose this job and any hopes of a new one."

They quietly left the office, not speaking until they were in front of the elevator leading to the underground parking.

"At least we know for sure Candy was on the job," Liz said.

While they waited for the elevator, Rory wondered what was going on at the hotel and if somehow Jade could have found out something that led to her death. An idea formed in her mind. She pulled a hotel keycard out of the pocket of her jeans and held it up. "Do you have time for a side trip?"

Liz's eyes lit up. "Is that what I think it is?"

"Yep. Keycard to the hotel room from Friday night. I was cleaning out the clutch I used and found it. I was going to return it to the hotel today. Kind of glad I forgot."

"Do you think it still works?"

"There's only one way to find out."

Instead of going down to parking, they took an elevator up to the guest floors. Rory was relieved to find the hallway deserted. When they got to the room they'd used Friday, they found a door that looked like all of the others, except for a tiny scrap of yellow crime scene tape that still hung off its frame. They stood uncertainly in front of the room.

"No more crime scene tape," Liz said. "Looks like the police are done with it."

"That's good. We won't be screwing up their investigation." Rory knocked and pressed her ear against the door, listening for any sound of movement inside. "I don't hear anything. Here goes." She inserted the card and a green light appeared. Surprised the card still worked, she turned the handle and they slipped inside.

They quickly got to work. Liz took the bathroom while Rory searched the bed area, looking through every nook and cranny for anything the police might have missed. She found the trash can empty, guessing the police had taken away its contents to sort through. Rory felt behind the dresser drawers to see if anything had been shoved or fallen back there, coming up empty-handed each time. She'd almost given up when she spotted something red peeking out from behind one of the nightstands.

"Nothing in the bathroom," Liz said when she walked into the bed area. "Did you find something?"

"Maybe." Her back to the door, Rory contorted her body and extended her fingers to reach into the tight space. "Got it." She'd just pulled the item out when she heard the door open. Clenching whatever it was in her fist, she turned around. Liz had a deer in the headlights look on her face. Rory suspected she did as well. She raised her hand in greeting and in a small voice said "hi" to the newcomer.

"I should have known," Martin said in a resigned tone.

"Just looking for an earring I lost Friday," Rory said.

"You weren't wearing any."

"That's right, um, I was going to, but I lost one, so I took the other one out."

"You never mentioned it to me."

"She didn't want to ruin the magic of the evening," Liz said.

He raised an eyebrow. "And you didn't think to look for it Friday when you picked up your bag?"

Rory looked down at her tennis shoes. "Forgot?" The word was more a question than a statement.

"What am I going to do with you two?"

Liz jutted her chin out. "The crime scene tape wasn't up. We figured you were done with the room."

"We are. We were just seeing who else had a keycard. The hotel staff alerted me when you used it." He held out his hand.

Rory took the card out of her pocket and gave it to him.

"Did anyone else borrow it?"

"I forgot I even had it until today."

"What did you find?" His gaze focused on the hand she still clenched by her side.

"I'm not sure." Rory opened her fist and stared at a red truffle wrapper. "That's disappointing."

"Looks like one of the wrappers from the candy box we had at the makeup party," Liz said.

"Guess it's not important then."

"I'll take it anyway. Where did you find it?" Martin carefully placed the wrapper in an evidence bag.

Rory pointed to the nightstand. "Behind that."

"Could've been there a long time."

"I don't think so," she said. "I think these wrappers were new for Valentine's Day."

"I'll look into it." He motioned toward the hotel room door. "After you, ladies."

They left the room one at a time, satisfied they'd searched everywhere but disappointed they hadn't learned more.

Chapter 10

Monday morning, Rory was hard at work when the receptionist at I Do For You called saying they had an opening later that day. After getting the meeting details, she relayed the information to Liz who volunteered to pick her up, in her Lexus sedan this time, half an hour before the appointment.

Later, after she put the finishing touches on a client's website and sent them a link for their approval, Rory leaned back in her desk chair and rubbed her eyes. She was about to go into the kitchen to get a Diet Coke before turning to her next project when a deliveryman in a brown uniform did a knock and run. By the time she got to the door to retrieve the package, he was already back in his truck and pulling away from the curb.

Her face softened when she saw the return address. Sekhmet wandered into the work area and gave an inquiring meow.

"It's from Martin. What do you think it is?" She opened the box to find a handwritten note on top of a flat box of mint chocolate Frangos and a small bag containing a catnip mouse. She glanced down at the cat. "There's something for both of us." She read the note to Sekhmet who listened attentively. "For my two favorite ladies."

Rory unwrapped the toy and placed it in front of the cat who cautiously sniffed it before pushing it across the wood floor. Before long she was running up and down the hallway, batting the toy between her paws as she ran. While Sekhmet played, Rory sampled the box of chocolates, giving a contented sigh when she took her first bite. After enjoying a second Frango, she called Martin.

"I got your box," she said as soon as she heard his voice come on the line. "Thanks. Sekhmet thanks you too. We're very happy with our presents."

"You're welcome. I'm glad you like them. I thought she could use a replacement for the mouse we got her for Christmas."

"I'm not sure I'm going to be allowed to get rid of the old one," she said when she saw her cat run by with the old toy in her mouth.

Martin laughed.

"How's your day going? Any leads on Jade or the bank robber?"

"Nothing concrete."

"She must have encountered the robber and that's what got her killed. It's sad."

"That is the most likely scenario," he said after a short pause.

"What about Xander? Is he still under suspicion?"

"We haven't ruled anyone out. But his story about throwing away the knife holds up. His staff verified what he said about having a meltdown on Friday. Apparently, that wasn't particularly unusual. I didn't realize how true the stereotype of the temperamental chef was until now."

"Stereotypes come from somewhere," Rory said. "We were right about Candy. She has been working undercover at the Akaw, looking into something for Nell." As soon as she said the words, she groaned inwardly, remembering too late her promise to keep the information to herself.

"Did you find that out when you were at the hotel last night?"

"About that..."

"It's fine. I should have asked if you had a keycard before that."

"So, we're okay?"

"Yes, but I wish you'd leave the investigating to us. I know you want to help your friend, but this is dangerous."

"I know."

"So, Candy. Do you know what she's investigating?"

"Not really. But it sounds like it's over now."

"I'd better get back to it. Talk to you later."

As Rory hung up, she wondered if she should have told him about their afternoon plans. She told herself the ball was already rolling. They couldn't cancel now.

On the way to the agency for their appointment that afternoon, Rory and Liz went over their roles for the upcoming meeting. Liz would play a bride reluctant to use their services while Rory would be the maid of honor who was pushing her to hire a bridesmaid.

When they pulled into the parking lot of I Do For You, they found a nondescript single-story office building. A discreet sign directed them to the appropriate suite where they stepped into a comfortable and soothing environment. Instrumental versions of popular love songs played softly in the background. Plush chairs and elegant end tables covered with magazines dotted the lobby. A display case on one side was filled with caps in varying colors, all with *I Do Crew* embroidered on them. Rory guessed this was where Solange had purchased the ones they'd all worn at the race.

While Liz flipped through the pages of a recent issue of a bridal magazine, Rory checked out the photos of smiling couples that covered the walls. She hoped her friends would look just as happy on their wedding day.

"Ms. Dexter, Ms. Anderson? Mrs. Tilcox will see you now."

They followed the receptionist down a short hallway to an office where an elegantly dressed forty-something woman waited for them. Their footsteps made no sound on the plush carpeting as they made their way toward her.

"I'm Edwina Tilcox," she said warmly, shaking their hands. "Welcome to my pride and joy."

"You own this place?" Rory said, a note of surprise in her voice. "I didn't realize we'd be speaking with the owner."

"I try to meet as many new clients as I can. May I get you anything to drink? Tea, coffee, water? Perhaps some champagne?"

"We're fine, thanks," Rory said.

At a nod from the owner, the receptionist left, closing the door behind her. Mrs. Tilcox sat down behind a French provincial desk of off-white finished wood and gestured toward the matching guest chairs upholstered in a brown and tan fabric. Rory sat down on one while Liz took the other.

"Remind me, please. Which one of you is the bride?"

"It's me. Rory's my maid of honor. She's the one who suggested we call you," Liz said, doing her best to put as much reluctance in her voice as possible.

"I see. May I ask how you heard about us?"

"A friend of a friend."

When neither of them elaborated any further, Mrs. Tilcox continued. "How many bridesmaids are you looking for?"

"Just one. To round out the numbers," Rory said. "You know, even number of groomsmen and bridesmaids." At the same time, Liz said, "We haven't settled on anything yet. I'm exploring the possibility."

Rory feigned annoyance. "You said you were okay with this."

Liz waved her hand in a shushing motion.

"I understand your reluctance. Let me assure you we are very discreet. If you don't want anyone to know you're using our services, that's fine. All of our employees know not to talk about the specifics of any job with anyone other than the person who hired us, but I will caution you that it's not always the best to keep it a secret. There's no shame in hiring a bridesmaid."

"Do many people keep it a secret?" Rory asked.

"Only one recent case comes to mind, but we're happy to go along with whatever you decide." Mrs. Tilcox folded her hands on the desk in front of her. "Now, what did you want the bridesmaid to do for you? We have a full range of services from simply attending the wedding to putting together a shower or bachelorette party." She looked over at Rory. "Though I suppose as maid of honor you'll be handling a lot of those duties."

After a short discussion of what she expected from the imaginary bridesmaid, Liz said, "Do you have a list of employees? And can we see pictures? I didn't see any on the website."

Mrs. Tilcox selected a binder from a nearby bookcase and placed it on the desk in front of her. "We're pretty old school here. We don't put our employees on the site because we've had issues with some..." she cleared her throat "...overenthusiastic members of the public."

Rory and Liz exchanged startled glances.

"But don't worry," Mrs. Tilcox hastened to add. "All our employees are very professional. We do background checks on all of them."

"Are they all full-time employees?" Liz asked.

"Most work part time while they're pursuing other opportunities."

"Like acting?" Rory asked, thinking about Jade's website.

"We have a fair number of those. This is L.A., after all." She pushed the binder across the desk toward them. "Take a look through these. I'll do my best to answer any questions you have."

Liz leafed through the binder while Rory looked on. On each page was a full-length photo and a short bio of a bridesmaid, including age and height. When they reached Jade's picture, Liz paused long enough for them to study the bio, but there wasn't anything in it they didn't already know.

"Jade," Liz said. "The name sounds familiar. Is she the one your friend told us about?"

Rory pretended to consider the question. "I think so."

Liz turned the binder around and tapped a dainty finger on Jade's photo. "What about her? We've heard good things about her."

Mrs. Tilcox paled. "I'm afraid she's not available."

"Whatever the problem is, I'm sure we can work something out," Liz said. "If I'm going to do this, I want to have someone who comes highly recommended. I'm willing to pay extra."

"It's not that. She recently...passed. I'm sorry, I should have taken her photo out of the book."

Rory and Liz did their best to appear shocked.

"So young too," Rory said. "What happened?"

The woman looked even more uncomfortable. "It was unexpected..."

Liz clutched Rory's arm so tightly she winced. "Wait. McIntyre. Wasn't that the name of the woman who was found dead at the race last weekend?"

"I think you're right." Rory suppressed a sigh of relief when Liz finally let go. "That was her?" she said to Mrs. Tilcox.

"I'm afraid so," the woman said reluctantly. "Where did you see her name?"

"A post on *Vista Beach Confidential*. There weren't many details."

"I didn't realize her name had been released to the press. We only recently found out ourselves. I'm not sure any of us have processed the news yet."

"So sorry for your loss," Rory said. "You don't think it was one of those overenthusiastic people you were talking about earlier, do you?"

"I hope not. As far as I know, she didn't have any problems with that."

Rory tucked the information away in her brain. "Please give our condolences to the family." She mentally crossed her fingers, hoping they'd learn something about Jade's past.

"That's very nice of you, but as far as I know she had none. That's one reason why she enjoyed this job so much. She got to be part of a family for a while." Mrs. Tilcox wiped a tear from her eye. "Enough of that. We have many other people available."

They leafed through a few more pages and tried steering the conversation back to Jade, but the woman refused to take the bait. When Rory sensed they weren't going to get any more out of her, she touched Liz's foot with her own to indicate they should leave.

Liz closed the binder. "I need to think about it some more. I'm not sure it's for me." She stood up. "Thank you for your time."

They left the office, mulling over the little they'd learned. They had barely gotten outside when they met a familiar figure walking across the parking lot toward them.

Martin Green raised an eyebrow. "Fancy finding you two here. I know you're not getting married." He directed his attention at Rory who refused to look him in the eyes. "Or at least I hope not." His gaze shifted to Liz. "Are congratulations in order?"

Liz shook her head while Rory mumbled something about the agency needing someone to maintain their website.

"Uh-huh." He looked heavenward and took a deep breath. "If I asked the employees about your visit, they'd say the same thing?"

"Um."

"That's what I thought." He ran a hand through his hair. "You two aren't going to stop, are you?" He placed both hands on Rory's shoulders and looked into her eyes. "Be careful."

Once he was inside the building and out of earshot, Liz turned to Rory. "Awwwwkward."

"At least he didn't seem mad."

"Mostly concerned, I think. Hopefully he'll learn more than we did. Sure was a bust for us."

"Maybe not." Rory gestured to a woman getting out of her car. "Isn't that one of the bridesmaids from the book? Maybe she knows something."

Rory led the way across the parking lot. "Excuse me," she said, trying to visualize the page where she'd seen the woman's photo, finally coming up with the name. "Lola, isn't it?"

"That's right. Do I know you?" she said cautiously.

Rory introduced herself and Liz. "We were just in I Do For You talking to Mrs. Tilcox about hiring a bridesmaid and saw your name in the book."

Lola's face relaxed. "Did you settle on someone?"

"I'm not sure I want to go through with it," Liz said, once more playing the reluctant bride. "No offense, but it seems odd to me."

"None taken. I know a lot of people think that. Do you have any questions I can answer for you? Mrs. Tilcox is very thorough, but she's not right there in the trenches, if you know what I mean."

"We had a couple people in mind," Rory said. "What do you know about Jade McIntyre?" She hoped Lola hadn't yet heard about her fellow employee's untimely death. She doubted she'd talk about her if she knew.

"Jade? She's good. One of the best. Guess it's all those years as an actress."

"What can you tell us about her most recent job? Mrs. Tilcox seemed reluctant to talk about it."

"She's very protective of us. We all appreciate it. There are a lot of weirdoes out there, believe me."

"Did Jade have any problems with people like that?"

"Not that I know of." Lola stopped as if deciding how much to tell them. "This last job of hers was...odd. I don't have all the details, but I heard another girl was originally assigned to it and Jade paid her a lot of money to take her place."

"Any idea why?"

"No, but I wouldn't be surprised if it had something to do with this play she's been trying to get off the ground. She's always looking for a wealthy man to back one show or another. If she thought the family had money, she often lobbied for the job. But don't worry, she's really good. She always comes through as a bridesmaid." Lola glanced at her watch. "I'd better get inside. Nice chatting with you. Good luck." She walked across the parking lot toward the front door of the agency.

Rory and Liz waited until they were inside the car before saying anything.

"*That* was surprising," Liz said. "I wonder why she paid the other bridesmaid to switch jobs."

"Beats me. Xander and Solange don't have that much money, at least not enough to fund a play."

"Maybe she was targeting someone else." Liz's eyes widened. "What about Xander's dad? He's loaded."

"That might explain the conversation I overheard between Xander and Jade. Maybe someone did warn him about her like he said, and he was worried about her targeting his father. She could have come onto Xander to rattle his cage." Even as she uttered the thought, Rory wasn't totally convinced. She checked her phone, noticing a half dozen texts from Solange asking for an update. She showed them to Liz.

"You'd better get back to her before she stresses herself out more."

While Liz drove, Rory called Solange on her cell, arranging to meet her at the pier where she was helping Arika with the ad photo shoot.

"Just drop me off at your office," Rory said after she hung up. "I'll walk down to the pier from there."

When Rory arrived at her destination, she found the photo shoot in progress. Solange stood in front of the love locks while Xander knelt on one knee in front of her in classic proposal stance, offering her a painted padlock. Veronica took several photos while Arika stood off to one side supervising.

As Rory watched, Paris raced down the pier toward the group.

"Did I miss anything?" she said, a little out of breath.

"I jut got here. Did my mom rope you into this too?"

"Happy to help." Paris frowned. "I thought I was supposed to have a boyfriend in the photo. I don't see anyone."

"Maybe he's late. Let's go talk to my mom." Rory led the way over to Arika who was consulting a piece of paper she guessed was a list of the shots her mother wanted to capture. "How's everything going?"

Arika looked up at the two of them. "We're done with the pictures I wanted of Xander and Solange."

"Where's the guy who's supposed to be playing my boyfriend?" Paris asked.

Arika checked her phone. "Just got a text from him. Unfortunately, he can't make it."

"So you don't need me?" Paris said, a note of disappointment in her voice.

"Wait here. Let me see what I can do." Arika strode past Veronica who was checking out the photos on her camera and leaned over the pier railing, looking down at the beach below.

Xander kissed his bride-to-be goodbye, then waved at the others before heading back to his restaurant. Rory walked over to where Solange still stood in front of the locks.

"Well?" Solange said quietly once Rory was close enough to hear. "What did you find out?"

Rory glanced at Paris who'd joined them.

Solange seemed to sense her unease. "It's okay. You can talk in front of her."

"She knows?"

"No, but it's okay. People are bound to find out now."

A confused expression on her face, Paris said, "What are you two talking about?"

"Jade wasn't an old friend of mine. I didn't know her at all. I hired her to be a bridesmaid."

Paris's eyes opened wide. "Why?" was all she managed to say.

"We can talk about it later. Right now, I want to know what Rory found out."

Rory told them everything she'd learned including about Jade paying to be in the wedding party.

"Strange. I suppose she could have targeted Zeke. He does have a lot of money. He's not a huge patron of the arts, but he does have an eye for the ladies and could probably be charmed." Solange stared at the ocean. "Too bad Xander had to leave. He might know something."

"Did either of you notice anything at the party?" Rory said.

"Now that you mention it, I did see Jade talking to Xander's dad on the patio. I didn't think anything about it at the time." Paris paused as if trying to remember more details. "He seemed...agitated."

"I should never have hired her," Solange said. "What if my hiring her was the reason she was killed?"

"I doubt that's the reason. Did you know the company had assigned you a different bridesmaid?" Rory asked.

"No. I didn't have time to visit their office, so I gave them my requirements and told them to pick someone for me. They said she would contact me directly. So when Jade called I assumed she was who they'd selected. I had no reason to think she was a replacement."

Arika walked over to them with a twenty-something man dressed in shorts and a polo shirt. "This is Jonah. He's agreed to sub in."

While Veronica set up the shot with Jonah and Paris, Rory asked her mother, "How'd you get him to help out?"

"His mom's a regular customer at the store. I'm giving him gift cards for her."

"And he agreed to that?"

"He loves his mom. She's been sick so he wanted to do something special for her for Valentine's Day. Sweet kid."

Less than ten minutes later, the picture shoot was over, and Jonah was on his way to Arika's Scrap 'n Paint with Rory's mother to get the promised gift cards.

The rest of them all huddled around Veronica to check out the photos on the camera's display. They'd viewed the last shot when Rory noticed black ink peeking out from under the long-sleeved t-shirt Veronica wore. She pointed to the inside of the woman's wrist. "Is that new?"

"The tattoo? Just got it. What do you think?" Veronica pushed back her sleeve, exposing a procession of tiny skulls that crept up her arm.

"It suits you."

Paris sucked in her breath and a momentary look of panic came over her face.

"What is it?" Solange touched her gently on the arm.

"Sorry," Paris said. "I remembered something about the bank robbery."

"What made you think about that?" Rory asked.

Paris indicated Veronica's arm. "The robber, he had a tattoo on the inside of his wrist."

Rory's pulse quickened. "Do you remember what it was of?"

"Between the gloves he wore and the long sleeves, I couldn't see much."

"You're sure it was a tattoo?" Veronica looked up from the notes she was now taking. "Couldn't have been dirt or something like that?"

"Definitely a tattoo. Black ink."

"What else do you remember?"

"Not much."

"I don't remember seeing anything about the robber wearing gloves in the paper," Rory said.

"It's news to me too," Veronica said. "Did you tell the police about it?"

"I don't remember," Paris said in a small voice.

Rory turned to Veronica. "You've reported on bank robberies before, haven't you? Is it usual for them to wear gloves?"

"Not that I know. But you can check out the photos on the LA Robbers website to see."

"What's that?"

She explained the site was put together in cooperation with local, state and federal law enforcement in hopes a member of the public would provide a lead. It was full of actual surveillance photos taken during the commission of a robbery.

Rory brought the site up on her phone and looked through the dozens of photos, pausing to study each one. As far as she could tell, the Sweetheart Robber was one of only a few who'd bothered to wear gloves.

"He's smart," Veronica said after Rory reported her findings. "Wouldn't accidentally leave any prints."

"Can I see?" Solange asked.

Rory handed over her phone so the others could check out the photos for themselves.

"Can't really see the tattoo in any of the photos of the Sweetheart Robber," Solange said. "I wonder if any of the other tellers remember seeing it."

"You think I'm making it up?" Paris said in a defensive tone.

"No, not at all. I thought one of them might have seen more."

Paris shuddered. "It's hard to remember anything when a robbery occurs. Even if it doesn't involve a gun, it's still frightening."

"What else do you remember about him? I can't tell from the photos how tall he is," Rory said.

Paris screwed up her face in thought. "Short beard, dark in color. Couldn't really see his face because of the sunglasses and ball cap. On the taller side, but not super tall. That's all I remember."

"That could be a lot of people. Slap a beard on your fiancé and it could even be him," Veronica said to Solange who turned pale at the suggestion.

"Why do you say that?"

"He's about the right height and build. He has a tattoo. Lots of them." Veronica shrugged. "But so do a lot of people. Not sure how much it's going to help the police." She checked her cell phone. "I've got to go.

Let your mom know I'll send the photos to her ASAP." She popped her notebook and camera into her tote bag and started back toward town.

"Don't listen to anything she said," Paris said to Solange. "Can't be Xander. He was with you all morning. Right?"

Solange's gaze remained riveted on the photos on the phone she held in her hand. She handed it over. "I've got to get back to work." Without another word, she made her way down the pier toward town.

Paris and Rory exchanged worried looks.

"Did I say something wrong?" Paris said.

"I think she's finding everything overwhelming right now."

"It is a stressful time of year for her. Then throw in a wedding..."

"And a murder," Rory softly added.

Her heart went out to the bride-to-be. She didn't know how she'd react under similar circumstances. As they went their separate ways, Rory vowed to do everything she could to help.

Chapter 11

Later that day, Rory added mail to the stack on the table in the entryway of the two-story Mission-style house next door to her own and closed the front door behind her. She was on her way into the living room when the chirping of crickets alerted her to an incoming video call.

Liz's face appeared on the screen of Rory's cell. "Seems kind of dark. Where are you?"

"Mrs. Griswold's place. Hold on a sec. I'll turn on some lights." Rory flipped a switch, illuminating a room containing modern pieces with a few antiques mixed in. Tchotchkes covered almost every flat surface.

"What are you doing there? And how'd you get in?"

"Don't worry. It's legit." She waved a key ring in front of the screen. "I'm collecting her mail and keeping an eye on the place while she's gone."

"Granny G's never asked you to do that before."

"Mrs. Maldonado's out of town too," Rory said, referring to a neighbor who lived at the end of the block. "Otherwise she would have done it." She made her way past a couch upholstered in a flowered fabric reminiscent of the eighties and sat down at a desk covered with books and papers. "Hold on. I'm going to set you down." She leaned her smart phone against a pile of books and powered up Mrs. Griswold's laptop.

"What are you doing now?"

"She wants me to send her some pictures."

"But she's on vacation."

"She's nursing her sister back to health. I'm not sure she considers it a vacation," Rory said.

"So what are these photos that can't wait?"

"Pictures of the construction workers across the street."

"Why does she want those?"

"She said something about putting together a complaint to the city about the construction company."

"But they're no longer working."

"They'll be back some day." Rory rummaged through the desk drawers until she found binoculars with a picture taking function. She plugged it into a USB port on the laptop and started downloading the photos.

"Is that her binocam?" Liz's eyes sparkled. "Do you think we can borrow it?"

"Probably. I'd have to ask her first. What do you want it for?"

"Our investigation."

Rory raised an eyebrow. "How can it help?"

"I don't know yet. Think of it as another tool in our sleuthing toolbox."

"We should come up with a specific reason to borrow it before I ask her. Believe me, she'll want to know." Rory glanced at the computer. "The pics have finished downloading."

"What do you see?" Liz's face now filled the phone's screen.

"Hold your horses. Let me look." Rory scrolled through the photos. "Oh my."

"Let me see. Let me see."

Rory flipped her cell's camera screen to face the computer and the photo on the display.

Liz drew in her breath. "Is that guy doing what I think he's doing?"

"Yep. He's dumping a load of trash on Mrs. Griswold's lawn."

"You never saw him do that?"

"Didn't even realize they had a feud going. She must have cleaned it up right away."

"Guess someone didn't like her complaints."

Rory changed the camera so it faced her once again. She propped the phone up in its previous location on the desk and flipped through the rest of the photos. "Here's one of Xander's dad checking out the lot. Any idea why he'd be there?"

"No clue. Unless he's thinking about moving back to the area now that he's patched things up with his son."

"Do you know the guy he's with?" Rory changed the camera once more so it faced the display.

"Looks like an agent here in town. Zeke must be interested in buying the property."

"Doesn't he have a cushy job up north?"

"Maybe he's found a better one here."

"I'm going to hang up now."

"Wait. I wanted to ask you about the photo shoot."

"Let me take care of this first. I'll call you when I get home."

After hanging up, Rory emailed the photos to her neighbor, then put them on a flashdrive. If she needed to resend them, she could do it from her own house. She powered down the computer, tucked the flashdrive into the pocket of her jeans and locked up the house, calling Liz back as soon as she was at her own desk.

"Tell me about the photo shoot," Liz said.

Rory brought her up to date on everything that had happened at the pier.

"So that's where Veronica got that info."

"What are you talking about?"

"You haven't seen the latest post on *VBC*? You should read it. I'll wait."

Rory put the phone on speaker while she brought up the blog on her computer. Liz hummed to herself softly in the background. The latest post detailed the revelations Paris had made at the pier about the robber's tattoo and gloves.

"I should have realized Veronica wouldn't keep it to herself," Rory said when she finished reading.

"She is all about the scoop. At least she didn't mention the brides-maid-for-hire thing. I still can't believe Xander doesn't know about it."

"Makes me sad Solange felt she had to hide that from him." Rory set troubled eyes on the flowers and box of Frangos on her desk. As soon as she saw them, her spirits lifted. "I forgot to tell you. I got another gift today." She explained about the candy and cat toy she'd received that morning.

"Dashing D really knows how to make someone feel special. What are you doing for him for Valentine's Day?"

"I don't know. Anything I do won't be as good as the things he's come up with for me."

"You don't have to top him. It's not a competition. Just do something to let him know you care. I should get back to it. Think about what I said."

Rory tapped her cell phone gently on her chin and sat back in her chair, trying to come up with something she could do to show Martin how important he was to her.

She glanced at the time on her computer and realized it was getting late. She looked down at Sekhmet who'd silently appeared by her side. "Ready for dinner? You know, I bet Martin's hungry too. He probably skipped lunch. I think I'll bring him some food."

After feeding her cat, Rory drove to a local deli to pick up one of Martin's favorite meals. When she entered the police station, she found him working at his desk.

She held up the bag. "Thought you could use something to eat. Meatball sandwich and barbecue potato chips."

His face lit up. "You read my mind. I'm starving."

"Didn't eat lunch?" She sat down on the chair beside his desk.

"You know me."

They sat in companionable silence while he dug into the food. When he set down the half-eaten sandwich, she looked at him, a serious expression on her face. "I want you to know I'll always try to be honest with you."

"What brought that on?"

"I was thinking about Solange and Xander."

"Are you talking about the bridesmaid-for-hire thing?"

"She told you, didn't she? That's why you were at the agency today."

"Seems like you know too. Why didn't you tell me?"

"I couldn't betray her confidence, but I did encourage her to talk to you."

"I understand where you're coming from, but every bit of information could be vital to the investigation. You never know where it's going to lead. Murder trumps confidences. Always." Martin opened the bag of potato chips and offered it to her. "What did you find out at the agency?"

Rory munched thoughtfully on a chip. "Not much. We learned more from the bridesmaid we met in the parking lot." She told him about how Jade had paid another employee to take her place in Solange's bridal party.

"Hmm. Do you know the name of the bridesmaid she replaced?"

"No, but Lola's the one who told us about it. She would probably know."

He jotted down the information on a piece of paper. "You really should stop investigating on your own." He pointed to his head. "See these? I didn't have them before I met you."

Rory leaned forward and squinted. "You're complaining about a couple gray hairs? I can barely see them." She grinned, then her expression turned serious. "Solange asked me to help. I couldn't refuse. I promise from now on whatever I find out I'll tell you about right away."

"That's all I can ask for." He squeezed her hand. "But please be careful, and no more questioning witnesses. If you think you have a lead, call me and I'll look into it."

Rory nodded her agreement, hoping circumstances wouldn't force her to renege on the promise. "Has Paris talked to you? She remembered something more about the bank robber."

"She called earlier. She told you about it?"

"We were at the pier when she remembered."

"Veronica was there too, I suppose."

"I didn't expect her to blab about it on *VBC*."

"It's fine," he said. "Getting that information out might bring in more tips from the public and help us catch the robber."

Rory hoped they'd find the culprit soon before someone decided to fight back and the robberies turned violent.

As soon as Rory stepped inside Arika's Scrap 'n Paint the next morning, the tension eased from her shoulders and a sense of relief washed over her. She spotted her mother near the back of the store helping a customer pick out wood and supplies for a project.

Rory checked out the display of painted samples on a bookcase next to the cash register, all projects for upcoming classes at the store. She was studying a wood plate with a colorful dot art pattern when Arika came up beside her.

"That class is almost full. Better sign up soon if you want to take it."

Rory returned the piece to its place on the shelf. "I wish I could. I'll think about taking a class after this wedding is over."

"Is that why you're in town? Are you doing an errand for the wedding?"

"No, I had a meeting with a prospective client to create an app for their business. They saw what I did for the Akaw a few months ago and liked it. Just stopped by to say hi before I go home."

"How'd it go?"

"They're interviewing a few others, but I'm pretty sure I got the job."

"While you're here, let me show you the ad I created from yesterday's photo shoot." Arika took a piece of paper from underneath the cash register and placed it on the counter. "What do you think?"

Rory studied the ad mockup. In the middle was a picture of Xander and Solange in front of the love locks on the pier. Surrounding the photo were the words *Get your love locks at Arika's Scrap 'n Paint* along with a close-up of a painted lock and the address of the store. "Looks nice."

Arika sat down on the stool behind the counter. "What's wrong? Are you worried about your friends?"

Rory looked up from her perusal of the ad. "How did you know?"

"A mother always knows."

"It's Solange. She seemed off yesterday."

"She seemed fine to me."

"It was after you left. Something changed. We were talking about the bank robbery and a weird expression came over her face."

"Someone she knew did unexpectedly die."

"She didn't really know her."

Arika furrowed her brow. "Oh?"

Rory told her mother how Solange had admitted to hiring a bridesmaid to fill out the wedding party.

"Still, it can't be easy. I don't think you should worry too much. It'll all work out in the end." Arika picked a piece of lint off her embroidered top. "How's the next issue of *BrushToBrush* going?"

"It's getting there. I'm not worried about it. There's plenty of time before it's supposed to come out."

The bell over the front door tinkled. Rory looked over at the newcomer. "We were just talking about the magazine."

"All good, I hope." Solange walked toward them.

"My customers are eager to see the new issue," Arika said.

"I'm glad to hear that." Solange picked up the ad Rory and her mother had been looking at. "This turned out good."

"I'm pleased with it. Thanks for helping out."

"No problem. It was a nice break from taxes. Are you using the photo of Paris as well?"

"I'm working on that one next." Arika rested her elbows on the counter. "Did you need help finding some painting supplies?"

"I'm here to pick up the coasters and get more varnish."

"You know where the varnish is. The boxes of coasters are in the back room on my desk. Rory can get them for you."

Solange picked out her supplies and Rory brought the two boxes into the classroom where her friend was now sitting at one of the tables, waiting for her.

Rory placed the coasters on the table next to several bottles of brush-on varnish.

Solange stared at the boxes and sighed.

"There are a lot of coasters," Rory said. "Do you need help varnishing? I know you said no before, but the offer still stands."

Relief shown on Solange's face. "Thank you! I don't know why I said that. Pride, maybe."

"How about Liz and I do them all?"

"That's so nice of you. Right now, I could use all the help I can get." She shoved a bottle of varnish toward Rory. "Take this."

"No need. I've got some of the same kind at home."

"I insist. No sense in you using your own supplies."

"Thanks." Rory sat across from her, rested her forearms on the table and leaned forward. "Is everything okay? You seemed different yesterday when we were talking about the robbery. You know Veronica was just yanking your chain, don't you, when she talked about the possibility of Xander being the robber?"

Solange burst into tears. Rory hurried around the table and sat down on the chair next to her, hugging her until the tears subsided.

Solange wiped her face with the back of her hand. "I can't take it anymore. I lied to the police about Xan being with me for the entire race."

"Where was he?"

"I'd like to know the answer to that," a deep voice behind them said.

Rory twisted her head around to find Martin standing in the doorway that led to the sales floor.

"I didn't know you were there," was all she could find to say.

"Obviously." He walked into the room and took the seat across from them. He offered Solange a white handkerchief before getting down to business. "Now, tell me what's going on," he said gently. "From the beginning."

"I'm sorry I lied to you." Solange wiped her face with the handkerchief.

"It happens. Tell me about Saturday morning and the Love Run."

She explained she'd been with her fiancé all morning until about halfway through the race. "That's when he got a text from the restaurant, so he left for a while."

"How long?"

"I'm not sure."

"Can anyone else help with the time?"

"I don't think so. We'd split off from the group by then. So many people along the course stopped us to congratulate us we told the rest of the group to go on ahead."

"I remember." Martin jotted down something in his notebook. "Go on."

"I didn't worry about it at the time, but after seeing the photo of the robber yesterday and hearing about the tattoo..." Solange took a deep breath. "I checked with people at the restaurant, but they all said they didn't text him. As far as they know, he didn't even stop by. When I asked him about it, Xan clammed up and walked away."

"There's something else. What is it?"

"I think—I don't want to, but...I'm afraid he might be the bank robber and that he killed Jade when she saw him."

"Why do you say that?"

"He's the right build and height and he has a tattoo here." Solange pointed to the inside of her wrist.

"What about the beard? He's clean shaven."

She shrugged.

"Does he need money?"

"He's worried about spending too much on the wedding, but he wouldn't rob a bank for that." An inkling of hope appeared on her face. "What happens now?"

"Thank you for telling me the truth. I'll keep what you said in mind. Right now, I have no reason to believe Xander had anything to do with the robberies." Martin stood up and returned his notebook and pen to the inside pocket of his jacket, then looked over at Rory. "Care to walk me out?"

He led the way through the back room to the alley door. When the two of them were alone outside, Rory said, "Do you think he could be the robber? I know what you said to Solange, but—"

"You're not convinced that's what I really think."

"Something like that."

He ran his hand through his hair. "There's no motive as far as I can tell." He raised an eyebrow. "Unless...?"

"None that I know of."

"If he does turn out to be responsible in any way, you know what I have to do. Wedding or no wedding."

"I know."

Martin walked down the alley. Only after she was back in the store did Rory realize she'd never asked him what had brought him there in the first place.

Solange was no longer in the classroom. The boxes of coasters and a bottle of varnish remained on the table with a note next to them. After saying goodbye to her mother, Rory put the items in the trunk of her car. She was about to drive home when she decided there was one more place she wanted to visit.

She dialed a familiar number on her cell. When Liz answered, Rory said, "How'd you like to do some sleuthing?"

Rory and Liz stood in the alleyway where they'd found Jade's body only a few days before. Crime scene tape no longer cordoned off the area and, as far as Rory could tell, there was no evidence left a crime had occurred there.

"Where do we start?" Liz turned in a circle, taking in the block-long space between two buildings.

"You take that side..." Rory pointed to the right side of the alley. "I'll take the other."

They slowly walked up and down the alley, studying the area. Rory peeked into the trash cans on her side, but they were all empty. Either the police had taken their contents to sift through later or the garbage had been collected since Saturday.

"There's not much here," she said when they met in the middle of the alley less than ten minutes later. "I don't know what I was thinking, hoping to find something that would eliminate Xander. I don't see any security cameras either. Do you?"

Liz looked around. "No." Excitement shown in her eyes. "I know. Let's retrace the robber's steps."

"He would have come from that direction." Rory pointed to the street behind them. "That's closest to the bank that was robbed on

Saturday. And Jade was found there." She pointed to the opposite end of the alley.

Liz walked toward the street nearest the bank and went around the corner. Moments later, she reappeared at a run. "The robber sees Jade who confronts him."

"Or tries to get away."

"Either way, he needs to get rid of her." Liz stopped next to the trash can nearest Xander's restaurant. "He sees the knife, grabs it and catches up with her." She seized an invisible weapon from the trash can and made a stabbing motion. "Then where does he go?"

"Street?"

"Someone would have noticed him."

"Not necessarily. People might think he was participating in the race."

An employee came out of the back door of the business nearest to them and gazed at them curiously as he deposited a bag in the garbage.

"What about one of the businesses?" Rory asked. "If they're anything like my mom, they keep their back doors unlocked during business hours. He could have ducked inside one of them and gone out the front door."

"Wouldn't the killer have blood on their clothes? Someone would have noticed and reported it."

"I don't know how much blood there would be. Maybe Jade only bled internally."

They peeked inside each of the doors. Most of them led into the back room of a business. One led directly to the sales floor. When they opened the door to Zephy's, they found a hallway and heard the clang of pots and pans and the flushing of a toilet.

"It was somewhere between nine and nine thirty, right?" Liz said. "We don't know if the businesses were open."

"We know someone was inside Xander's restaurant. We'll have to check the others. Let's go and see if anyone saw anything."

They split up the businesses, going inside each one through the back door and going out the front as they supposed the robber would have done. When they regrouped in the alley, they compared notes.

"No one batted an eye when I came through," Liz said. "I checked and none of them were open Saturday morning. They were at the pier for the end of the race."

"Same here, except for the restaurant," Rory said. "I barely got in the door and they showed me out."

"So a stranger couldn't have gone through then."

"Unless it wasn't a stranger," Rory said slowly, not liking where her thinking was taking her. "Xander could have gone inside and they wouldn't have questioned him."

"But he doesn't have a beard," Liz said.

"It could have been fake. Maybe he threw it out in the garbage."

"There's no motive."

"Still, I'd feel better if we could find something that points to someone else."

"Unfortunately, the only prints on the knife are his."

"That's easily explained." She reminded Liz about what Paris had said about the robber wearing gloves.

Liz glanced at the door to Zephy's. "Maybe someone at the restaurant knows something they didn't want to tell the police."

"Maybe."

Rory had come hoping she'd find something to exonerate Xander, but all she'd done was demonstrate he could have robbed the bank. She'd even come up with a possible way for him to escape.

Chapter 12

Later that day, Rory peered into the refrigerator, studying its contents. Sekhmet brushed up against her leg and meowed.

"Not much choice, is there?"

The cat jumped onto the empty bottom shelf.

"I know. I know. I need to go to the store. At least *you* have food for dinner."

She picked up the cat and placed her on the floor, hastily closing the door of the refrigerator to prevent a repeat performance. She took a can of cat food out of the cupboard and put its contents into a bowl. Sekhmet started eating as soon as Rory set it down.

Rory was about to order pizza when Liz called, an excited tone in her voice.

"Drop everything. You've got some investigating to do."

Rory glanced at the clock on the wall. "It's after five. Aren't you supposed to be at that speed paint and date event tonight? Is this your way of getting out of it?"

"I'm still going. That's what I'm talking about. It's being held at Xander's restaurant. It's the perfect time for you to find out if anyone knows anything that could help."

"I already have a boyfriend. I can't very well sign up for a speed dating event even if it does involve painting."

"You're not participating. You're helping out."

"I thought Naomi was working all of the events at the restaurant."

"Change of plans. She's, uh, under the weather. They could use the help, so I suggested you."

"What do they want me to do?" Rory sat down on a kitchen chair.

"Just check people in. Easy peasy."

"My mom's coming over to drop off some painting supplies I ordered from her, and I still have some work to finish. Plus I have a date with Sekhmet to watch a movie."

"Doesn't your mom have a key to your place? You don't need to be there. The rest you can do later. Come on, it'll be fun. You can give me your opinion on the guys I meet while you're there."

"Since when have you ever needed my opinion on the men you date?"

Liz's voice took on a wheedling tone. "It's only a couple hours. You'll be helping out. You can take pics and do a write-up on the event for *BrushToBrush*. As a participant, I'll give you some quotes."

Rory thought about it. It would make a good article for the magazine. She didn't know if Solange would be interested in it, but she could pitch it to her later. It would give her a chance to hang out at Zephy's and learn more about the restaurant. "Okay, okay. What time should I be there?"

"Quarter to six. The event starts at six. I'll let Xander know you're coming."

Before Rory could ask any more questions, Liz hung up. She had less than twenty minutes to change and hit the road if she hoped to be there on time. After she put on dress pants and a lightweight sweater covered with small colorful hearts, she called her mother to let her know about the change in plans.

"I'll come pick everything up after I'm done," Rory said.

"No need. I'll drop it off at your place. I'm going that direction, anyway. I'll let myself in."

"Thanks, Mom. I appreciate it."

"No problem."

She'd barely hung up when Sekhmet padded over, her new toy in her mouth, and dropped it at Rory's feet. The cat sat down and looked up expectantly.

Rory patted the top of her head. "Sorry, I'm afraid we'll have to watch *The Secret Life of Pets* later. I'll only be gone a couple hours. My mom will be by to drop something off. Maybe she'll play with you."

Sekhmet meowed, then ran down the hallway with the toy in her mouth.

When Rory got to the restaurant, she made her way to the same banquet room where the wine and chocolate tasting had been held. Inside she found Xander and his staff setting up for the event. Ten easels were spread around the room with bins filled with brushes and paint next to each one.

"Rory, thank you so much for helping out on such short notice," Xander said as soon as he saw her. "I didn't know what to do after Naomi told me she had some last-minute plans."

"I thought she was sick."

A surprised look flitted across his face soon replaced by a more serious expression. "That's what I meant."

While the staff placed blank eight-by-ten canvases on the easels and prepared the rest of the room, Xander brought Rory up to speed. He led her over to a table near the room's entrance. "You'll be checking people in. We have twenty people signed up, ten men and ten women. If anyone asks, we don't have any room for walk-ins. Check people off as they arrive." He indicated a list on the table next to a stack of black aprons. "Next to their name is the easel number they'll be starting at. It's also on their nametag." He pointed to prepared nametags placed in neat rows on the table. "Don't forget to give them a dating card. The white is for the women, yellow for the men."

Rory picked up one of the white cards and studied it. In one column was a list of all the male participants. Next to each name was a column marked *Interested* with a space next to it to check *yes* or *no*. "So I pick these up at the end of the event? Is that how it works?"

"That's right. We'll look at them later and call the people who have matches sometime in the next day or so. We'll give them each other's contact info. It's up to them after that."

"So that's all I need to do? Check them in and collect the cards at the end? Sounds easy enough."

"You'll also be facilitating."

"What? You mean running the event? I thought you'd be doing that."

"I'm needed in the kitchen. Don't worry, there's nothing to it. I'll give a short intro at the beginning explaining the rules, so you won't have to worry about that. All you'll have to do is ring this bell—" he pointed to a silver bell that sat on the table "—every seven minutes and remind people to move on. I'll be back before the event ends. I'll have one of my staff check in on you in case you need help. I know it's a lot to ask. Do you have any questions?"

"Don't worry. I'll be fine."

Less than ten minutes later, participants started trickling in and a line began to form. She was kept busy checking people in and handing out black aprons, comment cards and nametags. When Liz stepped to the front, Rory said in a low voice, "You didn't tell me I was running the event."

"Oops. My bad."

Rory handed Liz a nametag along with the other items. "You're at easel number one." She pointed to the closest spot to the table.

"Right where you can keep an eye on me." Liz's gaze swept the room filled with excited singles putting on the aprons over their clothes. "Looks like quite a crowd." She lowered her voice. "Are you set? You know, for the other thing?"

Rory nodded even though she had no idea how she was going to investigate and work the event at the same time. Liz went over to her spot and the next person stepped up. Before long, all of the participants were standing at their assigned easel.

Xander rang the bell to get their attention. "Welcome to our speed painting event. The theme tonight is travel. Ladies, think of some place you'd like to visit or enjoyed visiting. You'll all be painting something that reminds you of that place. The canvases stay with the ladies and the men move from place to place. You'll have seven minutes for each date. When you hear the bell..." He rang the bell once again. "The men will move on to the next higher number easel. Be sure to mark your comment cards as soon as possible after each date. Any questions?" He looked around, but no one raised their hands. "Here we go. Your first date starts now. Have fun."

Xander handed the bell to Rory and went back to the kitchen. From her vantage point at the table near the room's entrance, she could see most of the couples. Snatches of conversation occasionally reached her ears. Talking about traveling proved to be a good icebreaker. Images of various destinations popped up on canvases around the room as the daters worked together on their art.

Rory guessed from the image of Big Ben that was taking shape on Liz's canvas that she'd selected England as her travel destination, a place that she had recently expressed an interest in visiting.

Every seven minutes, Rory rang the bell and the men walked to the next numbered easel. At one point, she noticed Liz having a particularly good time with a date. She made a mental note to ask about him later.

Three quarters of the way through the event, a restaurant employee stepped into the room and asked if she needed anything.

"I could use a bathroom break." Rory glanced at the timer on her cell phone. "But I only have six minutes before the next round."

The employee waved a hand toward the doorway. "Go ahead. I can handle this. You don't have to rush. Use the bathroom at the end of the hallway. It's the closest one. Hardly anyone other than Chef uses it so it should be available. I'm pretty sure he's busy in the kitchen right now."

Rory left her phone on the table and walked down the hallway, easily finding the single stall bathroom next to Xander's office. A nearby door led into the alley behind the restaurant. When she opened the bathroom door to return to her duties, she heard two voices coming from outside. She paused next to the partially open back door and listened to the conversation.

"...telling you we're not getting paid anytime soon," a male voice said.

"But Chef promised—" another, more feminine, voice replied.

"I don't care what he promised. When was the last time you saw any money?"

"Sure, it's been a couple weeks, but it's only a glitch in the computer payroll system."

"Is it? We work hard. We get to work on time. We should be getting paid on time. I don't know about you, but I can't afford to work for nothing."

In a pause in the conversation, Rory peeked around the door to see who was talking. The more belligerent voice belonged to an employee dressed in clothes that indicated he worked in the kitchen while the other was dressed as a waiter. The kitchen employee took a sip from the water bottle in his hand.

The waiter finally said, "Chef's been good to us. He'll make it right."

"I'm not so sure. Look at Saturday. The bathroom near his office was locked. Guess he didn't want his kitchen staff using his precious toilet. You'd think it was made of gold or something."

"I don't know what you're talking about. I used it."

"Still, I'm telling you if I don't see some money by the end of the week, I'm out of here. You should leave too."

Rory wondered how many of the restaurant's employees felt the same way. If enough did, Xander might soon have a full-scale revolt on his hands.

The kitchen employee took a final sip of water and threw the plastic bottle in a nearby recycling bin. "Break's over. We'd better get back inside."

Rory checked the nearby office to make sure it was empty, then ducked inside, closing the door behind her. While she waited for the employees to clear the hallway, she glanced around the postage-stamp-size room. A framed photo of Solange and Xander stood on the desk next to neat stacks of papers. Rory glanced at the top paper in each pile. One contained an overdue notice from a supplier, another held a notice regarding an increase in rent for the space the restaurant occupied.

Without her phone, Rory didn't know how much time had passed, but she decided she'd better get back. After making sure the hallway was empty, she hurried back to the banquet room, arriving in time to ring the bell for the next round.

As she sat at the table, she thought about the restaurant. Xander always talked about how well it was doing. The overdue bill on his desk and the conversation she'd overheard indicated otherwise. She was wondering if Solange knew about the issues when she sensed a presence next to her. She looked up to find the man himself standing beside her.

"How's it going?"

Rory shoved all thoughts of the restaurant's problems to the back of her mind. "Great. Everyone seems to be enjoying themselves." She glanced at the countdown timer on her phone. "Almost done with the final round."

"Let me take over." When the timer reached zero, Xander rang the bell. After thanking them for coming, he asked them to hand their completed dating cards to Rory and told them they'd be notified of any matches the next day.

When she was collecting the cards, Rory glanced at the one the man turned in who seemed to be enjoying Liz's company. She was pleased to note he'd indicated an interest in her friend.

Liz turned in her card last.

"Did you have a good time?" Rory asked.

"It was great. Not all of them were my type, but there was at least one I could see dating."

"Josh?"

"You noticed."

Rory glanced around to make sure no one was within earshot. "I probably shouldn't tell you this, but it's mutual."

Liz squealed with delight. "Really?" She glanced down at her cell. "Look at the time. You should go home. I'm sure Sekhmet could use the company."

Rory cast a puzzled glance at her. "Don't you want to know what I found out?"

Liz's face brightened. "You got a chance to do some sleuthing." She shook her head, a disappointed look in her eyes. "You should get home. You can tell me later. Why don't you walk me out to my car? I'm parked near you. We girls can't be too careful."

Liz had never worried about walking to her car alone before, but Rory could see the wisdom in the suggestion. Even a city as safe as

Vista Beach occasionally had problems, though not enough that she'd considered carrying pepper spray or a stun gun as some women she knew did.

"Sure, let me give these to Xander." Rory found him standing in the hallway deep in conversation with the waiter from the alley and handed the cards to him.

On their way to the front entrance of the restaurant, Rory and Liz passed the host stand.

Rory caught a glimpse of a familiar face in the dining area. "Is that Naomi? I thought she wasn't feeling well."

"Just popped in for a moment, I'm sure. Wouldn't want to catch whatever she has." Liz grabbed Rory's arm and picked up the pace, only letting go when they were outside. Before long, they were both safely in their own cars on their way to their respective destinations.

When Rory got home, she found the lights on in her house. She took a stack of letters out of the mailbox and went in through the front door. An enticing smell hit her nose as soon as she stepped inside. "Mom, are you making dinner for me?" she said as she walked toward the kitchen, dropping her mail on her desk along the way.

In the kitchen she found her mother and her boyfriend staring into an open oven. The table was set for two. A candle sat in its center alongside a bowl of mixed greens.

"What's going on?"

"Martin will explain." Arika picked up her purse. "I put the supplies next to your desk. I'll let you two be. Have a nice dinner."

"Thanks for your help, Arika," Martin said.

"Anytime," Arika said and left the room.

Moments later, Rory heard the front door open and close and the click of the lock. Her thoughts moved from the sudden request for her help at the event to her sighting of the supposedly ill Naomi to Liz practically pushing her out the door of the restaurant at the end, uncharacteristically uninterested in the results of her investigation.

"Naomi wasn't sick, was she? You wanted to get me out of the house. Did Xander know?"

Martin carefully took a quiche out of the oven and set it on the counter to cool. "He was happy to help."

"How many people were involved in this subterfuge?"

"Let's see. Naomi and Xander. Then there's Liz who was in charge of getting you to the restaurant and making sure you stayed there until I texted her everything was ready."

No wonder Liz was practically shoving her out the door of the restaurant. It must have been hard for her to not ask about what Rory had found out.

"And my mom?"

"She let me into your place and helped me cook." He pulled a chair out from the table. "Care to take a seat? Dinner's about ready."

As soon as she was seated, he laid a cloth napkin in her lap and poured a glass of Pinot Grigio for her. Before sitting down himself, he placed the quiche on a trivet in the center of the table to serve after the salad course.

"This looks really good. I didn't know you could cook."

"Your mom helped a lot. I've been practicing for weeks. Everyone at the station is tired of quiche by now."

Rory looked around the kitchen. "Where's Sekhmet? It's not like her to stay away so long when there's this much activity. She likes to be in the center of everything."

"Your mom played her out. I think she's sleeping it off."

Rory settled down to enjoy dinner, wiping all thoughts of the problems at Xander's restaurant out of her mind.

Chapter 13

Rory had barely settled down at her desk to work Wednesday morning when Liz called.

"So? How'd it go?" Liz said as soon as Rory answered.

"The dinner was very nice. I still can't believe how many people were involved. You didn't have to go to so much trouble. Martin could have told me he wanted to cook dinner for me. I would have turned over my kitchen to him and left for a couple hours."

"Where's the fun in that? Besides, he wanted it to be a surprise. You can't say you weren't happy to come home to a handsome man cooking dinner for you."

Rory smiled softly as she thought about the previous evening. "That is true."

Liz's voice took on a more businesslike tone. "Enough about romance. What were you able to find out at the restaurant?"

"I'm surprised you held out asking about it for this long."

"It wasn't easy, believe me. Practically killed me not to ask for all the details last night."

Rory brought her friend up to date on everything she'd learned about the financial problems Xander's restaurant appeared to be having.

"Sounds like he might have an employee strike on his hands soon," Liz said. "I wonder if Solange or the police know about this."

"I don't know about her, but Martin hasn't said anything. He probably wouldn't tell me if he did. What about the rent increase? Is that unusual?"

"Depends. The downtown area has become more popular. Lots of upscale shops and restaurants have been popping up. Rents have been going up like crazy in some areas. He may have negotiated a lower rent for the first six months or year while in his startup phase. It would go up after that. Usually isn't a problem if the restaurant's doing well."

"It always seems to be busy. I would have thought he'd be able to weather a rent increase."

"Maybe he's had some unexpected expenses."

Rory leaned back in her chair. "A part of me wishes I'd never found out about the problems at the restaurant."

"Why?"

"Because it gives Xander a motive to rob those banks."

"Oh, I hadn't thought of that. It doesn't look good, does it?"

"No, it doesn't. He's the right build, has a tattoo right where the robber does, and he was who knows where when that last bank was robbed. He could have put on a fake beard. Too bad we didn't find anything at the crime scene that would point to someone else."

"Did Paris remember anything else about the tattoo?"

"Not as far as I know."

"I hope it's not true," Liz said. "Did you tell Dashing D about what you learned last night?"

"No, I wanted to enjoy dinner. I probably should call him, but something tells me he already knows about Xander's financial problems." Rory rubbed the space between her eyes. "Have you ever thought about getting a tattoo?" She could almost hear her friend shudder over the phone.

"Never, ever going to do that. Sounds way too painful to me. One of those rub-on temporary tattoos is more my style. That would be kind of fun."

Rory's mouth dropped open and she stared at the phone. At the same time, they both blurted out, "Temporary tattoos!"

"The robber could..." Liz started.

"...have had one," Rory finished. "Do you know anything about them? Are they hard to apply?"

"I don't think so."

"I wonder how temporary they are."

"You mean, how hard are they to remove? No idea. I think they last several days, so might not be that easy. Listen, I have to go. I've got another call. I'll check with you later."

Before Rory went back to work, she looked at several websites that sold temporary tattoos. One of them featured short videos on their application and removal. They looked easy to apply and almost as easy to remove using readily available items like olive oil, transparent tape, rubbing alcohol and nail polish remover, leaving no indication a tattoo had ever been there.

It didn't exonerate Xander, but at least it widened the field of suspects, something that could work in his favor. She made a mental note to show Paris the temporary tattoos she'd found online to see her reaction.

Rory wondered if she was dismissing the possibility of Xander's guilt too easily. He'd always seemed a standup guy to her, but she'd only known him for little more than a year. His financial problems could have pushed him into doing something he wouldn't normally do.

She typed the restaurant name into a browser window and sifted through the results for anything that might explain its recent difficulties. Several pages in, she came across its name on a list of temporary restaurant closures. Three weeks ago, the health department had closed Zephy's for two days for problems having to do with water.

Rory sat back in her chair and thought about what she'd learned. She decided to stop by the restaurant later that day to see what she could find out.

On her lunch break, Rory stepped inside Zephy's front door and went up to the host stand where Naomi was seating customers.

"Rory, nice to see you. Are you here by yourself?" Naomi reached for a menu.

"I'm not here to eat. I think I lost an earring last night. Could you help me look for it?" Rory crossed her fingers, hoping Naomi would believe her.

"Sure." She motioned for an employee to take her place, then led the way to the banquet room.

"Must be a lot of work running a restaurant," Rory said as they searched the room.

"It can be, but it's also a lot of fun. It's been Xander's dream for a long time now."

Rory bent down to stare at a spot on the carpet. "I wouldn't want to have to deal with things like health inspections."

"Tell me about it. We had to close for a couple days a while back. Plumbing problems."

Rory straightened up and moved to another spot. "Really? I didn't hear about that."

"We tried to keep it quiet. Managed to get the problem fixed in two days."

"That must have been expensive."

"Money is a little tight, but we'll weather this storm like we have all the others. It's only a temporary setback." Naomi's gaze swept the room. "I don't see it."

"I must have lost it somewhere else. Thanks for helping me look."

Rory left the restaurant wondering how tight money was and if it could have led to Xander robbing banks.

Before she went home, she stopped at a grocery store to pick up supplies for the rest of the week. She grabbed a shopping cart from the rack outside the entrance and wheeled it inside. She'd checked most of the items off her mental shopping list when she spied Harmony Wells in the baby food aisle. Something about the woman's demeanor caused Rory to pause and watch.

Harmony looked around before reaching for containers of baby food and shoving them into the large purse slung over her shoulder. She hustled down the aisle and into the next one. Rory followed as surreptitiously as possible, watching as the woman reached for a can or box here and there. At the last minute she seemed to think better of each purchase and put the item back on the shelf. Finally, she hurried toward the front of the store. Instead of getting in line at the checkout counter, Harmony made a beeline for the closest exit.

When a security guard rounded a corner and walked toward her, her eyes widened and she stopped in her tracks.

Rory waved and called out, "Harmony! There you are. I've been looking all over for you. I started shopping without you."

Confusion and uncertainty written all over her face, Harmony said nothing as Rory looped her arm through hers and gently guided her into the depths of the store, only stopping when they reached a deserted aisle.

"Quick," Rory whispered. "Put the baby food in my basket before he gets here."

"I didn't—"

"There's no time."

Harmony paused for a moment, then pulled the baby food out of her purse and dumped it in the cart right before the security guard rounded the corner.

"Now, what else should we get, do you think?" Rory said, leading Harmony into the next aisle. Rory picked up the rest of the items she needed as well as a few she'd noticed the woman looking at earlier. She continued her chatter as they moved around the store, the security guard watching them from afar. As soon as they got in line at the checkout counter, he lost interest in them.

After they left the store, Rory handed one of the paper bags to Harmony. "Here you go."

"I can't." She pushed back her shoulders, a defiant look in her eyes. "I can buy my own food. I forgot my wallet, that's all. I've been such a ninny since the race, and you know..."

"I understand. Please, let me do this for you."

"Really?" Harmony's eyes filled with tears. "Thank you. I'll pay you back." Bag in hand, she walked across the parking lot toward her car.

Rory watched her for a moment before driving home.

"That was nice of you, buying that food for her." Liz's face filled the display on Rory's phone later that day.

"I could tell she needed it. No one tries to shoplift baby food unless they're desperate."

Liz crinkled her face in worry. "I hate to say this, but are you sure she wasn't playing you?"

Rory adjusted the phone in her hand. "She never asked me for anything. I had to convince her to take the food."

"Teresa did say Harmony was going through a rough time right now." Liz glanced at something off camera. "I know how we can help her." She waved a card in front of her face. "We can buy some makeup from her."

"Teresa said the same thing." Rory placed her phone in a holder on her desk while she brought up Harmony's website on her computer.

"What are you doing?" Liz craned her neck as if she could poke her head through the phone and see what was on the computer screen.

"I'm looking at her website." Before she could say anything else, she heard pounding on her front door followed by a woman's voice. "Rory, are you home? It's important. Open up."

Liz craned her neck even farther. "What's that?"

"Sounds like Solange. I'd better get that before she breaks down the door. I'll call you later."

As soon as Rory opened the door, Solange and Xander rushed inside.

Rory looked from one to the other. "What's going on? Did something happen?"

The couple took the couch in the living room while Rory sat down on a nearby chair.

"What did you need to see me about?" she asked.

Xander's cell phone rang. He ignored the call and scooted closer to Solange, putting an arm around her shoulder. She looked down at her hands. "The police are at the restaurant," she said in a hushed tone. "Searching it."

"Do you know why?"

He cleared his throat. "Remnants of a fake beard were found in a bathroom."

"One of his employees found it and called the police without telling Xan first," Solange added.

"I see," was all Rory could find to say. "Why did you come here?"

"Don't you see?" Solange's voice went up a notch. "Someone's framing Xan."

"You think someone planted the beard? Where was it found, exactly? In the men's or women's restroom?"

"Not the public restrooms," Xander said. "In the small bathroom near my office."

"And the back door," Rory said softly, mulling over the implications of the news.

"That's right. The one you used at the paint and date event last night."

"Is that why you came here? Because I used the bathroom?"

"We want to gather as much information as we can before we talk to the police," Solange said.

"If we can pinpoint when it was put in the trash, maybe we can figure out who did it," Xander added. "Or at least narrow down the possibilities."

"Did you notice anything last night?" Solange asked.

Rory thought back to the previous evening. "Sorry, I didn't. I don't even know if the beard was in the trash can. It has one of those swinging covers. I tossed in the paper towel I used and didn't look inside."

Disappointment washed over Solange's face.

"When was the last time the trash was emptied?" Rory asked. "That could narrow things down."

"I should have thought of that." Xander frowned. "Probably a week ago. That bathroom isn't used much. It's cleaned daily, but we don't empty the trash as often."

"That was before Saturday's race then."

"What are you thinking?"

"Liz and I checked out the alley where Jade's body was found. We were thinking the robber could have ducked in one of the businesses. He could have slipped in the restaurant's back door and gone straight into the bathroom, ripped off the beard and left the same way he came in."

"That means he knows the restaurant," Xander said slowly. "I can't believe it could be one of my employees."

"They haven't exactly been happy lately," Solange got out before he shut her up with a glance.

"It doesn't have to be one of your employees," Rory said. "Maybe the robber ducked in a random door and got lucky. Stranger things have happened."

"That doesn't help much," Solange said.

A cock-a-doodle-doo sounded from the direction of Rory's desk. "Let me get that call. I'll be right back."

When she answered the phone, the deep voice on the other end of the line said, "Is Xander there with you?"

"Yes. Did you need to talk with him?"

"Have him come down to the restaurant" was all Martin said before he hung up.

When Rory returned to the living room, the couple were already on their feet.

"I've been summoned?" Xander said.

"The police want to see you at Zephy's."

"We'd better get going then."

Solange laid a hand on Rory's arm. "Would you...would you come with us? We could use the moral support."

"Let me get my coat."

Moments later, the three left for the restaurant.

Chapter 14

After talking to the police with Xander and Solange, Rory left them at Zephy's and stopped at a Mexican restaurant downtown to satisfy her grumbling stomach. She was taking the last bite of her chicken tacos when Liz slid into the seat across from her.

"Here you are. You had me worried."

Rory wiped her hands on a napkin. "Why?"

"I called and called and you didn't answer."

"Sorry. I put my phone on silent." She took her cell phone out of her pocket and checked its display. "Four calls and half a dozen texts? I hope you haven't been wandering around town looking for me."

Liz waved her own cell in the air. "No need. Tracked your phone."

"You really were worried." After installing the tracking apps on each other's phones, they'd vowed to only use them in an emergency. Liz had obviously thought this was one.

"After that pounding on the door..."

"I'm sorry to worry you."

Liz put her elbows on the table and leaned forward. In a soft voice she said, "I saw some...unusual activity at Xander's restaurant. Do you know what's going on?"

Rory told her everything that had happened in the last couple hours from the moment the couple appeared on her doorstep to accompanying them to Zephy's.

Liz's mouth dropped open when she heard about the false beard. "Wow. Did the police find anything else incriminating besides the beard?"

"Not that I could tell when I was there. They were still searching when I left. I don't know if they'll be done before the restaurant is scheduled to open tonight. I told Martin everything I know, which isn't much. I wish I could help them pinpoint when the beard was put in the trash can."

Liz pursed her lips in thought. "What about those employees you overheard talking? Could one of them have planted it? They probably could use the money if Xander hasn't been paying them."

"That's assuming an employee's the robber. Or maybe someone planted the beard in the trash to make him look guilty out of spite." Rory cast her mind back to the speed paint and date event the previous evening. "In that conversation between those employees, one of them talked about the bathroom being locked on Saturday morning."

"Maybe the bank robber slipped inside and got rid of the beard." Liz mimed ripping off a false beard and throwing it away. "Then slipped out the back door when the coast was clear."

"That could have happened. I'm not sure that helps Xander. He could have been the one who put it there."

"If it was him, he would have taken out the garbage right away to get rid of the incriminating evidence."

"Good point." Rory sat back. "I found out more about the financial issues at the restaurant." She brought Liz up to speed on the plumbing problems.

"That probably cost a bundle. That happened about the time the bank robberies started, didn't it?"

"Exactly."

"Things are not looking good for Xander." Liz's face turned thoughtful. "I'm not sure how we can help him, but we can help Harmony. Have you ordered your makeup yet?"

"Not yet. I forgot all about it. What about you?"

"All taken care of."

"I don't think I can do as good a job applying the makeup as she did."

"She's got some tutorials on her site. They'll help."

"Does she?" Rory brought Harmony's website up on her phone and checked out the various videos. "Wow. She's got a whole YouTube channel. Even talks about how to do theatrical makeup."

"Didn't Solange say she did the makeup for a school play?"

"That was kids, this is much more professional than I expected." As she looked through more videos, one in particular caught her attention. "Oh."

Liz leaned forward, trying to get a glimpse of Rory's screen. "What is it?"

"Did you see this video on transforming a woman into a man?"

"What?"

Rory waited while her friend looked at the beginning part of the video which showed the before picture of Harmony and the after picture of what she looked like as a man.

"That could be a twin for the robber's photo posted on that LA Robbers website." Liz sucked in her breath. "You don't think...?"

"I don't know. She does need money, and she's the right height and build."

"Can't be her. She doesn't have any tattoos. The robber had one, remember?"

"Could be a temporary one like we talked about before."

"But we saw her at the race. She didn't have a tattoo then. I would have noticed."

Rory scrunched her eyes closed, trying to picture Harmony when they saw her on the street. Moments later, her eyes popped open. "The tape."

"What tape?"

"She was scratching the inside of her wrist when we met her on her way to the pier. I picked something up to throw in the trash afterward, but I forgot about it until I got home. It was a tissue with a clear piece of tape attached to it. I didn't think anything about it at the time. Clear tape was one of the methods used to remove a temporary tattoo. And this piece had some black marks on it."

Liz's mouth formed an O, but no sound came out.

They stared at each other while they digested the new theory.

"What should we do?" Liz finally said. "I'd hate to accuse her of being the robber unless we have concrete proof. That could ruin her life."

"There's a lot of evidence against her." Rory ticked each point off on her fingers. "She can transform herself into a man, a man that looks remarkably like the robber, and she was in the area not long after the latest robbery."

"Then there's the tissue and tape you found on the ground where she was standing," Liz added.

"We can't be sure that was hers, but I could swear it wasn't there when we stopped to talk to her and Teresa."

"She also needs money."

"She could have taken off the false beard and dumped it in the bathroom of the restaurant."

"Which was locked at some point that morning. Maybe that was when she was in there. But they would have noticed her come in."

"That's what I thought, but now I'm not so sure," Rory said. "She might've looked enough like their boss that the workers thought it was him."

"Did any of the employees say they saw him on Saturday?" Liz asked.

"No. Martin mentioned that when he questioned Xander at the restaurant."

"What did Xander say?"

"He pretty much clammed up at that point. Talked about getting a lawyer."

"That's not good. Maybe he's the robber after all."

"I don't like either option," Rory said.

"Are you going to tell Dashing D about our suspicions?"

Rory knew she should talk to Martin, but she was reluctant to do it until she was sure she was right. Her own experience had taught her how much damage a false accusation could do. "I don't know." She picked up her phone. "Right now, I'm going to order some makeup."

They were going out the door when they both received texts from Candy asking them to come see her.

"I wonder what she found out," Rory said as they walked toward the PI's office.

"Hopefully, something that will help us figure out who killed Jade."

When they entered the office, they found Candy standing by the receptionist's desk talking to a distinguished-looking older man dressed in a rumpled suit. The two of them abruptly ended their conversation when they spotted the newcomers.

"Ladies," the man said as he left.

Candy led the way into her office and sat down at her desk, indicating they should sit in the chairs across from her.

Rory noted how much cleaner the desk looked. A short stack of folders she assumed were current cases sat on one side. Everything else had been cleared off except for a newly opened box of heart-shaped chocolate truffles. She glanced at the labels on the folders, spotting Jade's name on one and *L. Hayward* on another.

As soon as they sat down, Candy picked up the top folder on the stack. "I had some time, so I looked into Jade McIntyre's background. I believe you know about her work for I Do For You. She's older than I expected." She looked at Rory. "Why did you think she was in her late twenties?"

"That's what someone told us, and it was the age on her bio sheet at the agency."

"How old was she?" Liz asked.

"A good ten years older than that."

"I wouldn't have guessed it."

"She's an actress so maybe she wanted to appear younger so she would get more parts. Forty is a little long in the tooth for Hollywood," Candy said. "No living family members that I could find, but I only did a quick search. I found something much more interesting. I checked with some of the actors she worked with over the years. Apparently, she had a thing for older men. They sent me some candids taken of her at parties. I printed them out. Thought you might like to see them." She took a stack of photos out of the folder and spread them out on the desk in front of them.

Rory and Liz leaned forward to study the five photos, all of Jade on the arm of a different man, all of them appearing to be on the older side.

"Do you recognize any of them?" Candy asked.

Rory's gaze zeroed in on one of the photos. She picked it up and studied it more closely, then angled it so Liz could see. "That's Zeke, isn't it?"

"Zeke?" Candy said.

"Axelrod," Rory said. "Xander's father. When was this taken?"

Candy consulted her notes. "Seven years ago, give or take. These were all taken within a year or two of each other. That one's the oldest."

"Can we keep this?"

"You can have them all."

Liz picked up the photos and stuffed them in her purse.

"Thanks for doing this." Rory's gaze strayed to the stack of folders. "Looks like work has picked up."

Candy looked at the stack. "Old cases. I work on them when I can. Unfortunately, doesn't bring in much money, but it keeps me busy."

"What do we owe you?" Rory drew her wallet out of her pocket.

"It's on the house. I didn't spend much time on it."

"That's awfully generous of you. Thank you."

"Glad to be of help."

Rory and Liz silently left the office, each taking in the unexpected news. Once they were alone on the sidewalk, Rory said, "So Zeke and Jade dated. I shouldn't be that surprised after what Lola told us about her penchant for wealthy men."

"Wasn't he married when that picture was taken?"

"Not sure exactly when he got divorced. Maybe his fling with Jade was the reason for it."

"I wonder if Xander knows," Liz said. "That could be why he had that argument with her at the party."

"Puts a different spin on it, doesn't it?" Rory frowned. "Zeke and Jade acted like they didn't know each other when Solange introduced them. I suppose neither of them wanted to reveal their past relationship. Maybe it ended badly."

"Or Zeke felt guilty about it," Liz said. "It would explain why she forced her way into the wedding party. Maybe he wouldn't take her calls and she wanted to get back together. Do you think he could have killed her?"

"I don't even know if he was in the area," Rory said. "I don't remember seeing him at the race."

"Didn't Xander mention something about him waiting at the finish line?"

"That's right. I'd forgotten about that."

"Too bad we didn't go there ourselves. We might have noticed him."

"Naomi must have been there. Remember, she ran ahead of us." Rory made a mental note to ask her the next time she saw her.

"Enough about the case," Liz said. "What did you think of Candy's sweetie?"

"Sweetie?"

"The guy in her office."

"You think they're dating?"

"Don't you?"

"Didn't even occur to me."

"Come on, can't you feel it? Love is in the air!" Liz spun around a few times, her hands raised to the sky. A couple walking toward them cast her amused glances and stepped out onto the street to avoid running into her. "I bet that box of chocolate truffles was from him." She glanced at her watch. "Got to get going. Places to go, people to see."

On her way home, Rory thought about Xander's father, wondering if he had enough of a reason to want Jade dead.

Rory worked into the evening, every once in a while giving her brain a break from code to focus on Zeke and his possible involvement in Jade's death. She was still mulling over how to find out more about him when she heard a faint knocking on her front door. She thought for a moment she'd imagined it until the noise came again, louder this time.

She opened the door to find Harmony Wells standing on the doorstep, a colorful bag with her website logo in one hand and a tote bag in the other.

She held out the colorful bag. "Your order."

"That was fast," Rory said. "I didn't expect you to bring it by yourself."

"I was in the neighborhood. Don't worry, I didn't charge you for shipping. And I took off what I owed you for the food."

"Thanks. I'm not sure I'll be very good at applying it, but I'll give it a shot."

"It just takes practice. Do you want me to give you a quick tutorial? It won't take long."

Rory opened the door wider. "Sure. Come on in."

The two sat down on chairs in the work area. Harmony dug around in her tote bag, producing a hand mirror and a few makeup brushes. While Rory watched in the mirror, Harmony made up her face with the products from the order, pausing to explain what each item was for and how best to use it. Less than ten minutes later, they were done.

"Do you have any questions?" Harmony said.

Rory felt the urge to ask her if she was a bank robber, but decided to take a more subtle approach. "I think I get it. I appreciate you taking the time. If I don't remember something, I can always look at the videos on your YouTube channel."

"You've seen those?" Nervousness shown in the woman's eyes.

"Some of them. You know, if you'd come by earlier you wouldn't have found me at home."

"Oh?"

"I was at Zephy's, Xander Axelrod's restaurant downtown." She lowered her voice even though they were the only two people in the house. "I'm not sure I should be telling you this, but it'll probably be public knowledge soon. The police found a fake beard there. They think it was worn by the bank robber."

Harmony's face paled. "Oh?"

"As soon as they analyze the DNA they got off it, the police should be able to identify them."

"That's good," Harmony said in a squeaky voice. "Can I use your bathroom?"

"Sure." Rory pointed her down the hallway. As soon as she heard the bathroom door close, she rummaged through the woman's tote bag, looking for incriminating evidence. Inside she found gloves and a stack of temporary tattoos. Rory had an unused tattoo in her hand when Harmony returned.

"What are you doing?" She grabbed for the tattoo, but Rory held on tight.

"This looks like the tattoo the teller described on the robber."

"What are you talking about? I didn't hear anything about a tattoo."

"You didn't see the article on *VBC*? The teller said there was a heart like this one on a tattoo on the robber's wrist." Rory mentally apologized to the universe for the white lie, hoping her face wouldn't betray her.

Harmony sat down heavily on a nearby chair.

"It's better if you turn yourself in."

"I don't know what you're talking about."

Rory's gaze strayed to the tote bag, noticing for the first time a red spot on its side. She pointed to it. "From the dye pack?"

Harmony glanced over and a defeated look appeared in her eyes. "I didn't want to do it."

"Why did you?"

"For my kids. I'll do anything for them." She sat up straighter. "They're not going to starve. Not if I have anything to say about it."

"What about your husband?"

"He got laid off some time ago. I have a part-time job and my makeup business. We were okay for a while, then my oldest got sick."

"Don't you have health insurance?"

"It's not the best and it doesn't cover everything. We took out one of those payday loans, but that only got us deeper in debt."

Rory cast a sympathetic glance at her. "I'm sorry, but why did you think robbing banks was the answer?"

"I was in a bank when it was being robbed once. It looked so easy and I didn't know what else to do."

"I'm sure the police will take it all into account." Rory cleared her throat. "But why did you kill Jade? Did she attack you?"

A look of horror appeared on Harmony's face. "No! I didn't kill her. She was waiting for someone in the alley when I left."

"You saw her?"

"I'd better start from the beginning. After the bank, I ran into the alley where I'd stashed my tote bag with a change of clothes in it. I was stuffing the cash in the bag when the dye pack burst. So I tossed it in the trash. Then I walked in the back door of the restaurant and slipped into the bathroom. That's where I took off the beard and tattoo and changed clothes."

"How did you know about the bathroom?"

"I know someone who works there. They took me on a tour right before the restaurant opened."

"Then what happened?"

"I went out the alley door and saw Jade leaning against the wall, staring down at her phone. It looked like she was waiting for someone. She didn't seem very happy."

"Why do you say that?"

"She was frowning and looked... awful."

"She was partying pretty hard the night before."

"That might explain it. I went out the alley the way I came. She never saw me, didn't even look up." Harmony looked at Rory, an appeal in her eyes. "You have to believe me. I didn't do it."

"What about the heart?"

"I must have dropped it when I took the money out of the bag."

"You need to go to the police and tell them everything. You don't want them to arrest an innocent person, do you?"

Harmony wiped a tear from her eye. "I don't know if I can do it. Walk into the police station and turn myself in."

Rory handed her a tissue. "Do you want me to call your husband?"

"How am I going to explain this to him? He has no idea what I've been up to."

"How about this? I can get Detective Green to come here and talk to you. Would that make it easier?"

"Thanks. I'd appreciate that."

"What about a lawyer? You really should have one."

"I'll be okay. I need to get this off my chest before I lose courage."

After making the call, Rory sat next to Harmony and held her hand until Martin arrived.

Chapter 15

A cock-a-doodle-doo pierced Rory's brain the next morning, jolting her out of a pleasant dream. She groped around on her nightstand until she found the incessantly ringing cell phone. Bleary-eyed, she checked its display, sighing when she saw the time.

"Mrs. Griswold. Is everything okay?" Rory did her best to sound alert, a hard thing for her to do at five a.m.

"Oh, my goodness. I didn't realize what time it is there. So sorry to wake you."

Rory sat on the edge of the bed and yawned. Sekhmet stretched and made her way over to her side. "It's okay. I was going to get up soon anyway. Is there something I can do for you?"

"I wanted to thank you for sending those pictures so quickly."

"No problem. How's your visit going?"

"It's fine, but if I have to listen to one more story about my sister's gall bladder operation, I'll explode. Still, she's family. How's everything there?"

"No problems with your house. I've been picking up your mail every day and making sure everything's okay."

"And the house across the street?"

"No changes there."

"And...?"

Rory racked her brain, trying to figure out what her neighbor wanted to know but wouldn't come out and say. Then something in her tired mind clicked. "You heard about what happened at the Love Run, didn't you?"

"I may have seen something on *VBC*. I like to keep abreast of everything that's going on in town while I'm away. Tell me everything you know."

Rory sat back on the bed and leaned against the headboard. With Sekhmet curled against her, she gave a bare-bones description of the discovery of Jade's body.

"Hmm," Mrs. Griswold said. "Of course, it had to be you who found her."

"Why do people keep saying that? It wasn't only me. It's not like I go out of my way to find bodies."

"You're a, what do you call it? A corpse magnet. Unfortunately, I don't know this Jade person so I can't help you there. But I might know someone who does. I'll make some calls."

"But you're all the way across the country."

"We do have phones here."

Rory rubbed her eyes. "Sorry. I mean you shouldn't have to worry about this when you're on vacation."

"Doesn't mean I can't help."

Rory heard a faint "Winifred" in the background.

"Hold on," Mrs. Griswold said. Rory heard her call out to someone, "Can't you see I'm on the phone?" followed by the sound of a door closing. A short time later, she was back on the line. "Sorry about that. We won't be disturbed now. Where were we?"

"Shouldn't you see what your sister wants?"

"She's fine. She just likes to complain. You were saying?"

"Maybe you can help. What do you know about Zeke Axelrod?"

"Is he a suspect?"

"No, maybe, I don't know. He was in one of the photos I sent you, checking out the construction site. Do you know why?"

Mrs. Griswold harumphed. "He's a piece of work, that one. Always has to be in control. His poor wife."

"You knew his wife?"

"Ex-wife. Poor Zephinia. Don't know what her parents were thinking, saddling her with that name. Lovely lady. She passed a few months back. That son of hers was very devoted to her."

"I figured that since he named his restaurant after her. Do you know when his parents got divorced?"

"Many years ago. Seven, eight. Something like that. Zeke got himself a younger model. A cute petite little thing."

An image of Jade flashed into Rory's mind.

"Didn't last long," Mrs. Griswold continued.

"Any idea why?"

"She wanted more than he was willing to give is what I heard. That's something I never understood."

"What?"

"He'd had affairs before. Lots of them. Zephy could handle the others, but not that one."

"Do you know what was so different about it?"

"She wouldn't say. She took the money from the divorce and ran."

"That's when Zeke moved up north, isn't it?" Rory said.

"That's right. Sounds like he might be coming back. I heard him talking to a real estate agent at the construction site. He was asking about buying the place."

"Really." Rory tried to imagine having Xander's father as a neighbor. "Wait a minute. How'd you hear them? Weren't they all the way across the street?"

"I have a..." Mrs. Griswold's voice lowered to a whisper. "...special helper."

"What do you mean?"

"I bought a listening device. Got it online. I'm always amazed how many things you can buy there. I keep it close at hand in my bedroom. I can hear all the way across the street and then some from my balcony. Unfortunately, that means hearing badly sung opera as well. I should have a talk with him sometime. It would be doing the neighborhood a service, really."

Rory suppressed a gasp. "Do you listen to everyone?" she said in a much higher tone than usual.

Mrs. Griswold's voice turned huffy. "I am the Neighborhood Watch block captain. It's my *duty* to know what's going on. I hope, if Zeke does buy the house, he hires a more suitable contractor. Listen, I'll see what else I can dig up. I'll call you if I find out anything."

After she hung up, Rory thought about the conversation. She didn't know if what she'd learned had anything to do with Jade's murder, but she did find it interesting as well as moderately disturbing. She vowed to herself to watch what she said around the house, then put the ringer on silent and snuggled up with Sekhmet for a few more minutes of sleep.

Less than three hours later, Rory settled down in the passenger seat of Liz's sedan for the short drive to the pier for the first phase in the transfer of the love locks. An overnight rain left a freshness in the air and dampness on the ground.

Rory peered out the window at the partly cloudy skies, put her hand in front of her mouth and yawned.

"Late night?" Liz looked over at her friend from her place at the wheel.

"Sorry. Mrs. Griswold called me at five this morning."

"That's awfully early. Is everything okay?"

"She forgot about the time difference. She said she called to thank me for sending the photos, but I really think she wanted the scoop on the murder."

"How'd she hear about that?"

"Where do you think?"

Liz stopped at a light and turned astonished eyes on Rory. "She keeps up with *VBC* even when she's out of town?"

"You know how seriously she takes her Neighborhood Watch duties. She doesn't want any surprises when she gets home."

They started moving again, turning at the next light to head down the hill toward the pier, now in sight.

"Did she have anything useful to say?" Liz asked.

"Not about Jade, but she did talk about Zeke's interest in the house across from mine." Rory shared everything she'd learned from the conversation with her neighbor. "Not sure it has anything to do with Jade's murder."

"Maybe it does. Maybe he didn't want her complicating his return to Vista Beach. Did you tell Granny G the latest about the bank robbery?"

"She never asked, and I didn't even think to mention it."

Liz slid the car into a parking spot in the lot nearest the pier and turned off the engine. She twisted in her seat to face Rory. "Before we go down, we need to talk about Harmony. How is she?"

"I'm not sure. She told Martin everything at my place, then they left together." Rory looked at the waves rolling onto the beach. "It makes me sad that she felt she had no other choice."

"I can see her protecting her family, but I can't see her killing anyone. Unless her kids were in danger."

"She insists she didn't. Said it looked like Jade was waiting for someone."

"If we find out who that was, we'll probably find the murderer."

"I'm sure the police are looking at her phone records. Maybe they'll find something. Let's go."

They each grabbed an empty plastic bin from the trunk and crossed the sparsely populated bike path onto the pier. The padlocks that graced the railings on both sides seemed to have doubled in number since their last trip to the area a few days ago.

"Looks like a lot of people ignored that." Rory gestured to a prominent sign on a pedestal near the entrance to the pier asking that locks be placed on the structure now set up in front of city hall.

"More locks for us to take care of." Liz set down her bin and cracked her knuckles. "I like the challenge."

"Where's your group?" Rory's gaze swept the area, taking in the people walking down the pier as well as those standing around watching the waves crash down on the beach.

Liz pointed to two men and a woman of varying ages clustered on one side of the pier. "There they are. Come on, I'll introduce you."

They were steps away from them when the youngest man turned around. "Here she is now," he said to the rest of the group.

Liz blushed as soon as she saw him.

Rory leaned down and whispered into her ear. "You didn't tell me about him. He's cute."

After introductions were made, Todd, the twenty-something man who'd greeted them, went over the procedure. Each of them would take a section of the railing and work on those locks, putting them on the ground. Rory would place the freed locks in one of the plastic bins, making sure to keep them unlocked, for later transport to city hall.

"Thanks for helping out," Todd said to Rory. "It'll go a lot faster if we can place them on the ground next to where we're working."

"No problem," Rory said. "I'm curious to see you work. Is anyone else coming? There are a lot of locks here."

"One or two others are joining us later. This'll be a challenge. But we're all up for it, right?" He looked over the group, getting shouts of agreement in response. "Okay, let's get to work."

The lock-pickers fanned out on both sides of the pier, brought out their lock-picking tools and began their task. Before long, Rory was picking up locks and putting them into the two plastic bins. She was standing in the middle of the pier watching Liz work when a hand thrust a digital recorder in front of her face.

"What can you tell me about this illegal activity?" a raspy voice said.

Rory turned her head to find Veronica Justice standing beside her. "No comment."

"You have nothing to say?"

"I don't want to be quoted. Put that away," Rory pointed at the recorder, "and I'll talk to you. Off the record."

Veronica turned off the recorder and shoved it in her tote bag. "Well?"

"First, this isn't illegal. The city knows about it and agreed to it. Second, if you want an official quote you should talk to one of the lock-pickers."

"What's your role in this?"

"I'm gathering up the locks when they're off the railings and helping to transfer them to the structure next to city hall."

Veronica jotted down something in a notepad she whipped out of her bag. "Who do you think is the best person for me to talk to?"

Rory considered the question. "I'd say Todd. He seems to be in charge." She pointed him out to Veronica. "Before you go, can I get a look sometime at the pictures you took at the finish line of the Love Run?"

"What's in it for me?"

"Does there have to be something?"

"You scratch my back, I scratch yours. That's the way the world works."

"What do you want?"

Veronica screwed up her face in thought. "Nothing...right now. You'll owe me one."

Rory reluctantly agreed, wondering what she was getting herself into.

"I'll be at the office later today. Come by and I'll show you what I have."

Veronica pulled out her camera and took several photos of the group before walking over to talk with Todd. A crowd soon gathered on the pier to watch, some of them using the stopwatch on their phones to unofficially time the participants.

After half of the locks had been rescued, they all took a break. Todd and most of the other members of the lock-picking group sat on benches that faced the beach, sipping water and talking while Rory and Liz sat down on the pier beside one of the plastic bins.

Rory carefully sifted through the locks they'd freed so far, happy to see a number of them had been purchased at her mother's store.

"A lot of these aren't decorated. I like the ones your mom is selling the best. Have you and Dashing D thought about getting one?" Liz held up a pair of intertwined padlocks. "This is pretty cool. You could buy two and do this with them."

"I'm not sure we're at the point of declaring our undying love for each other yet. It's only been six months. Going to a wedding together is a big enough step right now."

Between sips of water, they continued looking through the box of locks. They'd examined half of them when a deep voice behind them said, "How's it going?"

Rory twisted her neck and looked up to find Martin standing next to them dressed in black biking shorts and a blue short-sleeved jersey, holding onto the handlebars of his bicycle. She smiled up at him. "Pretty good. We're about halfway done. Are you getting back from a ride or just heading out?"

"I'm at the tail end. I saw you and thought I'd stop to say hi." He took off his helmet, hung it on the handlebars, and leaned his bike against an empty part of the railing. After taking a water bottle off the clip on the bike's frame, he sat down cross-legged next to Rory. "Quite a few locks here. Have you counted them?"

"No time to. We've been taking them off as fast as we can. There's another bin over there." Liz pointed to the other side of the pier where an identical plastic bin rested next to the railing.

"Have you found any locks for people you know?"

"I saw one for Xander and Solange." Rory rummaged around in the bin and withdrew a padlock with *XA* and *SF* painted on it. "I'm pretty sure this is theirs."

Martin examined it. "Can't be too many couples with those initials in the area. I'm sure they'll be happy to have it rescued." He returned the lock to the bin and looked at a few others.

"How's Harmony?" Rory said.

Martin rested his hand on the edge of the bin. "Her bail hearing is later today. Lawyers are sorting everything out."

"What do you think is going to happen to her?"

"I can't say for sure, but in a similar case in San Diego, the robber got three years."

Rory sucked in her breath. She couldn't imagine spending that much time away from her family.

"You don't think she killed Jade, do you?" Liz asked.

"I very much doubt it."

"Why are you so sure?" Rory said. "I mean, I don't think she did it either, but you tend to be more suspicious of people."

He raised an eyebrow.

"I know, I know, it's part of your job."

He took a sip of water. "Call it a gut feeling."

Rory suspected there was more to it, but she let it go.

"It must have been whoever she was meeting who killed her," Liz said.

"Do you know who that was?" Rory asked.

"Not yet," he said.

"From what Harmony said, Jade was practically glued to her phone in the alley. There weren't any texts that could tell you something?"

"If there were any, they were deleted. We're working on getting access to her records now. We should know something soon."

A short while later, Todd stood up and clapped his hands. "That's enough of a break. Let's get back to work."

"That's my cue." Martin stood up and offered a hand to Rory to help her up. Once she was on her feet, he gave her a peck on the cheek, then turned his back and picked up his helmet.

Liz glanced at his butt and giggled. "You're right," she said to Rory in a soft tone. "Bootylicious."

Rory blushed as Martin eyed the two of them. Amusement spread across his face. He waved a hand in farewell, then wheeled his bicycle the short distance to the bike path.

Two hours later, all of the locks were off the railings. They lugged the now much heavier bins to an SUV parked in the lot. Todd and his group piled into it while Rory and Liz followed in their car to city hall.

Soon they were all standing in the courtyard in front of the building where a tree-like frame made of painted green steel stood next to the fountain. The circular structure, sixteen feet tall topped with a finial, held six mesh panels, each seven feet high. A nearby sign indicated love locks could be affixed to the mesh and requested that keys be discarded in the nearby trash can.

"Wow," Rory said. "I didn't realize it was going to be so tall."

"Holds twenty-five thousand locks," Todd said. "If that's not enough room, the city can always spring for another one."

"Maybe we'll have a love lock forest." Liz seemed pleased at the idea.

Rory pointed to a half dozen locks already on the tree. "Didn't take long for people to find this place."

"Soon there'll be a lot more. Let's get to work." Todd set one bin on one side of the tree while another member of the group put the second one on the other side.

Liz sat on the ground next to one of the bins and handed locks to the much taller Rory who randomly fixed them to the metal structure, glancing at the names and initials on each one as she placed them on the tree. They'd barely started work when Solange arrived.

"There you are," she said. "I checked at the pier, but no one was there."

"We started early," Liz said. "What brings you by?"

"I wanted to make sure our love lock didn't get lost in transit."

Liz rummaged around in the bin and found the lock with the couple's initials on it. "Here it is. Do you want the honor?"

Solange affixed it to the tree, selecting a spot at eye level. "So it's easy for us to find." She sat down on the edge of the fountain. "I wanted to thank you for finding out who the robber was. I still can't believe it was Harmony. She seemed so sweet."

"Desperate times call for desperate measures," Rory said.

"I feel better now that we know who killed Jade. She can finally rest in peace."

Liz placed a hand on the edge of the half empty bin. "I'm not sure we do."

"What do you mean?"

"Harmony insists Jade was still alive when she left," Rory said.

"She would, wouldn't she?"

"You said yourself you weren't sure the robber was the murderer."

"I know, but I was so hoping this was all over." A miserable expression on her face, Solange stared at the spot on the tree where her lock now hung.

The other two women exchanged glances.

"There's another possibility," Rory said in a low voice. "I'm not sure you'll like it."

Liz took a photo out of her purse and handed it to Solange.

"What's this?"

"Proof Zeke and Jade knew each other...before," Rory said.

Solange studied the photo, a mix of emotions playing across her face. "When was this taken?"

"About seven years ago. They were dating back then."

Solange sat quietly, absorbing the new information. "That's about the time Xan's parents divorced," she finally said in a subdued tone. "He told me his father had an affair, but I never knew who the woman was."

"Do you think Xander knew about them?"

"He would have told me at the party as soon as he saw her, wouldn't he?"

"Maybe he didn't want to ruin it for you," Liz said. "Or he didn't know what she looked like."

"Do you think she was trying to get back with Zeke? That's why she paid to be part of the wedding party? To get close to him?"

"It's a possibility."

Solange stood up. "Let's go and see what Xan knows. He's at the restaurant."

"We can't leave right now," Rory said. "We still have locks to put on."

Liz made a shooing motion with her hand. "Go. I can finish this. Todd can help me. Come back after."

"You're sure?"

"I'm sure."

The picture of Zeke and Jade clutched in the bride-to-be's hand, Solange and Rory left city hall for the short walk to the restaurant.

Chapter 16

When they arrived at Zephy's less than fifteen minutes later, Solange and Rory found Xander and his sister in the banquet room.

"...put tables there and there." Naomi pointed to spots in the currently empty room.

Solange knocked on the door frame. "Sorry to interrupt, but it's important." She stepped forward while Rory hovered in the background, unsure of her role in the upcoming conversation.

"What's wrong?" Xander said.

Solange silently gave him the photo of Jade and his father.

"What's this?" He looked at it, surprise written all over his face.

"We think this is why Jade paid to be in the wedding party."

"Let me see," Naomi said.

"I can't help what my father has gotten up to in the last couple years," Xander said as he handed over the picture. "What does it matter now, anyway? We know who killed her."

"It wasn't the bank robber," Rory said. "She saw Jade in the alley, waiting for someone, but that's it."

Xander's face turned pale. "Do you think my dad did it?"

"We don't know, but the photo is suggestive."

"When was it taken?"

"Seven years ago," Solange said.

"What?" Shock written all over his face, his gaze rested on his sister who didn't seem surprised at what she saw or heard.

"You knew? You *knew*?" he said to her.

"He swore me to secrecy," Naomi said in a small voice.

Rory wondered why Xander was getting so upset. He'd known the reason for the divorce even if he didn't know the name of the woman his father had an affair with.

"What's going on?" Solange said.

"You'd better tell her," Naomi said.

"I suppose I can't avoid it any longer." Xander took a deep breath and plunged in. "Many years ago, long before I met you, Jade and I were...engaged."

Solange stared at him open-mouthed as the information sank in. "She's the one you were engaged to?" She turned to Naomi. "You knew about this and didn't tell me?"

Naomi took a step back. "It wasn't my news to tell."

"She's not the one you should be upset with," Xander said. "I should have told you as soon as I saw her."

"Why didn't you?"

"That chapter in my life was over years ago. I never thought I'd see her again. And I certainly didn't expect her to be one of your bridesmaids. I was confused, didn't know what to think. I know you couldn't have known each other in high school."

Solange took a deep breath. "Who broke it off?"

"Jade. We got engaged when I was in medical school. Worst mistake of my life. The engagement, not medical school, though that was a close second. As soon as I told her I was quitting to become a chef and she realized she couldn't change my mind, she told me we were done."

"What about her and Zeke? They were obviously together in that picture. Was she dating both of you at the same time?"

"I have no idea. I knew nothing about their relationship." He looked pointedly at his sister. "But she obviously did."

"Dad started dating her right after she broke up with Xander. Apparently, they'd been discreetly flirting while she was engaged, but they never did anything about it until after. He and Mom wanted me to keep it quiet," Naomi said. "That was the straw that broke the camel's back for her. She could take Dad's other affairs, but not when it was with her son's ex-fiancée."

"What about that conversation you had with her at the party, Xan? What was that really about?" Solange said.

"I wanted to know what was going on. Why she was there, masquerading as an old school friend of yours. From our conversation, it seemed like she was trying to get back together with me. I would never do that. You're the one I love." He brushed his hand across her cheek.

"Could you two leave us? We have a lot to discuss."

"I'll walk you out, Rory." Naomi led the way down the hallway toward the front door. "We didn't tell him out of love, you know." Her eyes pleaded for understanding.

"It's a tough situation. I hope they work it out," Rory said.

"The police are positive the bank robber didn't kill her?"

"Seems so. If we only knew who Jade was meeting. You ran ahead of us at the race. Did you see anything that could point the police in the right direction?"

"No, nothing," she said quickly. "I've got work to do." She left Rory standing by the front door wondering what Naomi was holding back.

When Rory got back to city hall, she found the bins empty, the lock-picking crew gone, and all locks attached to the metal tree. Liz stood on tiptoe, testing the secureness of each one she could reach. A single lock lay on the edge of the fountain.

Rory pointed to it. "You forgot one."

"I kept it out to show you. Take a look at it."

Rory examined the lock. In the middle were a crudely painted *XA* and *JM* and the word forever surrounded by hearts.

"Looks like she was after Xander, not Zeke," Liz said.

"Makes sense," Rory said. "They were engaged once."

"Whoa." Liz's hands formed a T. "Time out. What's this about Xander being engaged before?"

"It was years ago when he was in medical school. Jade broke it off when he quit to become a chef. He told us about it at the restaurant."

The silence stretched out as Liz took in the unexpected news. "Sounds like she didn't really love him if she couldn't support his change in careers. Is that what they were arguing about at the party? Their engagement."

"Something like that."

"And he never told Solange?"

"He told her he had been engaged once before, but never told her who it was."

Liz sat down on the edge of the fountain. "Now that we know about the engagement, it makes sense Jade would want to get back with Xander. He's a famous chef now. On his way to becoming the next Gordon Ramsay. Did you ask Xander if he knows who she was meeting at the race?"

"Didn't get a chance to. I asked Naomi if she saw anything, but she said no."

Rory thought about everything she'd learned. If Jade really was trying to get back together with Xander, maybe he was the one she was meeting in the alley. The one who'd killed her. She stared at the lock still in her hand. She didn't like the idea, but she knew she had to turn it over to the police. With a heavy heart, she stood up. "Before I hand this over to Martin, let's go and see Veronica and look at the photos of the finish line of the race. Maybe that will tell us something."

Rory stuffed the lock in the pocket of her jeans and led the way to the newspaper office.

When they reached the offices of the *Vista Beach View*, they found Veronica at her desk in the far corner. They made their way around the dozen desks scattered around the large room toward her.

Veronica looked up from her phone. "You're here." She grabbed a couple chairs from neighboring desks, and they all settled down around the computer screen.

"You wanted to see the pics from the finish line, right? Let's see..." Veronica flipped through the photos she'd taken at the Love Run until she found the right ones. "Here we go."

Rory exchanged places with her. Liz pulled her chair in closer and peered at the screen while Veronica sat behind them and observed. They'd looked at a couple dozen photos before finding one with Xander's father in it.

"That's him," Rory said. "Talking to the mayor."

"Do you know what time it was taken?" Liz asked.

Rory checked the photo's properties. "It says 8:55 a.m." She twisted around in her seat and addressed Veronica. "Is this time stamp accurate?"

She looked insulted to even be asked. "Obviously."

"That was before the bank robbery," Liz said.

"Maybe he left." Rory examined a dozen more photos. "Looks like a long conversation with the mayor."

"And several city council members," Liz said. "That's a heck of an alibi."

"Alibi?" Veronica leaned forward and rested her elbows on her knees. "Why does he need an alibi? Oh, you think Zeke Axelrod is the killer. Why?"

"He's not, so it doesn't matter." Worried that Veronica was going to call in her favor and ask her to spill the beans on Xander's father, Rory stood up. "Thanks for letting us look at the photos."

Rory breathed a sigh of relief when Veronica didn't stop them from leaving. As soon as they were far enough away from the newspaper office, she drew the padlock they'd found out of her pocket. "I need to take this to the station."

"Do you want me to go with you? I did find it."

"No. I can do it on my own. Someone will call you if they need any more information."

Liz waved goodbye and Rory texted Martin she had something to show him before taking the short walk to the police station.

The first thing Rory noticed when she stepped inside the station was Solange and Xander standing in the middle of the lobby, talking quietly to each other. Anger written all over her face, Solange strode toward Rory as soon as she saw her.

"This is all your fault," she said in a loud voice. "You couldn't keep your mouth shut about the engagement, could you? It doesn't matter. That was years ago."

Before Rory could say anything, a deep voice said, "What engagement?"

Solange swung around and stared open-mouthed at Detective Green who was now standing in the doorway that led to the interior of the station. She collapsed into a nearby chair and covered her face with her hands.

Rory sat down beside her and gave her a side hug.

Xander took a step toward them, stopping when the detective addressed him by name.

"Let's talk. Don't worry, she's in good hands."

Martin and Xander disappeared down the hallway into the bowels of the station.

As soon as Solange calmed down, Rory said, "Tell me what's going on."

"I'm not sure. Xan got a call from Martin and here we are."

"Do you know why?"

"He said it was about Jade. I assumed..." Solange looked down at her hands, now neatly folded in her lap. "Sorry. I should have known you wouldn't blab to him about the engagement. But I didn't know what else the police would want to talk about."

Rory patted her shoulder. "It's okay. I understand."

"What's that?" Solange reached out to touch the padlock Rory had forgotten she still held in her hand.

Rory's fist closed tighter around it.

"Oh, it's a love lock." A smile spread across Solange's face. "For you and Martin? You don't have to show me. I'm sure you want him to see it first. Let me know when it's on the tree."

Moments later, the outside door flew open and Zeke strode into the station looking what Rory's grandmother would have described as spitting mad.

"Where is he? Where's my son?" he said to the world in general, his voice booming off the walls. His gaze zeroed in on the two women who cringed and tried to make themselves as small as possible.

He strode toward them, his face softening when he realized the impact he was having. "Where's Xander? Do you know what's going on?" he said in a quieter tone.

"They know about his previous engagement," Solange said.

"How?" Zeke glared at Rory.

"It wasn't her," Solange said in barely a whisper. "It was me. I thought they already knew."

He mumbled something about "worthless woman" and "even in death," then stomped over to the counter and demanded to see his son. One officer tried to calm him down while another went down the hallway, presumably to get Detective Green.

When Martin appeared in the lobby, Zeke walked over to him, stopping within inches of the detective's face. Martin merely raised an eyebrow and held up his hand. In a quiet voice, he said, "Your son can leave anytime he wants. He's not under arrest." An unspoken *yet* hung in the air. "He gave me this note for you." He handed over a piece of paper, then turned to talk to an officer who had entered the lobby.

Zeke glanced at the note, then sat down on the other side of Solange and patted her hand. "He says he's okay. Wants me to take care of you."

Solange looked at him. "Could I talk to Rory for a moment in private?"

He moved to the opposite side of the lobby to study a display of historical photographs.

"I'm so sorry to drag you into this," Solange said. "And for...before."

"It's not a problem. Are you and Xander okay?"

"We still have some talking to do, but we'll work it out. Don't get me wrong. It was a shock to learn he'd been engaged to Jade. But that's not what I wanted to talk to you about. Could you do me a favor?"

"What do you need?"

Solange reached into her purse and brought out a Post-it note. "I made an appointment with Jade's landlord tomorrow morning to get into her apartment. She'd already bought some decorations for the shower. Could you go there for me?"

"But you cancelled the shower."

"I paid for them already. I figure I shouldn't let them go to waste. I'll find a use for them."

"The police don't have any problem with that?"

"They're done with her place. I think they got everything they want from it."

"What about her landlord?"

"She was very understanding. The address is on the paper. The apartment manager knows someone's coming. He's in apartment one."

An idea formed in Rory's mind. The errand would give her a chance to see if she could find out anything else about Jade that would point to her killer. She might even find a phone bill with phone numbers she could investigate. "No problem. It'll give me a chance to...explore."

Solange looked confused for a moment, then understanding dawned on her. "Exploring is a good thing."

Rory stood up when Martin motioned for her to follow him. She remained quiet until she was sitting in the chair beside his desk.

"Don't you have to go back to Xander?" she said.

"He can wait." Martin allowed a touch of frustration to appear in his voice. "Did you know? About the engagement?"

"Not until today. Are you going to arrest him?"

"Haven't decided yet, but it's not looking good for him." His face relaxed. "What do you have for me?"

Rory reluctantly handed over the love lock with Jade's and Xander's initials on it.

He studied it. "This was one of the locks you transferred today?"

"Liz found it. We don't know if it's important but thought you should have it. It came from my mother's store, but I doubt anyone there put on the initials. Too sloppy."

"Any idea which one bought it?"

"I assume it was Jade in an attempt to get back with Xander."

"Never assume anything. I'll check with your mother and see what she knows. Thanks for bringing it to my attention."

When Rory passed through the lobby a few minutes later, she found it empty. As soon as she was outside, she phoned Liz. "We've got work to do."

Chapter 17

"So you still don't know why Dashing D called Xander in for more questioning?" Liz said as Rory opened the front door to Mrs. Griswold's house the next morning. "He didn't even give you a hint when you saw him at the station?"

"No clue. It wasn't about him being engaged to Jade. Martin didn't even know about that until Solange let it slip." Rory dropped the mail on the table in the entryway.

"I still think if we find out who Jade was meeting, we'll have her killer."

"Maybe we'll find something that will tell us who that was at her place. Let me take a quick look around to make sure everything's okay before we go. I'll take the downstairs while you take the upstairs, okay?"

Rory had finished a circuit of the first floor when Liz raced down the stairs.

"Everything okay?"

"Nothing's wrong upstairs," Liz said. "But Zeke's at the construction site."

"Let's go talk to him." Rory opened the door at the same time a car screeched to a halt, parking haphazardly on the street nearby. Xander slammed the car door and strode toward his father.

Rory closed the front door and leaned against it.

"What's the matter?" Liz said.

"Xander just showed up. He doesn't look happy. I think we should stay out of it."

Liz stood stock still. Rory could almost hear the wheels turning in her friend's brain.

"Where's the binocam?"

Rory pointed toward the living room. "I left it on top of the desk. Why?"

Liz ran into the living room and grabbed the combination binoculars and camera, then motioned for Rory to follow her up the stairs into Mrs. Griswold's bedroom and onto a balcony that overlooked Seagull Lane.

Rory caught a glimpse of Xander and his father facing off in front of the construction site before they crouched down on their knees. Liz hid behind a potted plant and trained the binocam on the scene. "Lots of hand waving and glaring," she reported in a whisper. "I wish I could read lips."

Her conversation with Mrs. Griswold popped into Rory's mind. "I have an idea." She hurried into the adjoining bedroom, her gaze sweeping the area until she spotted what she was looking for on the dresser. She grabbed a device with headphones and what looked like a miniature satellite dish attached to a handle, then sat down cross-legged on the balcony. Liz looked wide-eyed at her as Rory placed the headphones over her ears and pointed the device at the arguing pair. In the background she heard a man's voice singing opera, then her ears focused on the conversation taking place across the street.

"I'm getting something now."

"...a mistake. I freely admit it," Zeke said. "I'm not the one to blame. She came on to me."

"You could have told her no. Why you thought that relationship was appropriate...You broke Mom. You know that, don't you?"

"She made out okay. We need to put this all behind us. Family should stick together."

Xander's snort came in loud and clear. "Since when has that been your motto?"

"They're talking about Zeke and Jade's affair," Rory said, trying to keep Liz up to date on the general direction of the conversation while still listening.

A truck rumbling down the street momentarily drowned out the next few words.

"...keep on going over the same ground again and again, but you're not listening," Xander said.

"I don't know why you won't take my help," his father replied.

Rory looked between the posts of the balcony railing in time to see Xander sweep his arm over the construction site.

"We don't need *this*," he said. "We have our own place."

"That grubby little house? It's not someplace my son and my future grandchildren should be living."

"It's not grubby."

"You'd be doing me a favor. I'm buying this place as an investment whether you like it or not. You'd be living in it rent free once it's finished. How can you turn down a deal like that?"

Liz tugged on Rory's arm. "What are they talking about now? Xander's pacing."

"Zeke wants them to live in the house after he buys it," she whispered back. "Rent free."

"But Zeke would still own it?"

"I think so." Rory went back to concentrating on the conversation between the two men.

"...may not matter," Xander said. "The police have it in for me."

"Don't worry. I'll take care of them," Zeke replied.

"You can't 'take care' of them."

"What do they have on you that's got you so worried? Fingerprints on a knife that people saw you throw away? An engagement that happened years ago? That's nothing."

"She was trying to sabotage the wedding. Cancelled some hotel reservations and called the florist with the wrong information. I wanted her to stop before she did something worse, so I agreed to meet her."

"So? You couldn't have killed her. You were walking the Love Run with Solange. Countless people saw you."

"Not the entire time," Xander said. "I was supposed to meet Jade in the alley behind the restaurant, but I was a few minutes late. When I got there, she was already dead."

Rory listened wide-eyed to the confession.

Zeke's voice took on a sharp tone. "Do the police know?"

"That's why they brought me in for questioning. They found texts I sent her."

"Why didn't you delete them?"

"I did, from both our phones. Or thought I did, but it wasn't enough."

"They haven't arrested you. That's a good sign."

"Maybe not good enough. I can't talk about this anymore. I've had it. I don't know why I thought you'd ever listen."

"Xander's leaving," Liz said, the binocam once again trained on the street.

The only sounds coming through the microphone now were normal neighborhood ones. Rory took off the headphones and peered at the construction site. Moments later, Xander's car took off at a fast clip down the street and Zeke climbed into his Tesla parked nearby.

"They're both gone." Liz put down the binocam. "Tell me everything."

Rory related as much as she could remember of the conversation between father and son.

Liz gasped at the part about Xander's appointment with Jade. "So that's why he left the race. That's so bad."

"Definitely not good for him, but he sounded sincere when he said she was already dead when he got there."

"Still, he's got the means, motive and opportunity. He could even have staged the throwing away of the knife so it would be there when he needed it."

"That would mean he planned to kill her," Rory said. "I don't want to believe that, but I think we should look into Xander more."

"He is the obvious suspect."

"Whoever killed her did it after Harmony saw her," Rory said. "That's something."

"Unless Harmony is lying. I wonder why the police are so sure she didn't do it."

"Skewering that paper heart to Jade's chest only brought attention to the bank robberies. Harmony wouldn't have done that." Rory shuddered as her mind flashed back to the scene in the alley. "Someone wanted to point the finger at the robber."

A thoughtful expression appeared on Liz's face. "Jade was a bridesmaid-for-hire. Maybe one of her clients did it."

"Why? Other than this wedding Jade seems to have done a good job. Lola thought so. She didn't say anything about complaints."

"Jade probably wouldn't have kept her job for long if there'd been many."

"Or it could be one of those overly enthusiastic members of the public Mrs. Tilcox was talking about," Rory said.

"Or the guy you saw in the lobby."

"Wish we knew who he was."

"What about Zeke?"

"Couldn't have been him. He was at the pier talking to the mayor and city council members when she was killed, remember?" Rory said.

"Maybe he did that on purpose. Sought out public figures so he'd have an iron-clad alibi. He could have paid someone to do the dirty deed."

Rory's eyes opened wide. "Do you think he'd do that?"

"He has money, and he seems the kind of guy who wouldn't rest until he gets what he wants. The kind of guy who doesn't like getting his fingers dirty." Liz glanced at her watch. "We should go if we're going to make it on time."

They returned the binocam and listening device to their places, then drove to their appointment with the apartment manager at Jade's building.

When they reached the apartment building in the eastern section of town, Rory and Liz found a well-maintained complex that gave off a 1960s vibe. They walked through an archway into an interior court-yard dominated by a kidney-shaped pool, more suitable for a casual dip than swimming laps. Rory glanced up at the two-story buildings surrounding them, wondering which apartment was their destination.

Sitting on the bottom of stone steps leading to the upper floor was a thirty-something man dressed in board shorts and a long-sleeved t-shirt with a wave logo on it, twirling a set of keys. Blond hair pulled back in a man bun, he stood up when they approached and introduced himself as the apartment manager.

"You're here to get into Jade McIntyre's place, right?"

"That's right," Rory said. "We're here on behalf of our friend, Solange. She made the arrangements."

"Cool, cool. This way."

As they followed him up the stairs, he said, "I was sorry to hear about what happened to your friend."

"Did you know her well?" Rory asked.

"Not really. She was nice enough. Sure was popular, especially with the men." He stopped in front of a door at the top of the stairs. "Here we are." He opened it and gestured for them to enter.

"Did anyone come by recently?" Liz said.

Man bun leaned against the doorframe. "Sure did. Some guy asking to get into the apartment. Didn't let him in. Wouldn't do that without the resident's or my aunt's permission."

"Your aunt?" Liz said.

"She owns the place."

"This was after Jade...passed?" Rory asked.

"Before. Said she borrowed something from him and he needed it back. Told him no can do. He tried shoving money at me. When that didn't work, he left."

"He didn't say what it was she borrowed?"

"Nope. Not sure she borrowed anything. The whole thing seemed sketchy."

"What did he look like?" Liz said.

"Some old dude." He handed the key to Rory. "Take as long as you want. Lock up when you're done and return the key to me. I'm in apartment one below." He walked down the stairs, whistling a tune.

"Sound like Zeke to you?" Rory asked after they were inside with the door closed.

"Couldn't have been him. He didn't even know she was in town until Friday evening."

"We don't know that for sure, but whoever it was, I wonder what he was looking for."

"Who knows." Liz put her hands on her hips and surveyed the room. "Where do we start?"

Rory's gaze swept the area, taking in the living room and adjoining kitchen. Everything appeared as neat as a pin. The only reading material was a stack of scripts and another of fashion magazines. Two doors led into what Rory presumed were the bedroom and bathroom. "In here."

Liz set her purse down on the couch and walked around the room. "She liked nice things."

Rory pointed to a small desk in one corner. Unplugged cords dangled where a laptop had most likely been. "No computer. The police must have taken it with them."

"I think I found the bridal shower stuff." Liz pointed to a box in one corner of the living room labeled with Solange's name on the side. She set the box on the coffee table and they examined it, verifying that it contained the items they were looking for.

"While we're here, let's take a quick look around," Rory said.

She searched the living room, while Liz took the kitchen.

"She had a sweet tooth, that's for sure," Liz said a few minutes later. "Her cupboards are full of cookies and candy."

"I'm not surprised. She practically wolfed those chocolates down at the makeup party." Rory looked through a neat stack of papers on the desk. "Here's a receipt from my mom's store for a padlock. That confirms she was the one who bought it."

Liz looked up from her perusal of the refrigerator. "You didn't really think Xander did, did you?"

"Not really, but weren't you the one who said we should assume nothing?"

"True."

"No phone bills. She must get her bills online."

Rory was looking over the living room to see if she missed anything when a squeal came from the direction of the kitchen. She spun around to find Liz leafing through a black book lying on the kitchen counter. A plastic Ziploc bag lay next to it along with a pile of packing peanuts.

"Where'd you find that?"

"In the freezer. In this." Liz held up a package that at first glance looked like your average half-eaten bag of mixed vegetables. "It was way in the back."

"How'd you even think to look inside?"

"Lucky guess. I know someone who keeps her jewelry in a bag in her freezer. She puts it in a Ziploc bag, then packs it in an old frozen veggie bag. She adds packing peanuts to round it out. It's not entirely unbelievable someone would have a half-empty bag of vegetables shoved to the back. That's what makes it a great hiding place. I thought Jade might have done something similar."

Rory stood beside her friend and watched as she turned the pages on the palm-sized book. Each set of pages displayed a week of dates with many of them filled with names. "Why would she keep her appointment calendar in the freezer?"

"Does seem odd." Liz flipped the page, uncovering the first of several photos tucked inside. She pulled out all of them and spread them across the counter. "Look at these."

Rory looked down at the pictures, all of Jade with a different older man, several of them in compromising positions.

"So it's blackmail?" Liz said. "Do this for me and I won't send this photo to your wife?"

"Maybe." Rory pointed at one of the photos. "This is the guy I saw arguing with Jade in the lobby before the engagement party. They could have been talking about this photo. Is there anything else in the book?"

Liz returned her attention to the appointment book, finding nothing of interest until she came to the Notes section in the back. In it was a list of men's names. All had a *yes* or *no* next to it. Some had a checkmark along with a date. "I wonder what these mean."

"Maybe the *yes* or *no* indicates if she has a photo of them."

"The checkmarks could mean she talked to them and showed them the compromising picture." Liz held up a flashdrive. "What do you think is on this? I found it in a canister full of tea bags."

"Digital versions of the photos? She probably printed these out to show to the men. Might have wanted to keep this separate in case someone found her appointment book. I wonder which one tried to bribe his way into the apartment."

"Could have been any of them."

Rory busied herself taking photos of each of the men with her phone as well as the relevant pages of the appointment book. "Let's put it all back and let the police deal with it."

While Liz repackaged everything, Rory called Martin, leaving a message on his voicemail about their finds. After they had finished their tasks, she said, "Let's look through the rest of the apartment."

They moved into the bedroom. Rory searched the drawers while Liz took the closet.

"She had expensive taste in clothes." Liz sucked in her breath. "Look at all of these shoes."

Rory glanced up from her search and looked in the closet. Boxes of shoes piled high to the ceiling stood on the shelf above the rod for hanging clothes. "That's a lot of shoes."

Liz pointed at two boxes. "These and these are one thousand a pop."

"Dollars?" An incredulous note crept into Rory's voice.

"Yep. They're my size too."

"Can't imagine buying shoes that are that expensive. I'd rather travel or donate to a local charity."

They finished looking through the bedroom and bathroom, finding nothing else of interest.

"That's it." Liz picked up the box of bridal shower decorations. "Can we go check out the love locks on the way to your place? I want to see if any new ones were added."

"Sure," Rory said as she locked the apartment door behind them.

When they dropped the key off with the manager, Rory said to him, "What's going to happen to Jade's things?"

"Depends on what her sister decides."

"Sister?"

"Guess I forgot to mention she stopped by the other day. I wasn't here at the time. Auntie let her in."

"Did you get a name?"

"Not that I heard. I gather she wasn't real happy about the idea of being responsible for clearing out the place. She has until the end of next week. After that, we'll chuck it all."

"All those lovely shoes," Liz whispered, more to herself than anyone else.

"What?" man bun said.

"Nothing." Liz handed him her business card. "If she stops by again, could you let us know? We'd like to talk to her. Oh, and call me if she doesn't come back. I'll help you get rid of it all. I've dealt with a lot of great charities over the years. I can find good homes for everything."

"One more thing before we go," Rory said. "Have you ever seen any of these men hanging around?" She showed him the photos she'd taken. When she came to the one of the man from the lobby, he pointed at it and said, "That's him. That's the one who tried to get into her apartment."

They thanked him and drove toward downtown Vista Beach to check on the love locks, talking about what they'd learned along the way.

"At least we identified the guy arguing with Jade in the lobby," Rory said.

"We didn't get his name, but Dashing D should be able to figure that out now. What about the sister? I thought Jade didn't have any family," Liz said. "That's what Mrs. Tilcox said."

"Candy didn't find any either, but she said she'd only done a cursory search. Maybe the sister has a different last name. Could be why she didn't find her."

"That explains it, I suppose." Liz didn't seem convinced.

Rory had her own doubts as well. As they made their way toward city hall, she wondered who this mysterious sister could be and if they'd ever see her again.

Chapter 18

When Rory and Liz reached city hall a short time later, they spotted a woman with purple hair, her back to them, examining a section of the love lock tree.

"Isn't that Candy?" Liz said. "Do you think she put up a lock for her sweetie?"

"I don't see anyone else around. Aren't you supposed to do it together?"

"It's not written in stone."

They walked across the courtyard toward the green metal structure. The number of locks on it seemed to have grown considerably in the last day. By the time they reached it, Candy was sitting on the edge of the fountain, staring forlornly at the tree. When they called her name, she wiped a tear from her eye and turned to greet them.

"Ladies. Pretty impressive. I hear you had a hand in this. Sit a while and tell me all about it."

Rory sat down on one side of her, Liz the other.

While Liz animatedly recounted the tale of the rescued locks, Rory studied Candy, coming to the conclusion the woman hadn't been placing a lock on the tree when they saw her. Her face reeked of sadness, not at all the demeanor she expected to see on someone who, only a moment ago, had completed such a romantic gesture.

"Is everything okay?" Rory said after Liz had finished.

"What makes you ask that?"

"It's just that, well, you look sad."

"Happy tears. Happy tears." Candy waved her hand at the locks. "All of these expressions of love make me happy. In my business, I usually see the messy end of relationships."

"I suppose you do deal with a lot of divorces," Liz said.

"Too many. Way too many. It's enough to make you despair of anyone having a relationship that lasts. Seeing these locks helps."

Rory cleared her throat. "We owe you an apology."

"For what?"

"We were nosing around the Akaw and, well, I think our actions got you fired."

Candy harrumphed. "Don't worry about that. Believe me, that job was going nowhere."

"So you never saw anything criminal going on there?" Liz asked.

"As far as I could tell, the place runs like clockwork. Some of the employees were a bit odd, but that's it."

"That's good to hear," Rory said. "What did Nell hire you to look into?"

"Sorry, can't tell you that. Client confidentiality." Candy slapped her thighs with her hands. "Now, what's this I hear about you and the bank robber?"

Rory and Liz took turns describing the path that led to them identifying Harmony Wells as the robber.

"That's good detective work. Sometimes it takes imagination to get to the truth. You've both certainly got that."

"Too bad we can't figure out who killed Jade," Rory said.

"Leave that to the police." Candy stood up. "I've got to get back to it. If either of you want some extra work, come see me. I should be able to come up with a case or two for you." She waved and headed in the direction of her office.

Rory eyed Liz. "You're going to take her up on that, aren't you?"

"I could use some excitement in my life."

Rory stood up. "Come on, Sherlock. Let's go see what Candy was looking at."

They studied the section of the tree the PI had been standing in front of, examining both sides of each lock without finding one with Candy's initials on it.

"What about this one? I don't remember seeing it before." Rory pointed to a plain padlock with *Laith* printed in black Sharpie on one side and *RIP Forgive Me* on the other. "Maybe this is the name of the man we saw her with. But I don't know why she'd write *Forgive Me* and *RIP* on the other side."

Liz studied the lock. "Definitely odd to have *RIP* on it. He seemed pretty alive to me. Must be a tribute to someone."

"Could be a case she couldn't solve."

"She obviously feels bad about it if she put it here."

"We don't know she's the one who put it here. But, come to think of it, I do remember seeing the name on a picture in her office. Maybe it's one of the old cases she's been working on."

"This could be the very first case she couldn't crack."

Or one that was personal to her, Rory thought, but didn't say. "Let's get going. We've both got work to do."

Saturday morning, Rory and Martin walked hand in hand toward the pier along the walk path that paralleled the ocean, silently enjoying each other's company.

"It's nice spending time with you even if it's only a few minutes," Rory said.

"Sorry about that."

"Don't feel guilty about it. I know you're doing important work. I have plenty to do. Liz and I are having lunch today at the diner downtown and we're varnishing coasters after church tomorrow. But I wish the investigation was over."

"We're doing everything we can," he said as they crossed the bike path onto the pier, now devoid of love locks. They stopped midway and leaned against the railing, staring down at the sparsely populated beach below.

"Have you had a chance to look at the stuff we found in the apartment?" Rory said.

"We're still processing it."

"Do you think Jade was a blackmailer?"

"Too early to say, but the photos are...suggestive."

"I wonder what she'd want in return."

"Let *us* figure that out," Martin said.

"Has anyone contacted you claiming to be Jade's sister? Maybe she was in on the scheme."

"As far as I know, she doesn't have one."

"That's what we thought too, but someone stopped by her apartment saying she was her sister."

"Haven't heard anything about that. Did you get a name?"

"Unfortunately not. What about the guy she was arguing with in the lobby?"

"Him we have a name for. Andrew Fletcher. Does it ring a bell?"

"Never heard of him."

"He's CEO of a bank here in town."

Rory tucked the information away in her brain and zipped up her hoodie. "Do you want coffee or hot chocolate?"

"Coffee would be nice." He pushed himself away from the railing. "I'll be right back."

"Let me. You've done enough for me already."

Rory left Martin leaning against the railing, staring at the ocean, to stand in line at the café at the base of the pier.

When she returned with the drinks, she found Martin talking with Zeke Axelrod. She sat down on a nearby bench and waited for the two men to finish their discussion. She sipped her hot chocolate while she listened to the words that drifted over to her on the ocean breeze.

"...can't possibly think my son had anything to do with that woman's death," Zeke said.

Martin stared at him with an expressionless face. "Oh?"

"Sure, they were engaged, but that was years ago. She hasn't had anything to do with my family in quite a while."

"She wasn't trying to get back together with you or your son?"

"Me? What are you talking about?" Zeke did his best to appear shocked, but Rory could hear the uneasiness in his voice.

"I've seen pictures of you and Ms. McIntyre looking quite...cozy."

"That was a mistake. Nothing to do with the present."

"You're sure?"

"Forget about me. My son had nothing to do with her death."

"He had an appointment with her."

"He said he found her dead."

"And didn't tell anyone."

Zeke ran a hand through his hair and paced. "There must be something I can do to convince you." He stopped his pacing and stood close to the detective, lowering his voice a notch. Rory scooted to the end of the bench nearest the two men.

"How about a donation to your favorite charity?"

Martin held up his hand. "Stop right there."

"What about that girl of yours? I hear she develops software. I'm sure I could find some work to send her way."

Rory suppressed a gasp. She didn't like being used as a pawn in Zeke's game.

A hint of anger showed on Martin's formerly expressionless face. "I'm going to pretend you didn't say that. It's best if you walk away. Right now."

"Come on. Tell me what you want. Everyone has a price. What's yours?"

Rory was so focused on their conversation, she didn't notice Naomi until the woman grabbed her father's arm. "Dad, stop."

Zeke scowled and shook off her hand. "Stay out of this."

"Listen for once."

"Leave. Now."

"I did it," Naomi blurted out. "I stabbed Jade. I'm the one who killed her."

Chapter 19

Naomi's announcement of her guilt got their attention. All pretense of minding her own business gone, Rory stared open-mouthed at the scene before her. A series of emotions flitted across Zeke's face from shock to disbelief to anger while Martin watched father and daughter intently.

"Nonsense," Zeke finally said. "Don't listen to her." He turned his back on Naomi and addressed the detective. "See what your misguided suspicions are doing to my family? Now my daughter's lying to save her brother."

"I'm not lying. I'm telling the truth."

Martin held up his hand to stop Zeke from saying anything more, then turned his attention to Naomi. "Why have you waited until now to talk?"

"I have no excuse. I guess I was hoping to get away with it."

"Refreshingly honest."

"I don't want Xander to take the blame for something I did."

"Does he know?" Martin asked.

"He has no clue."

"Stop talking." Zeke brought out his cell phone. "Don't say another word until I get you a lawyer."

"I know what I'm doing. Let me be honest for once."

"You foolish girl."

Naomi stuck out her chin. "I'm an adult, not a girl. You can't order me around. This is the right thing to do."

"Let's go down to the station," Martin said. "We can finish our talk there."

"No. I need to do this here. Now." Before anyone could say anything else, she launched into her account of what happened in the alley the day of the murder.

"I found out about the meeting between Xander and Jade so I left the race to talk to her before he arrived. When I got there, she was leaning against the wall across from Zephy's back door. Looked like she was about to throw up. I figured she was hung over."

Martin jotted something down in the notebook he'd drawn out of his pocket. "What happened next?"

"I tried talking to her, but she waved me away and moved farther down the alley. That made me even madder. I wasn't going to let her ruin my family again. I saw the knife on top of the garbage can and grabbed it. Then I went after her."

"It didn't matter to you that the knife implicated your brother?"

"I didn't realize it was his. I wasn't in the restaurant when he had his blow up."

"Go on."

She continued in a quieter voice. "I stabbed her in that cold heart of hers and she went down." A triumphant gleam showed in her eyes for a moment soon replaced by a look of defeat. "I panicked after I realized what I'd done. The knife was still in my hand. I saw the paper heart nearby and remembered the bank robber. I figured I'd blame it on him. I speared it with the knife and stuck it in her chest, then ran in the back door of the restaurant. I always keep a spare t-shirt in Xander's office in case I spill when I'm working. Then I rejoined the race. Ran all the way to the pier."

"What did you do with the top you changed out of?"

"I rolled it up in a ball and stuffed it in a trash can a few blocks away." She looked at Martin. "You believe me, don't you?"

"I do," he said gently. "Let's go down to the station."

Martin mouthed *sorry* to Rory as the three of them passed by. She waited until they were out of sight before pulling out her phone to call Liz with the startling news.

A couple hours later, Rory walked in the front door of Buddy's Rockin' Diner, the only twenty-four-hour restaurant in Vista Beach, to meet Liz for lunch. As soon as she stepped inside, she was transported back to the 1950s. Customers filled the restaurant, eating their burgers and blue-plate specials while Elvis Presley's "Love Me Tender" played in the background.

Liz looked up from her perusal of a menu and waved from a red vinyl booth in the back.

Rory moved across the black and white checkered floor and slid into a seat across from her. "I still can't believe what Naomi said."

Liz put down her menu. "Do you think she's telling the truth?"

"I do. More importantly, so does Martin. As soon as she gave the details of her attack on Jade, his face changed. Any skepticism he had seemed to go away, just like that." She snapped her fingers. "Something she said convinced him."

She barely had time to glance at a menu before a gum-chewing waitress dressed in a uniform typical of a fifties diner approached the table, notepad in hand. "Ready to order?" she said, her words punctuated by the occasional snapping of gum.

After the waitress went off to put in their orders, Rory sipped a glass of water and looked around the diner, her gaze zeroing in on a distinguished-looking man in a rumpled suit and a woman with purple hair sitting in a booth near the entrance. Her eyes widened and she leaned across the table. In a hushed tone, she said, "Look who's here. Near the front door."

Liz glanced over at the couple and grinned. "Candy and her sweetie."

"We don't *know* they're dating."

"What else?"

"You've got love on the brain."

They drank their sodas and talked about the case while they waited for their food to arrive. Rory occasionally glanced over at Candy's table, trying to decide if their body language indicated they were in a romantic relationship. On one of those glances, she spotted Martin entering the restaurant. He stopped inside the front door, his gaze sweeping over the tables. He inclined his head as soon as he spotted her and started toward them.

"Martin's here," Rory said.

"Were you expecting him?"

"No." Her face crinkled in worry. "I hope he doesn't have more bad news."

They watched as he stopped at Candy's table and talked to her lunch date.

"Ooh, Dashing D knows him. He can give us the scoop." Liz barely waited for Martin to slide into the seat next to Rory before beginning her interrogation. "Who's the man you were talking to? Tell us everything you know."

Martin cast an amused glance in her direction. "Hello to you too. I'm fine, thanks."

"Come on. Spill the beans."

"His name's Orson Huddleston. He's a retired detective. Left the department before I joined, but I still see him around the station from time to time. Helps out with cold cases. Is that enough or do you need his age, weight, marital history and shoe size?"

"So Candy's dating a detective," Liz said in a sing-song voice. "Marital history would be nice."

"What makes you think they're dating?"

"Aren't they?"

Martin glanced over at Rory. "Is that what you think too?"

She held up her hands, palms forward. "I have no opinion what-soever. *She's* the one who has love on the brain."

"You have to admit, they make a cute couple," Liz said.

"I doubt they're dating," Martin said. "Looked more like a work-ing lunch to me. He had some notes spread out on the table."

"Maybe Candy's helping him with a cold case," Rory said. "Do you know what they were talking about?"

"No idea. Whatever case it is, it was probably before my time."

Rory wondered if it was one of the old cases Candy had men-tioned working on.

Their waitress set plates of food in front of the two women. "Can I get you anything?" she said to Martin.

He waved a hand. "Thank you, no. I'm not staying."

As soon as the waitress left, Martin took a piece of paper out of his jacket pocket. "I didn't come here to talk about cold cases. Naomi asked me to give this to you."

He handed the note to Rory who read it and passed it over to Liz. It briefly asked if they'd come visit her whenever it was convenient.

"Is she still at the station?"

"For the moment. Let me know if you want to see her."

Rory picked at her fries. "She really did it, didn't she?"

"Stabbed Jade?" Martin said. "I have no doubt she did."

She found his choice of words curious.

"What convinced you?" Liz said.

"She knew something we never made public," he said.

Rory thought back to the conversation on the pier, trying to remember every word. "The knife was inserted twice," she whispered, more to herself than the others. She turned to Martin. "That's it, isn't it?"

"I can neither confirm nor deny." His face creased into a frown.

"What is it?"

"Something about this case doesn't sit right. Call it a gut feeling. There's something I'm missing." His phone rang. "Excuse me, I've got to take this."

While he listened intently, Rory took a bite of her burger. She strained to hear the other side of the conversation but couldn't make out a word.

As soon as he hung up, he said, "I've got to go. Have a nice lunch."

Rory watched him as he hurried across the floor toward the front door.

"What do you think that was about?" Liz said between bites.

"Something unexpected, that's for sure."

They finished lunch and had barely stepped outside the restaurant when someone thrust a folded copy of the *Vista Beach View* in front of Rory's face. "What's that PI friend of yours up to?"

Rory pushed the paper away. "It's the weekend. Don't you ever take a day off?" she said to Veronica.

"The world doesn't stop spinning, so I don't stop working. Come on, what's she up to?"

"What about Candy? What do you mean?"

"She put an ad in the newspaper."

"People still do that?" Liz said.

Veronica tapped a circled classified ad. "What do you know about this?"

Rory and Liz examined the ad that asked for any witnesses to a murder to come forward. It gave the date the crime took place as well as the names of the victims and two phone numbers. Rory recognized one as Candy's cell phone and assumed the other was her office number.

"She hasn't said anything to you about it?" Veronica said.

"Not a word. Why would she?" Rory said. "What's the case?"

Veronica gave them a brief overview of the murder that had taken place in Vista Beach around twenty years ago. A couple had been stabbed in their home and died before they could reveal who'd attacked them. A man had been convicted of the crime, largely on the basis of a witness who'd seen him running from the scene. The man had since been exonerated of the murders with the help of DNA.

"That's sad he spent so much time in jail for something he never did, but we don't know anything about it," Rory said. "You'll have to ask Candy. If she's looking for a witness, I'm sure she'd be happy to talk to you."

"You'd think so, but she hung up on me when I called." Veronica tucked the newspaper in her tote bag. "Thanks for your time. Let me know if you hear anything."

Rory and Liz walked down the sidewalk in the opposite direction from the reporter, discussing the new development.

"Do you think it's the case Candy was talking to the retired detective about?" Liz said.

"Could be. I wonder why she refused to talk to Veronica. You'd think she'd be ecstatic to get that call."

"Veronica can be overly aggressive at times. Puts people off. Should we have told her Candy was in the diner?"

"If Candy wanted to talk to her she wouldn't have hung up on her."

They continued down the street, their minds full of everything that had happened that day.

At church on Sunday, Rory sensed something was going on when, after the service, several people were staring down at their phones and talking excitedly to one another. She joined a group and, as soon as she found out what they were talking about, called Liz with the news.

"The twitterverse is blowing up about Naomi's confession," Rory said. "There's talk of boycotting Zephy's. Let's go over to the restaurant to show our support. We can work on the coasters after lunch. And we can ask Xander about Jade's sister. Maybe he knows how to get in touch with her."

"I'll meet you there."

A short time later, Rory's gaze swept the dining room, taking in the sparsely populated restaurant. "Isn't Sunday morning one of their busiest times?"

"Guess people have started boycotting already," Liz said. "At least we didn't see any protesters outside."

"I don't understand why people think they should avoid this place. It's not like anyone died from eating the food."

They stepped up to the podium and were immediately seated at a table in a quiet corner. After a waiter took their order, they gave their names and asked if Chef Axelrod had time to stop by. They were halfway through their brunch when Xander appeared at their table with two mimosas.

Dark circles under his eyes, he set the glasses in front of them. "Thought you might enjoy these. On the house."

"That's nice of you," Rory said, "but you didn't have to."

"It's a thank you for having the courage to eat here."

"We noticed things were quieter than usual. Do you have time to sit?"

"I can spare a few minutes." A dejected look on his face, Xander sat down in an empty chair at their table.

"How are you doing?" Liz said.

"As well as can be expected. Naomi's still in jail. We're working on getting her out on bail. This is all my responsibility now." His gaze swept over the dining room. "What's left of it, anyway. I hope we won't have to close."

"Is that a possibility?" Rory asked.

"Only time will tell if the talk of boycotting us on social media will have much of an impact. I got more bad news today. My TV deal is on hold. They're seeing how this all pans out."

"It's a minor hiccup," Liz said. "Soon people will forget all about the recent drama and be back in droves." She speared a piece of Scallops Benedict with her fork. "Who can resist this food?"

"I hope you're right. Thank you for visiting Naomi yesterday. Is that what you wanted to talk to me about?"

"We just wanted to see how you're doing and show our support," Rory said. "This must be rough on your family."

"It hasn't been easy, but we'll survive."

"How are you and Solange?" Liz asked.

"Honestly, in a strange way all of this has been good for us. It forced us to really talk. We both feel like we're going into our marriage with everything laid out on the table. No more secrets."

"That's good to hear," Rory said. "I'm curious about something else. Did you ever meet Jade's family?"

"Didn't have any as far as I know."

"Not even a sister?"

Xander shrugged. "Honestly, I have no idea. She didn't like talking about her past. She was always focused on the future. I do know she'd been on her own since she was sixteen. Why are you asking?"

"Just curious."

"I'd better get back to work. Enjoy your food."

They stared at him as he made his way across the dining room, greeting customers along the way.

They ate the rest of their food in silence.

Rory laid her napkin on the table. "Are you finished? We should go and work on the coasters." She glanced at the time on her phone. "I don't see how we're going to get all of them done today. Not with multiple coats of varnish."

"We'll do as much as we can. We can finish at lunch tomorrow if you're available."

Rory indicated her agreement, vowing to get up earlier than usual the next day so she could fit everything in.

Chapter 20

Rory was hard at work Monday morning when she heard a knock on the front door. She opened it to find Mrs. Griswold on her porch, a small shopping bag in her hand.

"I didn't expect you back for a few days," Rory said.

"I decided to come home early. My sister's on the mend. Nothing more for me to do there."

"Let me get your keys." Rory grabbed them off her desk and handed them over.

"Thank you for looking after my place." Mrs. Griswold held up the bag. "A little something I thought you'd like, to show my appreciation."

Rory pulled out a snow globe with twin dolphins frolicking in the sea and the word *Florida* written across its base. "How nice. Do you want to come inside for a few minutes?"

"All right, but no fussing. I don't need tea or anything like that."

Rory set the snow globe on her desk and joined her neighbor in the living room.

As soon as Rory sat down, Mrs. Griswold said, "Tell me about the poison."

"Poison?"

"You don't know? Did you and that detective break up?"

"No."

"Oh. I thought he would have told you."

"I have absolutely no idea what you're talking about," Rory said.

"Really. I'm surprised. I've been back less than a day and I know what's going on. You're not as plugged in as I thought. That woman who was killed. Jade or some such nonsense of a name." Mrs. Griswold leaned forward and stared at Rory intently before delivering her news. "She was poisoned."

"But Naomi stabbed her. She confessed."

"Poisoned first. Stabbed when she was almost dead. If you can be almost dead."

"Do you know what kind of poison?"

"The police are keeping that quiet. I was hoping you'd heard, but I guess not." A disappointed look on her face, she stood up and headed toward the door.

Rory followed, still trying to wrap her mind around the news. "Where did you hear about this? Are your sources reliable?"

"Reliable enough. If you don't believe me look online. The story's making the rounds."

Rory bid her neighbor goodbye and closed the door. She sat down in front of her computer and did a quick search, finding an article on the *View*'s website as well as one on *VBC*. Neither mentioned what kind of poison was used.

She sat back in her chair and thought about what she'd read. She cast her mind back to the phone call Martin received on Saturday at the diner. That must have been when the tox screen came back and he learned about the poison.

She was still mulling over the unexpected news when lunchtime rolled around. As soon as Liz arrived to finish varnishing the coasters, Rory told her about Mrs. Griswold's visit.

Liz stared at her open-mouthed. "Poison? And I thought this was all over."

"I'm surprised you didn't see the post on *VBC*."

"I haven't gotten around to checking it today. What do you think this means for Naomi?"

"No idea. She did stab Jade, so they have to charge her with something."

"Maybe Dashing D will know. You'll have to ask him." Hands on hips, Liz stared at the coasters laid out on the kitchen table. "We got more done yesterday than I thought. Shouldn't take more than an hour or so to finish these."

They sat down across from each other. Rory poured varnish into two bowls and they silently got to work.

Rory finished the final coat of varnish on a coaster and placed it to one side, then picked up another. "We're making good progress here."

"What we need to make progress on is finding out who poisoned Jade," Liz said.

"Unfortunately, that means Xander is once again a suspect."

Liz looked up from her work. "I suppose it does. You don't think he did it, do you?"

"I don't want to, but we have no idea what kind of poison was used or when or how it was administered. The field is wide open. Anyone could be to blame."

"Might be one of those men she was blackmailing. Do you know anything about poison?"

"Only what I've seen on TV or read in mysteries."

Liz started on another coaster. "Maybe it was in something she ate."

"It's possible. But she could have been poisoned some other way. I've heard of ones that can be absorbed through the skin."

"Could have been in her makeup then. That brings Harmony back in the picture."

"She has no motive. At least none that we're aware of. I don't think we can make an informed guess without knowing what kind of poison was used. We don't know how long it took for her to feel the effects."

Liz screwed up her face in thought. "What did Naomi say about seeing her in the alley?"

"She found her leaning against the wall. Thought she looked like she was going to throw up, but that could be a sign of a bad hangover. We'll have to see what the police say."

The two bent over their work, varnishing coaster after coaster in companionable silence. Half an hour later a knock sounded on the front door. Rory laid down her brush and went to answer it.

"Do you have time for some questions? Official business," Martin said.

"Sure. Liz and I are in the kitchen varnishing coasters."

"Good. I can talk to you both at the same time."

Martin joined them at the table while Rory got him a glass of water. "Thanks," he said when she set it down in front of him. "Looks like you've gotten a lot done."

"We've a ways to go yet, but we're getting there."

He took a notebook and pen out of his jacket pocket. "Go ahead and continue working."

"I think we could use a break," Rory said.

They put aside their work and gave him their full attention.

"Is this about the poison?" Rory said.

"Who told you?"

"Mrs. Griswold stopped by this morning and I saw mention of it online."

Martin rubbed the space between his eyes. "That wasn't supposed to get out."

"How did it?" Liz said.

"Someone at the station leaked it to Ms. Justice." He took a sip of water. "Let's start with the makeup event before the party. Did you see Jade take anything?"

"What do you mean?"

"Pills, prescription drugs, vitamins, anything like that."

"Slow-acting poison then?" Liz said.

"Something for a headache, maybe?" he said.

"Not that I saw," Rory said. "You could ask Mrs. Tilcox or someone at I Do For You. She worked there long enough they might know if she took any medications on a regular basis."

Martin jotted something down. "Back to the makeup event. What food was there?"

"We had some appetizers, but I don't remember her eating any of those. Do you?" Rory looked at Liz for confirmation.

"Not that I saw."

"Nothing?" the detective said. "You're sure?"

Rory sat up straighter. "Wait. The chocolates."

"That's right. She wolfed down a bunch of those." Liz sucked in her breath. "Do you think they were poisoned?"

"I have no reason to think that right now. I'm just collecting information, trying to get a complete picture," Martin said in a soothing voice. "Can you describe them?"

"Heart-shaped chocolate truffles in a flat box with red wrappers like the one I found behind the nightstand in the hotel room," Rory said.

"Did anyone else eat them?"

"We all had at least one." Liz looked relieved. "That means they weren't poisoned. Otherwise we would have...you know."

"Do you know where they came from?"

"They were on the dresser when we got there," Rory said. "Before Candy delivered the appetizers. I assumed they were a gift from the hotel."

Martin raised an eyebrow. "Candy was there?"

"She was playing room service waiter as part of her cover," Liz said.

He made a couple more notes, then gently tapped his pen against the page.

The silence was long enough, Rory wasn't sure if he'd finished with his questions. She picked up her brush to go back to work when he finally spoke.

"What was Candy investigating at the hotel?"

Rory felt uncomfortable talking about what they'd been told in confidence, but she decided the police needed to hear the little she knew. "Nell hired her because she thought there was a problem there, but she didn't give us any details."

"Not even a hint?"

"Nothing. We asked but she wouldn't tell us anything. I don't think it was drugs. She seemed surprised by the suggestion."

"Did Candy mention Jade at all? Talk to her?" he said.

"At the party?" Rory asked.

"Any time."

"Not that I saw."

"I didn't see them together either," Liz said.

"You'll have to talk to Candy," Rory said. "Maybe she noticed something the rest of us didn't."

Martin returned his notebook to his jacket pocket. "She's my next stop."

When Rory returned to the kitchen after walking him to the door, Liz said, "Shoot. We forgot to ask about Naomi."

Rory sank down on the chair across from her friend. "Maybe we'll hear something soon."

"Gives me the creeps to think someone put poison in something Jade ate or drank. Or that anyone would want to poison her at all. Who does something like that?"

"Someone who thought she was a danger to them. Doesn't sound like the poison was in any of the food at the makeup party, but we should still find out when it was taken away." Rory made a mental note to ask Nell the next time she saw her.

Liz produced a pen and pad of paper from her purse. "Here's the list of suspects we made last time. Before we knew she was poisoned."

"Or that Naomi had stabbed her." Rory leaned forward, trying to see who was on the list.

Liz turned the paper toward her and used the pen to point to each line. Xander, the robber, overenthusiastic member of the public, the man in the lobby and Zeke were all on the list. "We can cross out the robber now that we know Harmony has no reason to want Jade dead."

"I'm not totally sure we can cross her off. She might have a motive we don't know about yet," Rory said. "Zeke's still a suspect. We know Naomi didn't poison her, otherwise she wouldn't have stabbed her too."

"Xander's back on the list."

"I don't want to believe Xander poisoned Jade, but things keep on pointing back to him. We have to at least consider the possibility. What do we know about him?"

"He was once engaged to Jade and he wasn't happy with her coming back into his life."

"His restaurant is also in trouble, though I don't see why killing Jade would help him there," Rory said.

"He went to see her in the alley, but she was already dead."

"She was probably poisoned sometime between the party and the alley. Let's concentrate on that period."

"They were both at the party. I didn't see him talking to her then, but there's that conversation you overheard. Could he have poisoned her on the patio?" Liz said.

"I don't think so. They didn't have anything to eat or drink with them."

"Let's move on. There's this overenthusiastic member of the public."

"Plus the guy in the lobby. Andrew Fletcher. And we need to add the men from the appointment book we found in the freezer." Rory brought up a photo on her phone of the relevant pages from the book.

They reviewed the list of names, which included the man from the lobby, trying to decide if any of them other than Fletcher should be added to the list of suspects.

"If the *yes* means she has a compromising photo with the man, like we thought before, that means only the ones with yeses are candidates," Rory said.

"But probably only the ones with a checkmark and name. They're likely the only ones she showed the photos to. I see Fletcher's one of them."

"Seems reasonable. That leaves three names."

They added the three men to the suspect list.

"Let me see what I can find out." After a few minutes on her phone, Liz came up with little about the men other than two of them were both fathers of recent brides and they lived in other states. "Do you think their daughters or sons-in-law were clients of I Do For You?"

"Are you thinking the company could be in on the scheme?" Rory picked up her phone. "I'm going to call Teresa and see what she thinks."

After a short conversation with the wedding planner, Rory reported back. "She doesn't think so. Apparently, Edwina Tilcox has a solid reputation. Jade must have been doing this on her own."

"But what did she want in return?"

"The bridesmaid we talked to said she was always looking for someone to finance her plays. Maybe she wanted a backer."

"I wonder why Zeke isn't in her appointment book."

"Probably thought she'd never see him again. We'll leave these two on the suspect list, but they don't sound very promising if they live out of state," Rory said.

"They could have been in town at the time Jade was killed."

They checked to see if either was signed up for the Love Run. After finding neither of them on the list of participants, they each took one of the men, looking at whatever social media posts they could get access to.

"Mine was in Nevada," Rory said.

"Mine wasn't in town either. What about this Fletcher guy?"

"He's local. Manager of some bank. Married, two kids. On paper he looks pretty upright."

"Only there was that picture of him and Jade. Plus he was arguing with her in the lobby so he's still a possibility."

Rory studied the list. "I'm betting Jade was poisoned at the hotel. Maybe Nell can tell us something. Do you have time to visit her tomorrow morning?"

"I can make that happen."

Rory stared down at the unfinished coasters on the table. "We'd better get back to this. I want to finish today."

The two bent over their work, wondering which of the suspects on their list had killed Jade.

That evening, Rory was sitting on the couch with Sekhmet curled up on her lap, watching a movie and munching on popcorn, when she heard a soft knock on the front door. While Rory paused the movie, the cat perked up and ran to get into position to greet the visitor. On the doorstep Rory found a tired-looking Martin. His face brightened as soon as he saw her.

"I didn't expect to see you tonight." She led him into the living room where they sat side by side on the couch. "I thought you'd be working."

"I needed a break."

Sekhmet jumped up on the couch and settled down on Martin's lap. He petted the cat. "Did you finish the coasters?"

"All done. We're letting them dry before we pack them up."

"I'm sorry I haven't spent more time with you or been more supportive."

"What are you talking about? I think you've been supportive. Don't worry about me right now. You have a job to do. How's it going? Are you seeing the light at the end of the tunnel?"

"Hard to tell at the moment."

"I forgot to ask earlier. What does the bit about the poison mean for Naomi?"

"Not sure yet. By her own admission, Jade was still alive when she stabbed her."

"But she would have died anyway, right?"

"That's what the coroner says."

"What kind of poison was it?"

"Any medicine can be a poison if used improperly." He eyed the popcorn. "Can I have some?"

She held the bowl out to him. "How about Candy? Was she any help?"

"What do you know about her background?" he said before he grabbed a handful and munched on it.

"Not much really. Originally from Boston, I think. I met her a few months ago when she was working for that PI before she got her own license."

"Nothing else?"

"No. Why?"

"Just curious." He directed his attention at the TV where the movie was still paused. "What are we watching?"

"*The Secret Life of Pets.*"

"Trying to get insight into what this little one does when you're not here?"

Rory grinned. "Something like that."

She started the movie and, before long, Martin was fast asleep, one hand resting on Sekhmet's back, the other around Rory's shoulder. She snuggled up next to him and watched the rest of the animated film.

Chapter 21

The next day, Rory and Liz parked on the street near the Akaw and walked the short distance to their destination. They were almost at the main entrance when Veronica came through the automatic doors escorted by hotel security. The reporter glared at the man before stomping in their direction.

"What's going on?" Rory asked when she was within earshot.

"Just doing my job. *Some* people don't like it." Veronica glared once more at the hotel entrance.

"What story are you working on?" Liz said. "Something to do with the murder?"

"I'm not sure yet." Veronica lowered her voice. "How about doing me a favor?"

Rory looked at her uneasily. "No promises."

"Find out what you can about the thefts from rooms here."

"Thefts? What thefts?"

"Some guests have reported items missing from their rooms recently. An unhappy customer posted a complaint online. That's what brought the situation to my attention. You can learn a lot from social media. Can't believe everything, but it's often a starting point for a story."

"You're not going to write about this, are you?" Rory said, thinking about the damage such an article could do to the hotel and Nell's prospects for the new job.

"Not unless I can confirm it. That's where you can help me out. Remember, you owe me. I look forward to hearing from you." With that, Veronica walked down the street.

"What do you make of that?" Liz said.

"Not sure. We'll have to see what we can find out."

As soon as they walked inside, they spotted Nell at the front desk. Her face creased in worry lines, she hurried toward them. "Please tell me everything's been resolved."

"Not everything," Rory said. "Have you heard about the poison?"

"Not so loud." Nell led them to the far corner of the lobby. "I can't believe she could have been poisoned here. None of my staff would do that."

"It could have been a guest," Liz said.

"Do you think it could have something to do with the recent thefts?" Rory asked.

Nell sucked in her breath. "Where'd you hear about that? Candy said she wouldn't tell anyone."

"She didn't," Rory said. "It was Veronica."

"I should have known. She was bothering the guests, asking about something. I didn't realize it was about the thefts. Don't know how she found out."

"Is that why you hired Candy?" Rory said.

"I was hoping to keep it quiet. Deal with it without having to inform the police. She never discovered anything and no one's reported any thefts in the last couple days."

"Maybe having her poke around convinced whoever did it to stop," Liz said.

"Cross your fingers that's true. I gave Detective Green a list of everything that was stolen when he came by yesterday."

"Do you think we could have a look at that list?" Rory said.

Nell pursed her lips. "I don't think I can do that."

"Not even if it helps solve the murder?"

"The police have the information. I'm sure they'll figure out if it's related," Nell said. "Thank goodness the thefts have stopped, but I still feel awful about them and Ms. McIntyre's death. This hotel is my responsibility. Though not for much longer."

"You got the job?" Rory said.

"A bittersweet moment."

"When do you leave?"

"Soon. We're still working out the details. I'd feel a lot better if everything was resolved before I go. Do the police know how or when she was poisoned?"

"Not as far as I know," Rory said.

"Maybe it was at the party," Liz said.

"Unlikely. Too many people milling around."

"What about something in the room we used for the makeup party? I understand she spent the night there," Rory said.

Surprise shown on Nell's face. "Did she? I didn't realize."

"We had appetizers in the room earlier in the evening. Do you know when they were cleared away?" Rory said.

"I can see if my employees know anything. Follow me," Nell said.

They walked over to the front desk where the hotel manager spent a few minutes talking to staff and looking on the computer.

"The best anyone remembers, it was cleared away within half an hour of your event starting in the restaurant." Nell raised a finger. "But that gives me an idea. Someone could have ordered room service later that night."

After confirming the room number, she looked up the information on the computer. "Here it is." She stared at the screen. "I don't see any...wait a minute. Someone asked for a box of chocolates to be sent up."

"Does it say who delivered it?" Rory crossed her fingers, hoping this was the break they were waiting for.

"Oh. It was Candy."

"Candy?" Liz said. "You're sure?"

"Yes. Did she have a...problem with Ms. McIntyre?"

"Not as far as we know," Rory said.

Nell lowered her voice. "I didn't want to say anything earlier, but I saw the two of them having words during the party."

"Where was this?" Rory said.

"In the hallway by the ballrooms. I don't remember exactly when. I planned on talking to her about it, but I forgot. Can't have my staff arguing with guests."

"Did you hear any of the conversation?" Liz said.

"I was too far away."

"Did you tell anyone?" Rory asked.

"No. But now I wonder if I should have. I'd better call the police. I'm sorry. I know she's a friend." After a few more taps on the keyboard, Nell bid them goodbye and walked into her office.

Rory and Liz sat down on bamboo chairs in the lobby, each silently taking in the new information.

Liz finally said, "Why would Candy poison Jade?"

"She delivered the chocolates, but that doesn't mean she poisoned them. We don't even know for sure that's where the poison was," Rory said. "It didn't seem like Candy knew Jade when I talked to her, so I don't know why they'd be having an argument."

"Maybe Candy was only pretending not to know her."

"I don't know. I really don't know." Rory rested her arms on her knees, unsure what to make of everything they'd just learned.

"Too bad we couldn't get that list of stolen items. It might have told us something."

"We don't even know if the two crimes are related."

They were still mulling over the possibilities when Liz received a call from the manager of Jade's apartment complex. She had a brief conversation with him, then hung up. "He was wondering if we were still interested in helping dispose of her stuff. They want to pack things up so they can get the apartment ready for the next tenant. They decided they couldn't wait any longer."

"The woman who claimed to be her sister never came back?"

"Hasn't heard a peep from her."

"Somehow, I'm not surprised."

"I said I'd be right over. Why don't you come with me? Who knows, maybe we'll find something new."

When they reached the apartment building, they found the manager carrying empty boxes up to Jade's place. They followed him inside.

"Auntie says thank you for taking this off her hands," he said as he rested the collapsed boxes against the living room wall.

"She doesn't want to store it all somewhere and see if the sister returns?" Rory said.

"She doesn't think she will. There was no answer at the phone number she left us. And she never gave us her name."

"That is strange," Rory said.

He shrugged. "Takes all kinds."

"Can we have the phone number? We can try her later," Rory said.

"Sure. It's down in my place. I'll give it to you when we're done."

"The police don't have any problem with this, right?"

"They came by yesterday to take more of her stuff. Mostly food this time. They said we could move everything else."

"I plan on storing it for a while," Liz said. "We'll let them know where it is in case they want to look over it again."

He surveyed the room. "I don't think this will take too long. The furniture goes with the apartment. We only need to pack up the personal stuff."

Rory was relieved to hear that. She didn't relish the idea of moving the couch or bed down those stairs.

He started packing up the kitchen while Rory took the living room and Liz the bedroom. Rory placed scripts and magazines in a box, saddened to think of the roles Jade would never be able to take, making a mental note to ask Martin if anyone had contacted her agent. They'd only been working for a few minutes when the manager received a phone call from a tenant complaining about a clogged toilet.

"I hope it's not another tree branch in the sewer," he said. "That could get dicey."

"Go, deal with it," Rory said. "We can finish up here."

He placed the key on the kitchen counter and closed the door behind him, leaving Rory and Liz alone in the apartment.

"I thought he'd never leave," Liz said as she emerged from the bedroom, a shoe box in her hands.

Rory eyed the box. "Have you been trying on shoes?"

"Maybe one or two. You should be glad I did. Look what I found." She took a pair of sandals out of the box, revealing a small photo album underneath.

"Odd place to keep it," Rory said. "Are there any family photos in there? Maybe there's someone we could contact."

They flipped through the album, studying the pictures on each page, all photos of a teenage Jade, either by herself or with a younger girl and a man and a woman they assumed were her parents.

"This must be the mysterious sister," Liz said. "She does exist." She took out several of the photos and looked at the backs. "Only first names. We can try doing a search using McIntyre as the last name."

"There aren't any photos later than Jade's teenage years."

"Xander did say she'd been on her own since she was sixteen," Liz said. "I wonder what happened."

"Maybe she ran away."

"What about the desk?"

"I was just about to start on it."

They checked each of the drawers. Liz found a stack of playbills in one while Rory pulled out the usual office supplies from another.

Liz glanced at the cast list of several of the playbills. "Looks like these were all productions Jade was in. Would be a shame to throw them away. I hope we can find a family member to give them to."

They searched the rest of the drawers, putting the contents in a box as they went.

"No address book," Rory said when they'd finished. "Not surprising, I suppose. Probably has all of her contacts on her cell. I'm sure the police still have that."

She made a final sweep of the desk, finding a piece of paper shoved to the back of one drawer. She unfolded it to discover a yellowed clipping from a newspaper about a fire dated over twenty years ago. "Look at this. Jade's family died in a house fire. The names match the ones on the back of the photo."

"All of them, even her sister?" Liz said.

"Everyone except Jade. She wasn't home at the time. Out past curfew with friends."

"That saved her life."

"Explains why she was on her own since she was sixteen," Rory said.

"Then who the heck came by claiming to be her sister?"

"That's a good question."

They finished packing everything up. After Liz called to have someone pick up all the boxes and place them in her storage unit, they returned the key to the apartment manager and told him about the arrangements. He thanked them and gave them the phone number they'd asked for.

As soon as they were in the car, Rory called the number, but received no answer. Then she called Martin to tell him about the newspaper clipping and the moving of Jade's belongings. "Liz is putting them in her storage unit, so you'll have access to them whenever you need it."

"Thanks for letting me know. I'd appreciate it if you'd keep everything while the case is still open. We might want to look at it again," he said. "While I have you, I have a couple questions about the search you did of the hotel room."

Rory felt her face heat up. "Sorry about that. We didn't mean to screw up your investigation."

"You didn't. Turns out, it could be useful."

"Oh?"

"How thorough was your search?"

Rory thought back to the hotel room, visualizing it in her mind. "Pretty thorough. Hold on." She talked to Liz for a moment before getting back on the line. "Liz said she even looked in the toilet tank, and I know I looked behind and under all of the furniture."

"Including both nightstands?"

"Yes. I found that red wrapper behind one of them."

"Could you have missed a half-eaten piece of candy?"

Rory considered the question. "I suppose it's possible, but I don't really think so."

"Hmm," Martin said.

"What's so important about a half-eaten piece of can—Oh, it had poison in it, didn't it?"

"It's puzzling," was all he would say.

"Someone could have planted it later."

"I'm inclined to agree."

"One more thing," Rory said. "I have the phone number of the person posing as the sister."

After she gave him the number, he said, "Thanks. I'll see what I can find out. I need to go. Let me know if you think of anything else."

Rory hung up and told Liz about the rest of the conversation.

"The police think that's how she was poisoned?" Liz said.

"Seems so. She did wolf those chocolates down. Remember how she popped two in her mouth at the same time at the makeup rehearsal?" Rory cast her mind back to the scene in the alley. "There were some red bits of paper near Jade's body. I didn't look very closely at them, but I bet they were chocolate wrappers."

"That confirms it. She must have eaten them on the way to the race. Did Dashing D say what kind of poison was used?"

"No, but something he said the other day makes me wonder if it could have been a prescription drug."

"He did ask us if we saw Jade taking anything at the makeup party," Liz said.

All Rory could think about on the drive home was Candy delivering a new box of chocolates to the hotel room Friday evening. A box of chocolates that may have been laced with poison.

Chapter 22

Rory buckled down to work Wednesday morning, trying to keep her mind off what they'd learned. She was in the kitchen getting a Diet Coke when she heard a cock-a-doodle-doo coming from her work area.

"I need your help," Candy said without her usual greeting, her voice barely above a whisper.

"What's up?"

"I need to talk to you...in person."

"Your office?"

"No, not there. Come to the pier. I'll be near the public bathrooms."

The sense of urgency in the PI's voice convinced Rory to drop everything. "I'm on my way."

On the drive to the pier, Rory decided Liz would want to know what was going on. She left a message for her while she walked the short distance from her parking spot to the designated meeting place.

Rory had been standing at the base of the pier less than a minute when she heard a "Psst!" followed by her name. She turned in the direction the sound had come from. A head poked out from the entrance to the women's restroom. Candy emerged from the shelter of the building, wearing layers of old clothes, her purple hair tucked in a scarf that had seen better days.

Rory hurried over to her. "Is everything all right? Are you on a case?"

"Can't talk here. Follow me." Candy led the way down the stairs to the beach. They walked toward the relative shelter of a nearby lifeguard tower, locked up and unmanned at this time of year. They sat down on the ramp of the tower facing the ocean.

"Does this have to do with Jade?" Rory said. "Or is it something else?"

"I wish I'd never taken that job at the Akaw. It's been nothing but trouble."

"So it is Jade. Are you looking into her murder?"

"Forget about all that for now. I need you to do something for me. The police are searching my office. Could you stop by there and see what you can find out?"

"Why don't you go yourself? It is your office."

"My gut tells me to stay away. I always listen to my gut."

"Why me?"

Candy raised an eyebrow. "Do you really have to ask?"

"Just because he's my boyfriend doesn't mean I have any more influence or access to information than you do. I can't interfere in his investigation."

"I'm not asking you to. But you know him. You know how he thinks. You're my best bet at finding out what the police are doing. Consider this payment for my looking into Jade for you."

"How'd you find out about the search?"

"Sky, my receptionist, called me. Gave me a heads up. Join forces with her. See what you can find out."

Rory considered the request. She wasn't being asked to do anything illegal, only observe and report back. Candy had helped them out in the past. She owed her something in return. Rory exchanged texts with Sky before getting up to leave, promising to report back as soon as she knew something.

When Rory reached the building that housed the PI's office, she spotted a young woman sitting on the bottom of the stairs leading to the second floor. A uniformed officer stood nearby.

The woman gave an almost imperceptible nod toward the nearby clothing store. Rory walked inside, casually glancing at the outfits on display until Sky entered the store, grabbed a dress off a rack and walked toward the fitting rooms. Rory followed with a dress of her own. They squeezed into the largest room and talked in low voices.

"What's going on?" Rory said. "Do you know what they're searching for?"

Sky produced a search warrant from her pocket.

Rory scanned its contents. Outlined in it was the address of Candy's office and a list of items to be seized. Included were jewelry and medicine. "Have they found anything?"

Sky pocketed the warrant. "Not sure. They asked me to stay downstairs and wait to be questioned."

"Who's in the office right now?"

"I don't know who they all are, only that they're with the police. A detective's supposed to be by soon to talk to me."

Rory guessed that would be Martin. She thought about what to do next. "There's another office next to yours, right?"

"An insurance agent."

"I think I feel the need to get myself some insurance."

They hung the dresses on the rack outside the fitting room without trying them on. Rory stayed inside the store until she figured Sky had time to return to her place at the bottom of the stairs.

As soon as Rory stepped outside, she made a beeline in that direction, feigning concern when she spotted the officer. She glanced up at the second floor. "I have an appointment with my insurance agent. Is there a problem?"

"No, ma'am. Just routine police business. You can go up, but make sure you don't interfere."

When she reached the top of the stairs, she glanced into the open door to the PI's office. Several people were inside, opening cabinets and drawers in the reception area. She suspected the same thing was going on in Candy's office. Before anyone could ask her to move along, she walked down the hallway. She had barely reached the door to the insurance office when it opened and a rotund man in a suit emerged. Rory stepped aside to allow him to pass.

"Sorry," he said. "I didn't realize anyone was out here."

"No problem." She glanced down the hallway. "Do you know what's going on?"

"Whatever it is, it's annoying. I've been trying to ignore the sounds coming from next door, but it's been hard. The walls are so thin."

"I think the police are searching for something. They didn't tell you anything?"

"Not a word. But the woman next door is a private investigator. Maybe she got herself involved in some funny business." He held out his hand and introduced himself as the insurance agent whose name was on the door. "Let's see what we can find out, shall we?" A twinkle in his eye, he walked down the hallway, Rory trailing behind. When they peeked inside the doorway, one of the officers produced a medicine bottle from a desk drawer. Another held up a gold necklace and a hotel keycard.

Before she could see anything else, Rory spotted Martin coming up the stairs. She said to the agent in a whisper, "I was hoping to get a few minutes of your time. I'm thinking of changing my car insurance. Do you have time to talk now?"

His ears perked up, all thoughts of what was going on forgotten. They went back to his office. She endured a lecture on car insurance, finally taking the quote he'd prepared for her when the noise next door seemed to have quieted down.

With a promise to consider the policy, Rory left the office, happy to see the police were gone. She knocked on Candy's door, but no one answered. Guessing that Sky had gone to the station to be questioned, she walked back to the pier to give her report.

When Rory reached the beach, she found Candy sitting on a bench not far from the lifeguard station with Liz next to her.

Worry written all over her face, Candy said, "Well?"

Rory related everything she'd seen, giving as detailed a description of the bottle and the jewelry as she could. "Do you know anything about them?"

"Nothing. I don't keep anything like that in the office."

"Not even for a case you're working on?"

"I've never had a case involving either of those things."

"They found a hotel keycard too."

"I could have sworn I returned it." A stubborn look came over Candy's face. "Somebody planted everything. It's the only explanation."

"It's possible," Rory said, a cautious note in her voice.

"You don't believe me, do you? Is there something else?"

Rory told her about the half-eaten chocolate found in the hotel room. "I'm pretty sure it was poisoned. They think it came from the box delivered to the room Friday evening."

"The one I delivered?" Candy pondered the news for a moment, then stood up. "Thank you, ladies, for your help."

"What are you going to do now?" Rory asked.

"Not sure, but I'll think of something. Whatever they think I did, I didn't do it. I'm innocent. Remember that. Right now, though, I've got a job to do." She tightened the scarf around her head and walked away.

"She's in trouble," Liz said.

"I know. I don't want to believe she killed Jade, but it sounds like they're finding a lot of evidence against her."

"Doesn't look good, does it? Do you know why the police started looking into her in the first place?"

"She did deliver the box of candy, the one we assume was poisoned. I don't know if that's enough to convince a judge to give them a warrant, though."

Liz frowned. "We should see what we can find out, but I'm not sure where to start."

"What about the thefts from the hotel rooms? Jade could have seen something on Friday that put her in danger. Maybe someone sneaking into or out of one of the rooms."

Liz sucked in her breath. "Given her history, she may have tried to blackmail them. I wish Nell had given us that list of stolen items so we could start there."

Rory pursed her lips in thought. "How did Veronica say she found out about them? From some posts online, right?"

Liz whipped out her phone. "Let's see what we can find. I'll check some of the more popular review sites."

Rory brought out her own phone. "While you do that, I'll see if there have been any reports of thefts from other hotels in the area." She checked all of the news sites she could think of, but came up empty. "No luck here."

"Bingo! Here's a review that was posted in the last few days that mentions a theft." Liz handed the phone to Rory who read the complaint about a gold necklace being stolen while the guest was out of her room.

"The police found a necklace that matches this description in Candy's office." Rory checked out another review. "This next one complains about a bottle of liquid oxycodone being stolen."

"Do you think that's what they found in the office? Could that be what killed Jade?"

Rory thought back to the conversation with Martin and his statement that anything could be a poison in the right dosage. "You hear about people overdosing on oxy all the time. And the liquid form would be pretty easy to inject in a chocolate truffle."

"This is so not good for Candy."

"I agree it looks bad. She could have been stealing from the rooms and Jade caught her at it. If Jade tried to blackmail her, that could be what the argument Nell witnessed between the two of them was about."

"How would she get into the rooms?" Liz said.

"The hotel keycard. Could be one that allowed access to every room."

"Candy said she didn't find out anything when she was investigating the Akaw, but maybe someone got spooked and decided to frame her by planting the evidence in her office."

"It's possible. Maybe Sky has some idea who could have planted it."

"Or when."

"Let me see if she's back in the office yet." Rory sent a text and got an immediate reply. "She's there. Let's go."

When Rory and Liz arrived at their destination, they found the door open and Sky cleaning the surface of her desk. When they knocked, the receptionist motioned for them to enter. As soon as they stepped inside, Liz closed the door behind them.

"We heard about—" Rory began.

"If you're talking about Candy stealing things from rooms at the Akaw, I'll tell you what I told the police. No." Sky slammed the bottle of cleaner on the desk. "No." Another slam. "And no. She's a good person. She wouldn't do that. I don't care what they found on that flashdrive."

"Flashdrive?" Rory said.

"The police found it in that Jade person's place. There were pics of Candy in the Akaw's lobby and on the guest floors around the time things went missing from rooms. Just because she was in the hotel doesn't mean she stole anything. She's often at hotels when she's working a divorce case."

"Is she working one now?"

"No." Sky sat down heavily in her chair, the bottle of cleaner still in her hand. "Candy's been very good to me. I don't know what to do."

"Let's see if we can figure it out together," Rory said. "What can you tell us about the prescription bottle and the jewelry the police found?"

"Nothing. The police showed them to me, but I didn't recognize either one."

"Candy said she didn't know anything about them either," Liz said. "Could they have been planted? Do you have any idea who might have had the opportunity to do that?"

Sky considered the question. "The office is locked unless one of us is here."

"The items were found in this room." Rory indicated the reception area. "Could you have stepped out for a few minutes?"

Sky set the bottle of cleaner on the desk and stared at them thoughtfully. "I do sometimes make a coffee run. It could have been then. If Candy was on the phone with her door shut, she probably wouldn't have noticed anyone enter."

"What about Jade McIntyre? Did she ever stop by the office?"

"Never saw her. Why would she come here?"

"I wondered if they knew each other, or if she was looking to hire Candy."

"Not as far as I know, but I was out of town for a few days. She could've stopped by then." Sky gave them the dates of her absence from the office.

"What about appointments?" Rory said after she noted the information in her phone.

"You think one of the people she had an appointment with might have planted the evidence?"

"It's a possibility."

Sky consulted her computer. "How far back should I go?"

"Two weeks?"

"I really shouldn't be giving you this, but if it'll help Candy..." She wrote down the information on a piece of paper and handed it over. "Don't give this to anyone. Someone could have dropped in when I wasn't around. There wouldn't be any record of that, but Candy would know."

Rory and Liz looked at the paper.

"There are only half a dozen appointments on here," Rory said.

"It's been pretty quiet lately. Not all of our clients come into the office. Some people call instead."

"We can count those people out, at least," Liz said.

"We can't really talk to any of these people," Rory said. "They would wonder how we found out about a confidential appointment, but we can look them up online."

They split up the names and the three of them got to work. After half an hour, they hadn't found any obvious connection to Jade or the Akaw.

Promising to keep in touch with Sky, Rory and Liz left the office, waiting to talk until they were at the bottom of the stairs.

"I hate to say it," Rory said. "But I'm beginning to believe Candy might be guilty after all. She delivered the poisoned candy to the room. There are pictures of her in the hotel at the time of the thefts. The police found a hotel keycard in her office. Then there's that argument with Jade."

"Not to mention the stolen oxy and jewelry found in her office. It all adds up," Liz said glumly. "But why would she steal from the rooms?"

"Could be as simple as needing money." Rory sighed. "I like Candy. I don't want to believe it either."

"But what about Jade? Why would she kill her?"

"She probably couldn't afford to pay her off. If Jade talked to the police, Candy could be found guilty of stealing. She'd not only go to jail, but also lose her PI license. You know how important that is to her. It would devastate her."

As they made their way down the street, Rory thought about Candy, wondering if she really could have been so wrong about her.

Chapter 23

Rory went to sleep that night upset about the sudden change in course the murder investigation had taken. After tossing and turning for half an hour, she gave up on sleep and worked into the wee hours of the morning until she was so exhausted that she couldn't keep her eyes open. What seemed like only minutes later, a cock-a-doodle-doo woke her.

She groped around on her nightstand for her cell phone and mumbled a very sleepy hello into it.

"Did I wake you?" Martin said. "Sorry. I thought you'd be working by now."

"What time is it?"

"Almost ten."

Rory groaned and sat up on the edge of her bed. "I didn't realize it was so late. Guess I slept through my alarm."

"Sekhmet didn't wake you?"

She glanced at the foot of the bed where the cat was curled up, sound asleep. "She must have had enough food left over from yesterday."

"Do you want me to call back?"

"No. I'm up now. What did you want to talk about?"

"Candy. We've been looking for her. Have you seen her recently?"

"For a few minutes yesterday," Rory said. "Doesn't look good for her, does it? Those pics on the flashdrive, the chocolates plus the medicine and jewelry you found in her office. And that keycard."

His tone sharpened. "How do you know about the office?"

"I might have taken a peek inside when you were searching," she said in a small voice.

He said something she couldn't quite catch.

"Martin?"

"I'm here. How did you find out about the search?"

"Candy told me. She asked me to see what you were doing."

"And you didn't find that suspicious?"

"Not at the time."

"If you hear from her or see her, let me know, okay?"

"I will. Before you hang up, did you find out anything about the person who was masquerading as Jade's sister?"

"Nothing so far. The apartment owner wasn't much help. She could only give a general description. Not enough to go on. We looked into that phone number you gave me, but it was a dead end. At this point, she doesn't seem to have anything to do with the case," he said. "Jade's memorial service is this afternoon at two. Maybe she'll show up there."

"Who made the arrangements? I thought she didn't have any relatives."

"Mrs. Tilcox is taking care of everything."

"From I Do For You? That's nice of her."

He gave her details about the service before hanging up with another request to contact him if she heard from Candy.

Yesterday, Candy's gut had told her to stay away from her office during the search. Rory wondered if it was now telling her to avoid the police altogether.

As she began her day, Rory texted Liz with the information about Jade's memorial service, agreeing to meet for a late lunch before it.

Rory was waiting on a bench outside a restaurant on Main Street when Liz rushed up to her and handed her a copy of the *View*.

"What's this?" Rory said.

"Read it." Liz tapped a graceful finger on an article at the bottom of the front page before sitting down on the bench.

Rory frowned when she saw the headline: *Local PI Wanted for Questioning in Poisoning Death*. The article talked about the hunt for Candy, asking for the public's help in locating her. "I wish she would turn herself in."

"She must be lying low while she figures out how to prove her innocence."

"If she is innocent."

"Before we make up our minds, we should hear her side of the story. That's only fair. Maybe her disappearance has something to do with another case she's working on."

"Like that cold case Veronica mentioned," Rory said. "Do you remember anything about it?"

"Not a whole lot. A couple was murdered in their home years ago. Don't remember exactly when." Liz held up her finger. "Wait. That ad she put in the paper last week had a date in it. Maybe it's in this one too." She turned to the classified section and ran her finger down the page, reading out the information as soon as she found the ad.

"That should give us enough to find out more about the case. The library has back issues of the *View*." Rory checked the time on her cell phone. "We don't have a lot of time before the service. If we want to do this now, we'll have to skip lunch."

"That's okay, this is more important."

They walked the short distance to the library. Once inside they made their way to a row of public computers. With Liz looking over her shoulder, Rory searched the newspaper archives for information on the cold case. In a quiet voice, she read the short account of the tragedy. A couple returning from their honeymoon had surprised a burglar in their home and been shot to death. A man was seen running away from the scene. At the time it was written, the police were still searching for the killer and the gun. An article in the *View* two weeks later detailed the arrest of a suspect, Laith Hayward.

"Laith," Rory said. "I remember seeing that name on the back of a picture in Candy's office."

"And on that love lock on the tree at city hall," Liz said.

BRUSH UP ON MURDER   213

"Right. I forgot about that." Rory studied the newspaper photo. "This is the same photo Candy had. Does he look familiar to you?"

Liz leaned forward and stared at the screen. "Not sure. Reminds me of someone." She shrugged. "Maybe I met his parents at some point."

"You do meet a lot of people in your business."

"Was he convicted?"

"Let me see." Rory searched the newspaper archive until she found a series of articles almost a year later that covered the trial and Laith's subsequent conviction. An eyewitness had seen him fleeing the scene, but he insisted he was innocent. The gun was never recovered.

"Someone must have hired Candy to look into the case. Someone who believed him."

"Odd after all these years. I wonder what triggered the re-investigation." Liz peered at the screen. "What about this witness from the trial? Maybe Candy went to see them. I don't see a name, though."

"There wasn't one in any of the articles. The police could have been keeping their identity secret for their protection. Sky might know something. Wait right here."

Rory went outside to make the call. Instead of a person, all she got was a message stating the office would open later in the afternoon. She reported back to Liz. "We'll have to check with her after the service. Who else might know something?"

Liz snapped her fingers, garnering a disapproving frown from a woman at a nearby table. In a hushed voice, she said, "That retired detective. Orson something or other."

"Huddleston."

"That's it. I bet he'd know more. He's familiar with a lot of cold cases. He might know about this one. Let's go talk to him."

"I'll find out where he lives." Rory swiftly found the address of the retired detective in an online Whitepages directory.

"Let's go," Liz said. "I'll drive."

A short while later, they pulled up in front of a single-story stucco home in the eastern part of the city.

"Let me do the talking," Liz said as they got out of the car.

When no one answered the front door, they walked down the driveway to check the backyard. They found Orson coming out of a building at the back of the property.

"Can I help you?" he said, a quizzical look on his face.

Liz handed him one of her business cards. "We were wondering if we could have a few minutes of your time."

After a quick glance at her card, he said, "I'm not interested in selling, Miss Dexter."

"Call me Liz. I don't want to talk about real estate."

"Then what?"

"We're interested in a cold case a friend of ours is working on. You know her. Candy."

"I'm sorry. I can't help you." He turned his back on them and started toward the door of the house.

"Please," Rory said. "We only need a few minutes of your time. Detective Green will vouch for us."

"Green?" he said, interest in his eyes. "You know Martin?"

"He's my boyfriend."

"He's a good man. Treats people with respect. I can give you a few minutes. Let's go inside." A short time later, they were all sitting in the living room.

"How can I help you?"

"We'd like to know more about a cold case." Rory described what they knew so far. "None of the articles in the paper mentioned the name of the witness. We thought maybe you knew who it was."

A puzzled look on his face, he studied the two of them before finally saying, "You really don't know?"

"Know what?"

"Candy was the one who witnessed the crime."

Rory and Liz exchanged surprised glances.

"Then why did she put an ad in the paper looking for witnesses?" Rory said.

"I'd better start at the beginning." Orson closed his eyes, gathering his thoughts. "Candy saw a man she later identified as Laith Hayward running away from a house where a couple was murdered. It was dark, but she was still absolutely sure of her identification. He was convicted of the crime and sent to prison, but he always insisted he was innocent. A member of his family campaigned for years to get his conviction re-examined. They finally convinced the Innocence Project to take up his case. A few months ago, DNA evidence exonerated him."

"That was twenty years ago," Rory said. "DNA was used in cases back then, wasn't it? Why did it take so long for the truth to come out?"

"The burglar had cut himself breaking into the house through a window. The sample was small and the technology didn't exist then to get anything useful out of it. Candy felt terrible, so she decided it was her duty to find the real culprit. She was hoping another witness would come forward."

"Where is Laith now? Maybe he wasn't very forgiving of her mistake. He could have come after her and that's why we can't find her," Liz said.

"Not possible. He died in a prison brawl before he could be released."

Rory and Liz both gasped.

"That's awful."

"I know. The police try to get it right, but it doesn't always work out that way." Sadness filled his eyes.

"You know Candy's wanted by the police right now?" Rory said, choosing her words carefully.

He pursed his lips. "I heard. The press have convicted her already." He eyed them. "Maybe you have too. I think you should leave now." At the door, he said, "She's innocent, you know, no matter what anyone says. I hope you have the decency to hear her out."

Rory and Liz quietly left the house, not saying anything until they'd reached the car.

"No wonder Candy wrote *Forgive Me* on that lock," Rory said.

"I know I'd feel awful if someone was convicted of a crime on my say-so and I turned out to be wrong."

"That's probably why she feels so strongly about looking into this case. But nothing we learned is helping us find her."

As they drove the short distance to the memorial service, Rory said a short prayer, hoping Candy was alive and well and that she'd be found soon so she could tell her side of the story.

When they arrived at the funeral home, they found Martin in detective mode, leaning against his car, watching people arrive for the service. Rory walked over and stood beside him while Liz joined a group near the entrance.

"I don't think she's going to be here," Rory said.

He cocked an eyebrow.

"Candy."

"What makes you think I'm waiting to see if she comes?"

Rory shrugged. "That's what I would do. But if I wanted to avoid the police, I wouldn't show up here."

"You never know. Stranger things have happened." He directed his attention to the entrance of the funeral home. "Not many people have arrived so far."

"It's early yet." Rory spotted a younger man with long curly hair looking uncomfortable in a jacket and long pants. She almost didn't recognize the apartment manager without the man bun. She pointed him out to Martin who confirmed the woman beside him was the owner of Jade's apartment building.

They continued observing the new arrivals until Liz gestured for her to come over.

"I'm being summoned." Rory said a quick goodbye and joined Liz while Martin remained at his observation post in the parking lot.

"Did Dashing D have anything new to say?"

"Not really. What about you? Who were you talking to?"

"Some of the women who work at I Do For You. Nothing new to add there. Nell's here. She's saving us seats."

When they entered the chapel, Rory's gaze swept over the sparsely populated room. Rows of chairs faced the front where a closed casket stood surrounded by floral arrangements in varying sizes. Lola and a couple other young women, all dressed in somber colors, walked down the aisle to take seats near the front next to Mrs. Tilcox. To their surprise, Zeke arrived and sat down near the back.

"There's Nell," Liz said.

They made their way down the aisle and sat down on chairs flanking Nell who had a solemn look on her face.

"Didn't expect to see you here," Rory said in a quiet voice while they waited for the service to begin.

"I had to come. I feel so bad that someone I hired could have..." Nell's voice trailed off. She dabbed the corners of her eyes with a crumpled tissue.

"We don't know that for sure," Liz said.

"Really? I thought the police...Didn't they arrest Candy? She's not in custody?"

"They're still looking for her."

"She's missing?" Nell mulled over the information for a moment. "I'm sure they'll find her soon. If there's a trial, I suppose I'll have to come back to testify. This is my last stop before leaving town."

"Congrats on getting the job."

"Seems odd to be happy about it...here." Nell's gaze swept over the room.

"I know what you mean," Rory said. "I hope Candy is found soon. I'd really like to hear her side of the story."

"You don't think she did it?"

"She never struck me as the type. Always seemed to be a good person."

"Sometimes good people do bad things," Nell said. "What about the thefts from the rooms? The police seem sure she's to blame."

"Maybe she was framed," Liz said.

"Really? Who would do that?"

"Not sure yet," Rory said. "It might have something to do with this cold case she's working on. A couple was murdered here in town about twenty years ago. Someone named Laith Hayward was wrongly convicted."

"Oh? That's sad."

A determined look on her face, Rory said, "Whatever the truth is, I'm going to get to the bottom of it. Even if it means Candy is to blame."

A man in a suit stepped up to the podium and raised his hands. After the murmur of voices died down and the room was silent, he began the short service.

Mrs. Tilcox praised Jade's professionalism and some of her co-workers shared anecdotes about working with her. At the end of the service, the owner of I Do For You stood in the lobby shaking hands with those who wished to express their condolences. Nell said her goodbyes and bypassed the line on her way out the door.

Rory and Liz were about to leave when the woman who owned Jade's apartment building walked up to them accompanied by her nephew. After introducing herself, she thanked them for helping out with Jade's belongings.

"Happy to help," Liz said. "As soon as the police give the go ahead, I'll make sure everything gets donated to worthy charities."

"Jade's sister doesn't want any of it?"

Rory gave her a puzzled look. "I thought the police would've told you, but no one's found her sister. The only one we know of died a long time ago."

"Wasn't she sitting next to you?"

"You mean Nell? She's not related."

"Oh, I thought..."

"She's the manager of the Akaw. Maybe you saw her there?"

"No, I'm pretty sure she's the one who stopped by." The apartment owner thanked them again and walked away with her nephew.

"What was that about?" Liz asked.

"A case of mistaken identity? She couldn't give a very good description to Martin of the sister before."

"She seems sure now."

"She does, doesn't she?" Rory said.

They waited until they were alone outside before continuing the discussion.

"Why would Nell pretend to be Jade's sister?" Liz asked.

"Could Jade have been blackmailing her about something at the hotel that could prevent her from changing jobs?"

"Her name wasn't on the list we found."

"Neither was Candy's, but there were incriminating photos on that flashdrive. It's odd the police didn't find it when they searched the place."

"You don't think..." they both said at the same time.

"That Nell planted those photos?" Rory finished the thought they both seemed to have. "Sky should be in the office now. Maybe she knows something that will connect Nell and Candy other than the case Nell hired her for."

They got in the car and drove toward the office, hoping Sky could provide some useful information.

Chapter 24

When Rory and Liz walked in the door to Candy's office, they found Sky sitting at her desk, staring at a fliptop phone lying on its surface, seemingly willing it to ring. She looked up, hope in her eyes that quickly faded when she recognized them.

"You're not Candy," she said in a dull voice.

"You haven't heard from her?" Rory said.

"Not a peep. Even if she wants to avoid the police, I'd expect her to check in to find out what was going on. We have burner phones to use in cases like this." Sky gestured to the phone on the desk. "I'm really worried. Did you find out anything new?"

"Maybe. Do you know of any connection between Nell Fremont and Candy besides the case at the Akaw?"

"The manager of the hotel? I can't think of anything. Why do you want to know?"

"Just an idea we had. Rather not say anything else until we have more info. We should concentrate on finding Candy. When we saw her at the beach, she said something about having work to do. Could she be chasing a lead on that cold case?" Rory said. "The one from twenty years ago."

"I don't know. She did place an ad in the paper."

"We saw it," Liz said. "Did she get any responses?"

"Not that I know of. At least no one called the office."

"What about family members?" Rory said. "Maybe she went to speak to one of them."

"Of the guy who was blamed for it? Or the victims?"

"Either one."

"From what I remember, the victims don't have any family left in the area," Sky said. "They didn't have any kids. Both sets of parents died and any other relatives they have live far from here. Candy has been looking for Laith's, though she doesn't want to make contact until she can tell them who the real culprit is. Whatever she found should be in the file." She opened the top drawer of a nearby file cabinet. "I shouldn't be letting you see this, but under the circumstances, I think it's okay." She riffled through the folders. "That's funny. It's not here. Candy must have taken it with her."

"Are her case files backed up online?"

"No. She deals with sensitive information. She figures the best way to keep it all confidential is to go old school. If she gets info electronically, she usually prints it out." Sky closed the file cabinet drawer and locked it.

Rory stared thoughtfully at the printer sitting on a nearby table. "Does your printer have the ability to reprint the last job?"

Sky held up her hands. "No clue. You're welcome to see what you can find out."

Rory sat down in front of the computer and a few minutes later the printer started working, spitting out a family photo of four people smiling into the camera, a mom, a dad, a younger man and a girl. Rory stared at the photo. "That looks like Nell, doesn't it?"

Liz's eyes widened. "That's the photo I saw in her office."

"So that's her brother." Rory studied the picture. "That's Laith Hayward. That's the connection between Candy and Nell." She paced the floor, putting it all together in her mind. Once she'd worked it all out, she explained what she came up with to the others.

"Nell had access to the rooms at the Akaw. She stole the items and poisoned the chocolates, all to frame Candy to get back at her for falsely identifying her brother."

"She doesn't seem like the kind of person who would kill an innocent person to get back at someone," Liz said.

"Her brother's death is a powerful motive."

"It doesn't explain the argument between Candy and Jade."

"Nell could have made that up. She was the only witness to it."

"That all fits," Liz said.

"What about Candy?" Sky said. "Do you think something's happened to her?"

"I hope not," Rory said. "She could be lying low."

"How can we be sure you're right about Nell?" Liz said.

"I'm going to call Martin and tell him our theory. He'll know what to do." Rory made the call.

The detective listened to everything she said. "I'll bring her in for questioning. Promise me you'll stay out of it."

"At the service she said she was leaving town today."

"We're on it. If you happen to see her, don't approach her. Call me. Don't worry, we'll find her."

Rory hung up the phone, hoping it wasn't too late.

Friday morning, Rory woke up looking forward to the wedding rehearsal that evening, but at the same time wondering if any evidence had been found to support her theory about the murder.

When Martin called her mid-morning, she immediately said, "Did you find Nell?"

"Not yet," he said. "We've got people looking all over the state for her."

"What about the job she took?"

"They haven't seen her yet. They'll let us know if she shows up."

"This waiting is killing me. I need to do something. What if she's got Candy?"

"We're looking for her as well. There's nothing you can do right now. How about some fun to take your mind off things?"

"I could use some right now. Worrying isn't going to help. What did you have in mind?"

"It's a surprise. You'll get a text this afternoon with details. Don't worry, we'll have plenty of time to get to the wedding rehearsal," he said before hanging up.

The rest of the morning, she kept wondering what Martin was planning. Even though he said she'd get details later in the day, she periodically checked her phone to make sure she hadn't missed a text. Eventually, she decided the best thing for her to do was to stop staring at her phone and settle down to work.

Rory was adding content to the March issue of *BrushToBrush* when her phone quacked, indicating the arrival of the anticipated text: *The Valentine's Day scavenger hunt starts now. Follow the steps, solve the clues and I'll be waiting for you at the end.*

A smile played about her face as she stared at the message. She texted back: *Okay, I'm game. Where do I start?*

Go outside and find the little man with the hat, Martin texted back. *See you soon.*

Sekhmet jumped up on the desk and gave an inquiring meow.

"It's a game," Rory said. "And there's a surprise at the end. I'm supposed to go outside. I wonder what he means by a little man with a hat."

The cat jumped off the desk and made her way toward the front door. When Rory didn't immediately follow, Sekhmet ran back to her and meowed.

"I'm coming, I'm coming. I need to finish something first." She took a few minutes to finish her task, then followed the cat to the front door. Sekhmet poked her head outside, turning back when a cold wind hit her in the face.

Rory looked up at the threatening skies, hoping the rain would hold off until she'd had a chance to finish the hunt. She stood on her lawn and stared at the front of her house. Her gaze swept the area, zeroing in on the flower bed to the left of the porch. A red hat poked out from behind a bush.

She brushed aside the leaves to find a garden gnome she'd never seen before. "Hello. Where did you come from?" she said as she picked it up and examined it. When she turned it over, she found a plastic sandwich bag duct-taped to the bottom. Inside the bag was a typed note. *Go to where paint and wood are king, where brushes and varnish wait for homes,* it read.

Rory puzzled over the words before realizing it was telling her to go to her mother's store. She brought the gnome inside and showed it to Sekhmet. "What do you think? Should I take it with me?" The cat meowed. "Right. Too bulky. Better leave it behind." She put the gnome on her desk before grabbing her keys and texting *on my way* to Martin to let him know she was starting the hunt.

She entered Arika's Scrap 'n Paint less than fifteen minutes later. Before she could say anything, her mother handed her another type-written note. Rory eagerly opened it and read *Go to the house of the men in blue*. Moments later, she was out the door on her way to the police station where the officer on duty gave her the next clue. From there she walked to Zephy's. Before long, a clue directed her to the Akaw where the concierge handed her an envelope. The typed note inside read: *Meet me at LG4*.

Rory puzzled over the note, unsure what to make of it. All the other ones had been less obscure and fairly easy to figure out. She looked around the lobby but didn't see anything that read LG4. When she asked the concierge, the man couldn't come up with anything either.

Once she was outside, Rory studied the clue once more and walked to an area where she had a view of downtown and the beach. Unwilling to give up, she texted Liz for help, explaining about the hunt Martin had sent her on. While she was waiting for a reply, her gaze zeroed in on a blue lifeguard tower on the beach below. Her face brightened and she swiftly texted Liz: *I figured it out*.

Rory stuck her phone in her back pocket and walked down the hill toward the beach. She walked along the sand until she found a lifeguard tower with LG4 painted on the side. Her gaze swept the area to see if she could spot Martin, but the beach was deserted, the threat of rain keeping people at home.

She studied the tower as she walked around to the ocean side. A wooden flap still covered its front window. Scattered rose petals created a path up the ramp to an open door at the top, inviting her inside. She walked up the ramp, calling Martin's name as she cautiously entered.

Rory couldn't make out anything in the dim interior. Gradually, her eyes adjusted. She'd expected a picnic laid out on the wood floor, but as far as she could tell the eight-by-eight-foot room was empty.

"Martin?" she said uncertainly and stepped forward, letting the door close behind her.

In the semi-darkness, she spotted a figure with hair styled in a bubble cut lying on her side on the wood floor, eyes closed, feet and hands bound, tape covering her mouth.

"Candy!" Rory hurried forward, intending to remove the duct tape from the woman's mouth. Before she could bend down, she felt a pressure on her back followed by a painful jolt. She tried to move away, but the pain continued until her muscles spasmed. She lost her balance and fell to the floor, her head hitting a hard surface right before darkness took over.

Chapter 25

Rory regained consciousness slowly, unsure where she was or how much time had passed. As her eyes adjusted to the dim lighting, she realized she was lying on the floor of a small room, her hands bound behind her, tape over her mouth. Panic set in. She closed her eyes and forced her breathing to slow.

Once she'd regained her composure, she listened for sounds coming from outside, but the rain pattered so hard against the roof it drowned out everything else. She struggled to a sitting position and examined the space around her. A small LED lantern sat on the floor in a corner of the room under a flat wood surface she guessed functioned as a desk, a chair next to it. She twisted her head to the right and spotted rolled up flags and a water dispenser.

Memories flooded in of the scavenger hunt, entering the life-guard tower expecting to find Martin inside, but instead encountering an attack from behind. An image of Candy sitting on the floor of the interior of the tower, bound and gagged, popped into her mind.

Rory turned her head to the left and spotted the woman lying immobile on the floor less than a foot away. She scooted over and nudged her with her foot, trying to say Candy's name, but all that came out was a muffled and unintelligible sound. A wave of relief washed over her when she saw the steady rise and fall of her chest.

Rory tested her bonds. No matter how hard she tried, the tape around her wrists wouldn't budge. She paused to think. She needed to get help. She didn't know how long it would be before their captor returned.

BRUSH UP ON MURDER 227

Rory was sure Martin would be looking for her when she didn't show up, but she didn't know how he would find her. Then she remembered her cell phone and the tracking app on it. She might not be able to call or text, but they could find her through the app. She brushed her hands against the back pocket of her jeans. Hope faded when she realized her phone was no longer there. Their captor must have taken it.

She was looking around the area for something that would help her free herself from her bonds when she heard a faint sound from outside, barely audible above the pounding of the rain against the roof of the tower.

The outer door opened, revealing darkness outside. Her heart lifted until she recognized the figure that stepped inside.

Her eyes sad, Nell shook her umbrella before closing it and leaning it against the wall. She sat down on the chair facing Rory. "You're awake. I suppose you're wondering why. I didn't want to, believe me." She raised her head, a defiant look in her eyes. "You gave me no choice. You couldn't accept Candy was the killer. Kept on pushing. It was only a matter of time before you figured out it was me." Her gaze shifted to Candy. "This is all her fault. She was supposed to eat the chocolates, not give them away."

With a start, Rory realized Candy was the intended target, and Jade an innocent victim.

Rory began to work her mouth in a desperate attempt to get the tape off.

Nell watched for a moment, then said, "I'll take it off if you promise not to yell. Otherwise..." She took a stun gun out of her pocket and held it up.

Rory nodded her agreement.

Nell ripped off the tape and Rory suppressed a cry of pain.

"You have something you want to say?" Nell said, keeping the stun gun visible.

"Why are you doing this?"

"You know why." She gestured toward the still unconscious Candy. "She lied on the stand. My brother went to prison because of it."

"She made an honest mistake. She's trying to make up for it."

"By finding the real culprit? Too little, too late."

"Your brother wouldn't want—"

Anger suffused Nell's face. "Don't tell me what Laith would want. You didn't know him." Her expression softened and a faraway look came into her eyes. "He was such a good brother. Always protected me. Even though he was seven years older, we were close. I wrote letters to him when he was in prison. I was only twelve when he was convicted. My parents wouldn't let me visit him. They meant well."

Rory figured the longer she kept Nell talking, the better chance she had that someone would find them. "Did you see him when you were older?"

"As often as possible. I tried for years to get someone interested in taking his case. I finally got the Innocence Project to look into it last year."

"They got the DNA retested, didn't they?"

"I was so excited when Laith was exonerated. Then he died." Nell cast an angry look in Candy's direction. "He wouldn't have been in prison if it weren't for her."

"How did you know she was the witness?"

"I'd heard my parents talking during the trial. I didn't know she lived here when I took the job at the Akaw. We moved away after the trial, but they wanted to move back. Then I saw Candy's picture in the paper. Some case she worked on."

"Did you decide to kill her then?"

"No," Nell said. "I was hoping to get her to change her story, but I couldn't get up the nerve to talk to her. Then Laith died."

"That's when you decided to kill her."

"An eye for an eye. Seemed fair. I took things out of a few guest rooms to create a problem I could hire Candy to look into. I didn't know how I was going to kill her until I saw the oxy in one of the rooms. I noticed that she loved chocolates so I gave her a box of spiked ones. So many of them were around the hotel, it would be hard to trace it back to me."

"Then she gave them away."

"At first, I was furious. Then I realized having her doing time for a crime she didn't commit was a better punishment."

"So you framed her."

"I planted the jewelry, medicine and a master keycard in her outer office when I went to give Candy a check for her services."

"Making sure to do it when the receptionist wasn't there."

"That was a lucky break."

"You planted the flashdrive in Jade's apartment, masquerading as her sister, didn't you?" Rory said. "And made up the argument between Jade and Candy."

"You know I went to her place?"

"The apartment owner told me. Did you put the half-eaten chocolate behind the nightstand too?"

"The police needed to know how she died. They didn't seem to be connecting the dots."

"Don't you feel bad about Jade?"

"Of course I do. I'm not heartless. That wasn't my fault." Nell pointed the stun gun at Rory. "Then you had to get involved. I've seen you solve other cases. You don't let go."

"What are you going to do now?"

"Make it look like Candy tried to kill you because you got too close." Nell brought out matches from her pocket. "But you managed to knock her out before she could get out of the tower, but not before she set a fire. You'll both die in it."

"Won't work. The police know everything."

A surprised look came over Nell's face, then she quickly recovered. "At least I'll be going to jail for something I did." She put the stun gun in her pocket, picked up the lamp and stood up. Her eyes focused on Candy, she walked over and knelt down on the floor.

"Don't do it." Rory scooted so she partially blocked Nell's access to Candy.

"Why are you protecting her? She's a liar and a murderer. She may not be the one who killed him, but she's still responsible for my brother's death. If it wasn't for her, he wouldn't have gone to prison in the first place. He died trying to break up a fight, you know. That's the kind of guy he was." Tears in her eyes, Nell raised the lamp, preparing to strike. "I *have* to do this," she said, as if trying to convince herself.

During the short time Nell had been in the lifeguard tower, the rain had stopped. Rory made out a sound coming from outside. She listened intently, unsure if she'd actually heard a footstep or only imagined it.

Apparently hearing the sound too, Nell turned her head toward the door.

At the same time the door opened, Rory shoved her shoulder into Nell, causing the lamp to go flying. Martin came through the door and grabbed Nell. After securing her with handcuffs, he handed her over to someone outside.

While he checked on Candy and removed both of their restraints, Rory told him everything that had happened.

He called for an ambulance, then held her in his arms for a moment. "It's all over now."

"Candy?" she said into his jacket.

"I think she'll be okay. We're getting help now. Let's go."

He helped her up and led her outside. The first thing she saw was Liz nearby, a worried look on her face. When she saw Rory, she gave a relieved smile and, arms open wide, ran over to them.

After being checked out by the doctors at the ER, Rory exited the treatment area. As soon as she appeared in the waiting room, Solange rushed toward her and enveloped her in a big hug.

"So, so glad you're okay. You had us worried," she said after she finally let Rory go.

"I'm fine. They gave me a clean bill of health."

"I'll let your parents know you're okay," Liz said and went outside to make the call.

Solange sat down on a nearby chair and patted the seat next to her. "Sit down."

Rory sank down on the seat, grateful to no longer be standing. "Sorry I missed the rehearsal and the dinner."

"It's okay. Liz explained everything. She and Paris will tell you what you need to know," Solange said. "I came over as soon as I could. Xander wanted to come too, but I insisted he take care of our out-of-town guests." She studied Rory. "How are you really doing? I'll totally understand if you're not up to being a bridesmaid, but I hope you can attend the wedding."

"Don't worry, I'm fine. A mild headache, that's all. A little rest and I'll be back to normal. I'm relieved to hear the wedding's still on. I was worried you'd call it off."

"It wasn't an easy decision, but we decided not to let everything that's happened derail us. I only wish Naomi could be there."

Liz returned and sat down next to them.

"I know it's not exactly what you planned," Rory said. "But we'll all do our best to make it a happy occasion."

Solange held her head high. "We've had to make some adjustments, but it'll be okay. Now, tell us everything."

"I never, ever want to be on the receiving end of a stun gun again, that's for sure," Rory began, then told them about being lured to the lifeguard tower and what had happened there. "I don't know how you found me, though."

Liz took up the tale. "Dashing D got worried when you didn't show up at the place he'd told you to go in the note he'd left at the hotel."

"Nell must have substituted a different one," Rory said.

"He called me and asked if I'd heard from you. The tracking app said the last location of your phone was on the pier. We went there but didn't see you or your phone."

"How in the world did you figure out where I was?" Rory asked.

"You texted me about that clue, LG4. I noticed the lifeguard tower near the pier had LG1 written on its side. Didn't take long for us to find the right tower."

"Has anyone heard how Nell is?"

"Why are you worried about her after what she did?" Solange asked.

"I feel sorry for her. She did lose her brother."

Solange shook her head. "Still doesn't make what she did right."

"No it doesn't," a deep voice behind them said.

Rory turned around and looked at Martin. "How's Candy doing?"

"She's recovering."

"She told you what happened?"

"The basics. She promised to fill in more details when she's feeling better. She wants to see you and Liz for a few minutes."

"Is that wise?" Rory asked.

"The doctor said it was okay if you make it short."

Rory hugged Solange goodbye, then followed Liz and Martin up the elevator to Candy's hospital room. After making sure Liz would get Rory home safely, he left them to get back to the station.

Rory held Candy's hand and softly called her name.

She opened her eyes and smiled weakly at the two of them. "Thanks for coming."

"How are you?"

"Tired, but fine. I wanted to thank you for saving me and say how sorry I am you got caught up in my problems." Candy took a deep breath and closed her eyes for a moment before continuing. "I really believed Laith was the culprit. All those years he spent in jail for something he didn't do because of me. And then his death. I'll never forgive myself."

"We don't have to talk about this now."

"I want to explain. As soon as I found out he was innocent, I started looking into the case."

"We saw your ad in the paper," Liz said.

"I had no idea Nell was his sister. She has a different last name because his father was her mother's first husband. Nell didn't attend the trial, so I'd never seen her before. Her parents thought she was too young. I only found out a few days ago when I saw the photo of Laith in Nell's office. I took a picture of it for my files."

"We saw you printed it out."

Candy looked surprised. "You'll have to tell me how you worked that magic later. I was walking over to the hotel to tell her I had a lead on the real killer, I figured I owed her that much, when I saw her on the beach. I followed her into the lifeguard tower, and she used her stun gun on me, then knocked me out. The next thing I knew I ended up here." Tears glistened in her eyes. "I'm so, so sorry."

Rory patted her hand and made soothing noises. "What about the poisoned chocolates? How'd the box end up in Jade's room?"

"Nell handed the box to me when I was delivering room service. She knew how much I liked them. I put it on the cart and forgot about it. Someone must have noticed it and put it on the stack in the kitchen. I grabbed it and took it up when I got the order."

Liz whistled. "Anyone could have died."

Candy looked down. In a weak voice, she said, "I know. All because of me."

"It's not your fault," Rory said.

"I agree," a male voice behind them said.

Rory turned to find Orson Huddleston standing in the doorway, concern written all over his face.

"Can I come in?" he said.

Candy gestured for him to enter. He stood on the other side of the bed and held her hand.

"We'll let you two talk," Rory said. "I could use some rest myself."

Candy said a hasty goodbye, all her attention now focused on Orson.

Rory and Liz slipped out the door.

"Told you," Liz said in a whisper, a satisfied smirk on her face.

Chapter 26

The afternoon sun beamed down on the group gathered on the beach for the Valentine's Day wedding. The bride and groom stood under a flower-covered archway set up near the water. Sixty guests watched as the officiant ended the brief ceremony with "It's my pleasure to introduce to you, for the first time as husband and wife, Solange and Xander." Clad in traditional wedding attire except for their bare feet, the couple kissed and turned to smile at their guests who were sitting in rows of white chairs facing the ocean. Amid enthusiastic applause, they walked hand in hand down the aisle between the chairs.

"Solange and Xander would like to remind you that the reception will take place at the Akaw just up the hill. You're welcome to go there now," the officiant said. "They'll be joining you shortly after taking some pictures here on the beach."

The guests began walking toward the hotel, stopping on the way to put on their shoes they'd left on a beach mat near the edge of the sand. A few stayed behind to watch the couple's photo session.

After making sure Solange didn't need anything, Rory and Liz made their way up the hill accompanied by Martin.

"Such a beautiful ceremony," Liz said, her eyes dreamy. "When I get married, I'm going to have a wedding like this one, only bigger."

"Do you have someone in mind?" Rory asked.

"I've got a couple possibilities. Too early to tell."

They stepped inside the Akaw where the new hotel manager greeted them. A brief moment of sadness washed over Rory. Determined to not let the events of the past couple weeks ruin the reception for her, she pushed all thoughts of murder out of her mind and joined the group going into the ballroom.

As soon as they entered, they found Veronica inside, pestering the guests with questions, not having much luck at getting any of them to talk to her. When she approached them, Martin frowned. "This is a private event. Please leave."

"What if I'm covering this for the society page for the paper?"

"What society page?" Rory said at the same time Martin said, "Are you?"

"I know when I'm not wanted." Veronica flounced toward the exit and disappeared into the hallway.

"She gave up too easily," Rory said. "She's probably going to hang out in the hotel lobby. I'm not sure we can do anything about that."

"We could talk to the new manager about it," Liz said.

"Leave it for now. Maybe she'll give up on her own." Rory looped her arm through Liz's. "Let's find our table. I think we're all at the same one." The three of them found their names on place cards at a table only steps away from the bride and groom's. Liz sat on one side of Martin, Rory the other.

By the time the happy couple arrived, the guests had settled down in their seats with glasses of champagne or sparkling cider in front of them.

They were in the middle of the main course when Liz leaned toward Martin and said in a low voice, "I keep forgetting to ask you...can I get rid of the stuff from Jade's apartment now?"

"You can. What do you plan on doing with it?"

"The personal stuff I'll give to Mrs. Tilcox. She seemed fond of Jade. The rest I'll give to charities I've worked with before."

"I'm sure they'll appreciate it," he said.

"Do you know how Candy's doing?" Rory asked. "I didn't get a chance to check on her earlier."

"She's getting out of the hospital today. Orson's going to take her home." He turned to Liz. "Seems you were right about the two of them."

"I can sense these things."

Rory thought back to their visit to Orson's house. Something clicked in her mind. "She was staying at his place when we couldn't find her, wasn't she?"

Martin nodded. "He has a separate guest house in the back."

"What about the person Candy found? The one she thinks committed the murders Laith was convicted of?"

"That was a group effort involving genetic genealogy. I don't pretend to understand every detail. I've seen a picture of the suspect. He has a remarkable resemblance to Laith. Wouldn't be hard to confuse the two of them in the dark."

"If only he'd been found sooner."

"Unfortunately, things work out that way sometimes."

"What was Candy's part in the search?" Liz asked.

"After the police got a list of potential suspects from a genealogist, she and Orson did a lot of leg work, investigating them. One was especially promising. We obtained his DNA and discovered it was a match."

"I'm glad he was found." Liz put her napkin on the table and caught Rory's eye. "I'm going to the little girl's room."

"I'll go with you," Rory said.

They were washing up at sinks in the multi-stall bathroom when Rory said to Liz, "It's weird not having Nell here. I half-expected her to come out from behind the reception desk when we arrived."

"I know. I'm still having a hard time wrapping my head around what she did."

Rory dried her hands on a paper towel. "If her brother hadn't died..."

"She wouldn't have felt the need to make Candy pay." Liz checked her makeup and hair in the mirror. "She must have decided to make her move when she got that job offer."

A toilet flushed. Rory glanced in the mirror and her eyes widened when she saw Veronica emerge from one of the stalls. She moved aside to allow access to the sink.

"Why'd she go after you?" Veronica said as she washed her hands.

"It's not nice to eavesdrop on people's conversations," Liz said.

"Kind of hard not to in here."

Rory was tempted not to respond, but she decided it would be better to answer the question. "She knew I'd helped solve cases before and was afraid I'd figure it all out, especially after I told her I wasn't going to give up. When Martin came to her to ask her to give me a clue for the scavenger hunt, she swapped it out with one of her own, sending me to the lifeguard tower." Rory cringed at the memory of entering the building and being zapped with a stun gun.

Veronica wiped her hands on a paper towel. "By the way, did you hear that Chef Axelrod's TV deal is back on?"

"I'm glad he isn't being penalized for something he had no control over," Rory said.

"Can't hurt that his name's been in the news so much either." Veronica threw her used paper towel in the trash and walked toward the door, tossing an "I'm glad you're okay" over her shoulder before she exited.

Rory and Liz looked at each other.

"Is she getting...soft?" Liz finally said.

"I think so."

They rejoined the reception in time for the cutting of the cake. When the celebration was winding down, Martin leaned toward Rory. "Would you take a walk with me? I promise we won't be gone long."

"Outside?" Rory looked down at her knee-length bridesmaid dress and the heels she'd paired with it.

"Don't worry, it's not far." He looked at her shoes. "You okay walking in those?"

"I've got a different pair." She took rolled up flats out of her clutch and put them on. "Liz got these for me to change into. She knows I don't spend much time in heels."

"Clever," he said. "Shall we?"

After draping a shawl around her shoulders, she put her arm through his. He led the way out of the front entrance of the Akaw. A blast of cold air hit them as they stepped onto the sidewalk. Rory shivered and pulled her shawl tighter around her shoulders.

"Are you cold?" Martin looked at her with concern.

"I'm fine," she said, then shivered again.

"No, you're not. Hold on." He stopped in the middle of the sidewalk and took off his jacket, removing something from a pocket before draping it around her shoulders. "Better?"

"Thanks." As they resumed their walk, she looked around to see if she could figure out their destination. Moments later, she spotted the metal tree structure filled with love locks in the plaza in front of city hall. "What are we doing here?"

"Recent events have made it clear to me how important you are to me." He reached into the pocket of his pants and pulled something out.

Rory's heart skipped a beat and panic began to set in.

Martin caught the look on her face and hesitated for a moment. It didn't take long before understanding filled his eyes. "I'm not ready for that...yet. Besides, I'd pick a much better location than in front of city hall to propose to you."

Rory felt a slight sense of relief. She wasn't ready for marriage yet, but she would've hated to turn him down.

"But I wanted you to know that I'm in it for the long haul. I do love you." He stared at her, an anxious expression on his face, and waited for her response.

Rory's face dimpled with pleasure. "I love you too." Happiness soared through her body as she said the words and realized she meant them.

"I wanted to make our first Valentine's Day together special."

"You've certainly done that."

He opened his fist and held up a love lock decorated with hearts and flowers as well as their initials.

"I painted that," Rory said, surprise evident in her voice. "How did you know?"

"Your mother saved it for me. She painted the initials on it herself." He gestured toward the metal tree. "Shall we?"

The two of them walked over to the tree. After attaching the lock to the metal structure, they threw the key in a nearby trash can.

Even with all the bad things that had happened, this was still the best Valentine's Day she'd ever had, Rory thought, right before they kissed.

Acknowledgments

I write stories I'd like to read. I'm always thrilled when others like them too. Thank you to everyone who has followed Rory and Liz on their adventures. To those who have reached out to me, I appreciate all your kind words. It means the world to me.

A special thank you goes to my editor, Erin George, who always tells me when I've gone astray in the gentlest way possible. Thank you, also, to the talented Stephanie Savage who created the wonderful cover that graces this book.

Thank you to everyone in the mystery community for their help, support and encouragement over the years. Special thanks go to, in part, Jennifer Chow, Laura Oles, Diane Vallere, Gigi Pandian and Cynthia Kuhn.

And, of course, the biggest thanks goes to my husband, Steve, who continues to support me on my writing journey.

About the Author

Sybil Johnson's love affair with reading began in kindergarten with "The Three Little Pigs." Visits to the library introduced her to Encyclopedia Brown, Mrs. Piggle-Wiggle and a host of other characters. Fast forward to college where she continued reading while studying Computer Science. After twenty years in the computer industry, Sybil decided to try her hand at writing mysteries. Her short fiction has appeared in *Mysterical-E* and *Spinetingler Magazine* among others. Originally from the Pacific Northwest, she now wields pen and paint brush from her home in Southern California. Read more about her and sign up for Sybil's newsletter at www.authorsybiljohnson.com.